THE
DEBTOR
CLA$$

a novel

THE
DEBTOR
CLA$$

a novel

IVAN G.
GOLDMAN

THE PERMANENT PRESS
Sag Harbor, NY 11963

For information, address:
    The Permanent Press
    4170 Noyac Road
    Sag Harbor, NY 11963
    www.thepermanentpress.com

Library of Congress Cataloging-in-Publication Data

    Goldman, Ivan G.
        The debtor class : a novel / Ivan G. Goldman.
            pages ; cm
        ISBN 978-1-57962-389-0 (hardcover)
            1. Ex-convicts—Fiction. 2. Collection agencies—Fiction.
        3. Collecting of accounts—Fiction. I. Title.

    PS3557.O3686D43 2015
    813'.54—dc23   2015000230

Printed in the United States of America.

For my lovely sister, Elayne Sidley

I went out full, and the LORD hath brought me home again empty.

—The Book of Ruth 1:21

I see my light come shining
From the west unto the east.
Any day now, any day now,
I shall be released.

—Bob Dylan
"I Shall Be Released"

CHAPTER 1

When they brought out the sidewalk chicken costume, Liz hoped they were pulling her leg, but every passing moment chipped away more of this hope. It was a one-piece outfit—bright yellow with red highlights and a gap-toothed smile sewn permanently into the chicken face. It occurred to her that she could pull on the suit, run straight out the restaurant door into traffic and be anointed the all-time queen of performance art: *'Chicken' Struck Dead Crossing Road: Critics Dazzled.* But declining posthumous fame, she assumed instead the persona of a bubbly game show contestant. "It's so cute," she exclaimed. Meryl Streep couldn't have been more convincing. And Meryl hadn't spent the last three days dragging herself up and down Pacific Coast Highway looking for a job. The manager, who smelled of cigarettes and whose nameplate said "Buddy," flashed a sardonic smile that told her he wasn't buying her act but wouldn't hold it against her either. Like Liz, he was Mexican. He claimed the suit had been washed after its previous tenant, but she wasn't so sure.

"Would you like me to try it on now?"

Buddy's face turned grave. "Yes," he said.

Crap.

Liz's road to chickenhood had been a long one. Along the way she earned a master in library science and stacked up $43,000 in student loans. As she started for the restroom, Buddy cautioned her: "Listen, I don't mean nothing by it, but if you can't pass a drug test, don't even bother. You need like thirty days for weed to clear your system. Everything else, it's less. I'm not like, judging or anything? But they send you down to this lab. And if you got one a those marijuana medical cards it won't do you any good. So if it's, you know, like a waste of time? Hell, don't waste your time."

Liz was tempted to ask how anyone could seek a job like this if they *hadn't* been doing drugs. "We're cool," she told Buddy. There was a time she'd have been shocked to discover you needed pristine pee to qualify as a sidewalk chicken, but she'd been scuffling out there so long nothing surprised her anymore. She felt a kinship with John Wayne in *The Searchers*, tramping across the plains day after day, season after season, in search of Natalie Wood whom he was probably just going to shoot anyway.

"Great," replied Buddy, who looked only a couple years older than Liz. Later she'd learn he was still paying off his wedding caterer from three years back. "I wouldn't wear more than just, you know, underwear underneath," he added. "It can get hot in there." In the bathroom she checked the label. One hundred percent polyester.

Most store managers treated her like she was selling dead cats, although in some instances she detected sympathy, the kind you might reserve for someone who'd fallen out of a speeding ambulance. But Buddy the fast-chicken manager had looked her up and down and called out to someone in back, "Hey Lonny, think she could fit into, you know, the suit?"

"Hang on, I'll get it!" someone yelled back. Moments later another young man appeared offering Liz the shroud for the last fragments of her dignity. She was already jealous of the other employees. They got to wear simple brown uniforms because they'd wandered in at a luckier moment. Timing was everything. "Might be a little loose," Lonny said, looking her over a little too closely. No sense objecting to his borderline-sexist observation. Whatever looks, brains, or decency she'd once counted on were about to disappear inside the folds of the chicken suit. Or so she thought. But after trying it on she checked herself out in the metal plate of a restroom mirror and an unrecognizable figure with a red beak looked back at her. Eureka! What's the difference? Her ignominy would be utterly anonymous. Even if she ran into someone she knew, so what? This was no speaking part. She was flooded with relief, even a bastardized thrill of inspiration. True, it must have been 113 inside, but at least nobody would *see* her sweat. Only one thing to do in an outfit like this—dance! It would make time pass and possibly even attract more customers. She sashayed out the restroom door to Buddy and Lonny and sprang up on her toes, one arm arched over her head. Applause. Those nineteen years of school paid off after all.

CHAPTER 2

Philyaw, driving down a coarse commercial street lined with strip malls and artless utility poles, tried to focus on Miles Davis's magical recording of "So What," but he'd been listening to it all week, and now it was just another unremarkable component of his surroundings, like the double yellow lines. Miles, Monk, Mozart, it didn't matter. Played too frequently, it lost its juju.

Suddenly he spotted an apparition, someone in a yellow chicken outfit dancing in place outside a gaily colored fast-food chicken joint. The solitary figure executed what might be a samba deftly and tirelessly in faultless rhythm. He recalled comic strips he'd seen as a kid that showed desperate sad sacks wearing sandwich boards from neck to knee. They were figures of fun. The costumed figures out there beckoning to drivers were their lineal descendants. Along this particular retail street you saw one every couple of blocks. Gorillas plugging payday loans, clowns hopping around in front of furniture stores. Only a minute earlier Chewbacca waved a sign offering cash for gold. What sort of motorists, Philyaw wondered, considered it a good idea to conduct a financial transaction generated by a Wookiee? He recalled seeing a particularly piquant penguin somewhere back there but had already forgotten its message. It was like e-mailing spam. If you hooked one or two customers out of ten thousand you'd make a nice score.

"We need the sixties back," one of his schmoes, a flower child now pushing seventy, told him during a routine collection call last week. "There's too much crap going on, and not enough people on the street." Next time he'd tell her she was mistaken. People were on the street—decked out as penguins and dancing chickens.

This chicken was clearly female. Narrow ankles, purple tennis shoes, fluid movements, and a slender figure under all that material. Philyaw caught a glimpse of a hand that was tan and smooth, almost baby-like. But now she was already in his rearview mirror. Which was when the idea came to him. A silly idea, which in his experience was often the best kind. He turned the corner to circle the block. It would ultimately cost him a weekend in jail. Odd how a quick decision that doesn't seem terribly important at the time can bear such sour fruit. Like stepping off the curb into the path of a cement truck.

After turning the second corner he was forced to stop behind a line of vehicles. He couldn't discern the cause of the holdup because the vehicle in front of him was one of those jumbo SUVs that obstruct everything ahead. An "Alumni College of Hard Knocks" bumper sticker identified the driver as less clever than he believed himself to be.

After a couple of minutes Philyaw stepped out to learn the cause of the holdup. Several cars ahead of him, a cop had stopped his patrol car to converse with the driver of a second police car facing the other way. They'd tied up traffic in both directions on the narrow street lined with low-rise condos and townhouses. He couldn't see their faces, but the more Philyaw watched, the less it smelled like an emergency and more like two cops gossiping across a figurative backyard fence. He returned to his seat and closed the door. The scene seemed eerily familiar, though not from personal experience, which meant it was *jamais vu*, in this instance a resurrection of all those movie scenes depicting kraut soldiers swaggering around Paris, Amsterdam or some other humiliated city. Officers in crisp uniforms barking orders, ordering the best wine, fucking the choicest women.

He switched from Miles to the radio. A correspondent interviewed state fairgoers about the previous week's acquittal of George Zimmerman, a Florida citizen who shot and killed a black teen he thought looked suspicious. Another station measured lingering effects from the global economic crash of five years earlier. A hospital commercial offered hope to listeners suffering from inoperable bowel disease. Back to Miles.

Another minute blinked on the digital clock. It's important to handle small inconveniences with patience and intelligence, but acting on that knowledge isn't as easy as acquiring it. Philyaw wished he had a newspaper. All this waiting to talk to a chicken.

Another oppressed civilian pulled up behind him, someone else living a life that the two cops ahead deemed insignificant. Suddenly Philyaw lost the war with himself. He tapped his horn once, twice, thrice. He knew it was dumb. A siren screeched momentary displeasure and blue lights flashed. It happened so fast he wondered if their fingers had been poised above the pertinent buttons. Their gossip suddenly ended, two new centurions, as policeman-author Joseph Wambaugh had affectionately dubbed them, were coming straight toward Philyaw, both scowling. One in uniform, the other in jeans and a long-sleeved pullover with running shoes. A plainclothes detective, beach style. "Couldn't you see we were conducting police business?" he said. Flashing his badge, he spoke in the flat tones of a man who was bored, upset, and particularly scornful of the shit-bird he was addressing. The bright ten A.M. sun was directly behind the cop, so when Philyaw looked up he couldn't make out the face, just the dark shape of a head framed in the glare. A long, tall guy now demanding Philyaw's license and registration. His voice was strangely muffled.

Philyaw was back inside the movie. *Your papers, please.* Curiously, in digitalized twenty-first century America there were more papers to keep track of than ever. Invoices, receipts, bank notices. HMO directives, enigmatic cable

TV and cell phone carrier statements, IRS fright bulletins. Entire regiments of tyrannical authorities not only spewed out tons of these documents (while pleading with you to accept them "virtually" instead), but might drag you through paper-mongering hell if you couldn't come up with some precise document you're not sure you ever saw. Mountains of these troublesome scraps of paper must be stored all across the land, everyone afraid to throw them out. What would Tom Paine do? Probably take his musket off the wall. In fact, it's what he did.

Philyaw, on the other hand, had a role to play—to grovel and squirm, thus allowing the cops to detach their hook and chuck him back as an obedient, chastised mackerel. He pulled his license from his wallet, and searching the glove compartment for his registration, he looked up from a different angle, allowing him to see the cop a little better now. He was a white man with elongated Clint Eastwood limbs and a hint of horse to his face, possibly from a touch of Marfan syndrome. Balding, short dishwater hair. Odd, but after Philyaw found the registration certificate and straightened up behind the wheel again, the cop's skin looked blue. Philyaw blinked and blinked again. Damn if the guy wasn't really and truly blue. The color of his complexion brushed a supernatural patina of madness over the entire scene, over everything Philyaw might see, hear, or even imagine. Because if there were blue-skinned cops in Hermosa Beach, California, anything was possible. Unicorns, elves. Leprechauns. Where did it stop?

The troll-like figure studied the license and registration awhile, then leaned in toward Philyaw, owning the situation. He was blue all right, though not precisely blue, just as people are never precisely white, black or brown, but a blend of dominant and lesser colors. This cop's leading hue was powder blue, more pronounced in some places than others. Probably several years younger than Philyaw, who was fifty, but already suffering from some improbable ailment. Blue jaundice or something. No wonder he had such a crappy disposition.

If it was such urgent police business, why weren't your roof lights flashing? "Sorry, officer, I wasn't sure what was going on, and I've got to be somewhere."

"You saw what was going on. I saw you get out of the car." There seemed to be a muffler on his voice because the cop barely opened his mouth. Could his jaw be wired shut?

"I just thought . . ." The cop looked at him expectantly. Although still emitting cold hostility, he seemed poised now to hand Philyaw back his miserable papers. But all at once Philyaw couldn't go on with it. His disgust was too deep. Not with the cops, but with himself, which was of course their goal.

"Look, what's my crime?" he asked. A not-so-silly question.

The blue cop tilted his head, looking at Philyaw and seeing something odd. "Ned? Look at this." He was smirking now, and suddenly Philyaw understood why. Sometimes he forgot about the family face. This tinted geek was talking about Philyaw right in front of Philyaw, as though he were a potted plant.

The other cop, moving up closer, was in the standard navy blue uniform with standard brown Hispanic skin. He had one of those cruel, vacuous expressions you might see on a male model. He was acutely beefy—one of those body builders who'd passed the point of sound mind. *I could crush you,* his mesomorphic resources announced. He checked out Philyaw and now both cops smirked, making sure Philyaw understood he was the joke. Philyaw, who'd endured a lifetime of school-yard taunts and amused references to his cursed countenance, required no exaggerated gestures to understand.

Breathing harder now, he stifled bluish-based insults. No matter what the provocation, you don't go around needling people about their medical conditions. Meanwhile two other patrol cars had shown up. They must have sped down the sidewalk so they could reach the scene of Philyaw's honking atrocity. Funny how this morning had seemed so ordinary.

He'd been planning to cold-call some doctors' offices for an hour or so and then help his employees stay on top of the schmoes. If it hadn't been for the chicken girl none of this would have happened. He'd be on time for a forgettable day.

Philyaw counted the expanding cluster of cops on the scene. One, two, three, four . . . Maybe next they'd bring up a tank.

"Okay, Bogey, listen up," the blue cop said to Philyaw. "We're—"

Bogey! That did it. "My name," Philyaw said, "is Spartacus." The brown cop turned his head toward the blue cop and took a deep breath, wordless moves to define Philyaw as a half-wit, then turned back to him. "Well you've got a problem here, Spartacus or Bogart or whatever your name is." He leaned over to read the license still in the blue cop's hand. "Philyaw? Is that how you pronounce it?"

"Wait a minute," Philyaw said, "you mean you're not shooting one of those reality shows? You guys are real cops?" The skirmish escalated. Somewhere along the line he complained about assholes in general. The words just flowed through him as though they'd originated elsewhere. Like the creative process described by countless artists. His cell phone rang. The little screen identified the caller as Beesling. Philyaw had been trying to reach him all week about the lease extension. A reminder that he still had a daily grind to grind.

"Excuse me," Philyaw said to the cops, ready now to debase himself again.

"Put your hands on the steering wheel."

To Beesling, he said, "Listen, can I—"

At that point a cop—he didn't notice which one—yanked open his door. The phone flew off somewhere as they grabbed him by his shirt, pulling him from his seat like a tub of laundry. Philyaw was surrounded by at least a half-dozen cops. Someone tripped him down to his knees. Sharp pain as they struck pavement. His arms were yanked behind him, and handcuffs snapped. They sat his ass on the curb for all the world to see. Now the other drivers had something to distract them, the fuckers. Was he driving drunk? Wanted for molestation?

Philyaw knew cops carried little digital gadgets to record arrest scenes. That's why they hadn't cursed.

"Looks familiar, doesn't he?" said the blue cop.

"You should see him in a trench coat."

"Here's looking at you, kid."

And they all laughed a dry laugh at Philyaw's expense, at the morning fool they'd bagged.

CHAPTER 3

Around the same time Philyaw honked his horn, Roland Sussman was pulling out of the airport in a taxi. He'd spent the last three years on a sparsely populated island, and Los Angeles assaulted him with its nervous energy. Billboards, traffic, impatience. Everything along the highway seemed poised to leap at him. Buy this. Do that. There was no mildness to it. Even the sunshine was intense.

When he reached home, he overtipped his Central Asian driver and stepped out into a caressing breeze. He'd given away possessions accumulated during his stay at the commune and carried only a small valise. His waiting house, though situated in a pricey beach neighborhood, was humble considering his status as an outrageously famous author. During his absence, Pick, a former girlfriend, had managed his worldly affairs, including his mutt, Lucy, who barked as he fumbled with the lock but recognized him as soon as he entered the vestibule. Jumping with delight, she was chubbier now. He pulled her down and calmed her. Good doggy. Everything looked convent clean, neater and more tightly organized than the way he'd left it. The plants burst with health.

Pick had already informed him she probably wouldn't be around when he arrived. Excellent. He needed depressurization, not conversation, certainly not questions. Dressed for the cooler clime of Puget Sound, he briskly climbed the stairs to wash off the plane stink and look for a clean T-shirt. He thought he might meditate a little, but first he opened the sliding door to his bedroom closet . . . and a stranger burst out waving a black commando knife. "Yahhhh!" Sussman heard himself scream. Well, if this didn't give him a heart attack, nothing would.

Lucy, who'd followed him upstairs, recommenced barking. Seventy pounds of portly indignation, she jumped harmlessly all around the intruder's legs, just as she'd done to Sussman at the front door. Submissive even to cats, she must have decided it would be impolite to bark at the intruder until *after* he sprang out at Sussman with a knife in his fist. Although everything was moving at lightning pace, Sussman's mind saw it all in slow motion. He expected his life to end within moments. He'd always assumed you receive advance notice in some way, a telegram or something, though there probably weren't any more telegrams.

The man from the closet was built like a redwood, his head a huge yellow moon, the nose squeezed flat into pig cheeks like something inside a jar. His eyes were tiny lizard eyes peeking out of an oversized baseball cap pulled down over his eyebrows. He was probably Asian or Hispanic, with hairless bull-moose shoulders exposed by a tank top. No discernible neck, the arms heavily tattooed. His cap bore Kelly green initials that Sussman didn't take time to read, color-coordinated with white athletic shoes and Kelly green laces. Coming forward, he waved his weapon left, right, left, like a snake head, his fingers fat coils of fiber. Nothing about this nightmare made less sense than the knife. Why bother with a weapon? This guy could tear a sofa in half. The blade had, if Sussman was not mistaken, a partially serrated edge and the knife appeared new, perhaps purchased specifically for this occasion.

With so much at stake here they should have much to talk about, but Sussman had the feeling that saying anything would defy etiquette. It all felt so strange and awful, incredible but starkly real. And true. The blade was truth.

Sussman hadn't expected to be knifed on such a cozy, sun-splashed, 72-degree afternoon, especially not in palmy, pastel Hermosa Beach, which teemed with trendy trust-funders. A lavish redoubt where 1 percenters could settle in with their jewelry, emergency gold bars and petty anxieties reasonably certain they were safe from subterranean sore losers harboring homicidal intentions.

Retreating, Sussman looked for something to use as a shield or weapon, but he stumbled over his own feet and hit the floor with a heavy thump. Oh God. That's when Pick, bless her, charged in from somewhere with a tennis racket raised in chopping position. Also strangely mute, she took a desultory sideways swing that missed. The invader reached out with his left to try to grab the racket but got his ear bonked by a second, quicker swing that made a hideous *thwak*. The intruder rubbed his ear and searched his fat fingers for blood. She swung again. *Thwak!* "Get away from me!" he shouted, the voice high-pitched and, not surprisingly, excited. If Sussman didn't know better he'd have thought the intruder was some poor innocent soul attacked for no good reason and that Pick was the stalking maniac. They stood facing each other, neither advancing, until the intruder suddenly turned and sprinted out and down the stairs with ape-like quickness. The retreat revealed an enormous fat braid hanging almost to the small of his back. Lucy licked the face of Sussman, whose ankle throbbed with white-hot pain. They assumed the prowler was gone but couldn't say for sure. Pick had never seen him before either. Obeying the 9-1-1 operator's instructions, they locked themselves in the bedroom and waited for the cavalry.

The cops who showed up five minutes later couldn't find the intruder or anyone in the neighborhood who'd seen someone of his description. It was as though a grizzly ran outside and blended in with the beach crowd. Police determined that he'd entered through an open window along the side of the house, but they found no usable prints.

Only an hour later Sussman saw an old photo of himself on the evening news over an emergency room TV screen:

Author Surprises Armed Intruder was the teaser. Eventually when he would see print versions of the episode some accounts referred to Pick as a girlfriend, others as an assistant, still others as a "friend." Her bare thighs hinted of sex, which spiced a story already made tasty by celebrity violence. Storyteller Sussman knew that only the element of betrayal was needed to give the story, as journalists liked to say, legs. Pick was in fact a compelling presence now that she'd grown her hair long and straight and dyed it black with hipster bangs and lipstick to match. It all diverted attention from the freckles and mild acne scars.

IF, AS the doctor feared, he'd suffered a third-degree tear to his ligament, Sussman might eventually need surgery. Pleased to be alive, he felt even more pleased after he scored a second Percocet off a nurse and felt his old friend the buzz. "You saved me," he told Pick as it kicked in. "You're my wench in shining armor."

"Tennis shorts," she corrected him.

Two detectives interviewed Sussman as he sat up in his curtained-off emergency room space. Repeating the same questions they and other cops had asked him in a hasty interview at the house, they didn't seem to have any new ideas. As he'd told them earlier, the attacker was a man of medium height, built like a Hummer, and probably around thirty, though he couldn't be sure. He couldn't recall specific images in the tattoos, and couldn't be sure of eye color. Nor, it turned out, could Pick. They vividly remembered the braid. Hanging between the man's massive shoulders, it somehow made him appear even more enormous. Yet Pick, seeing Sussman helpless on the floor, had attacked without hesitation, like trained infantry. Quite a babe.

The intruder's voice was high-pitched for such a big man, but alarm did that to voices. Sussman remembered no distinct accent or unusual speech pattern. All he had to go by were four words: *Get away from me.* Was Sussman sure he never said anything else? Yes. Sussman was terribly verbal. Words stuck to him like briars. What he remembered in this instance was the absence of words, as though they were all actors in a silent film. The man carried no discernible booty out with him. Pick would be a better judge of what might be missing from the house, Sussman said, explaining once again that he'd been up in the San Juan Islands of Puget Sound for the previous three years.

Sussman tried to pay no attention to the fact that one of the detectives was blue. It was as though a screeching monkey were bouncing around on his shoulder yet mentioning it was taboo. Sussman was pretty sure he knew the source of the man's pigmentation. He'd read about these blue people once or twice, but seeing one in the flesh startled him anyway. In most modern cases their condition originated with the Y2K scare, when fearmongers and crackpots predicted the first moment of the year 2000 would create a crippled, darkened planet swept by famine, plagues, cannibalism, and poor TV reception. Some of them worried that antibiotics and other medicines would be unavailable when digital clocks struck the Hour of the Wolf, which would quickly degenerate into Night of the Living Dead followed by a millennium or two of generic deprivation and horror. According to the theory, unchecked microbes would romp across earth, and, Glocks or no Glocks, even the most prepared survivalists could therefore end up dead. (Sussman had briefly considered writing a novel about the Y2K fanatics but ultimately consented to write an essay for the *New Yorker* instead. He never finished it.) Some Y2K extremists seized upon a preventive measure—silver! It was, they concluded, a time-tested antidote to lots of maladies. By ingesting it in carefully rationed doses, they'd float harmlessly above the death-dealing microorganisms that would thrive in the Road Warrior world to come.

It must have been a terrible disappointment to the silver-eaters when computers kept humming, civilization persisted, and the repeated doses turned their complexions blue. Sussman wondered whether there might be thousands more of these blue-skinned Chicken Littles scattered around—more than anyone suspected—bitterly hunkered down and praying for some apocalypse to come along and prove them correct after all.

Most of the cops who'd showed up to the house seemed genuinely concerned for Sussman and Pick. But this big blue one that followed them to the hospital, the tall one who kept his lips closed while he talked, treated Sussman with deadpan contempt, addressing him as though he were reading his words off a soup can. Over the years Sussman had run into a fair number of antagonists who despised him as the hippie Jew bastard who'd written *Marching with Kings*. Most of them despised the book so deeply that they could never bring themselves to read it. Or maybe Officer Blue just despised crime victims in general. Hard to tell. In the hospital he'd been paired with a muscled Latino in uniform. Now he was accompanied by a polite plainclothesman playing the role of good cop. Yet it made no sense. Wasn't good cop-bad cop supposed to be used against suspects? Sussman had to remind himself he was the victim, not the perpetrator. Perhaps he was fulfilling his role as the injured party inadequately, failing some test he knew nothing about, like that college nightmare when you're suddenly faced with the final exam and hadn't realized you were enrolled in the course. Sussman was impressed by the enormity of Officer Blue's disdain. He seemed to be biding his time, waiting for a predetermined signal to rise up with his confederates and, in a riot of blood and stymied passion, spring upon everyone that displeased them, especially Sussman. Sussman was disturbed to discover that after shutting himself off from the world for three years he might still carry a celebrity target on his ass, as had John Lennon, Lenny Bruce, and so many others brought down by madmen—in Bruce's case, government madmen. He'd hoped that the news media, which normally suffer from striking memory loss, would forget about him, even though his opus was still taught in college classrooms.

One of the cops asked him what the Kelly green and white worn by the intruder signified. They're probably some kind of team colors, Sussman said. You can check them on the Internet, he added. Officer Blue wrote something in his little spiral notebook, apparently considering this significant new information. Sussman found that discouraging, but his principal concern wasn't to catch the culprit anyway. He mainly wished to put the incident behind him and fade back into obscurity.

He couldn't understand how the gorilla with the giant braid down his back could escape notice, but Officer Blue's partner pointed out that braids could be cut or unbraided and massive muscles weren't so distinct either. "You know how many gyms we've got around LA?" he asked. "They're like Starbucks. Full of tattooed guys pumping iron." The partner was a tenor. His voice contained elements of Jay Leno and Mickey Mouse, which made him seem more nervous than he probably was. He looked close to retirement, a medium-sized man with a trimmed brown mustache and a too-obvious hair transplant, the hairs spaced evenly like rows of corn.

No, Sussman said, this guy was almost like another species, supernaturally thick. Officer Blue snorted. He talked more than the tenor, but he didn't talk a great deal for a man asking questions. He spoke as though the words were currency he was reluctant to spend. Anyway, Sussman told them what he could. No, he'd never seen the intruder before and had no idea of his motives. He doubted that his written works had anything to do with the break-in. The intruder didn't look much like a reader.

After Officer Blue folded his notebook, he said, "You know where the station is, right?" The words sounded like they were coming from inside a locked trunk.

Sussman nodded.

"Stop by in the morning. Your girlfriend too."

Although three years of commune time and his recent helping of Percocet had boosted Sussman's serenity, he was fed up with this goofy cop. "Pick isn't my girlfriend," he said.

Reading Sussman's displeasure, the tenor cop jumped in. "We'll come pick you up if you like. How's nine thirty?"

Sussman assured him they'd get there on their own. Later he would learn from Pick that during her separate interview Officer Blue hadn't been terribly nice to her either.

As soon as the cops left, two employees in hospital greens showed up and loaded Sussman onto a gurney. "Off you go," said one, wheeling him to an unknown destination. He was pushed through sad corridors that smelled of chemicals, uneaten food, silicone wiring—a range of disagreeable hospital odors that lurked beneath all the disinfectant. Patients attached to bags of fluids that hung from skinny wheeled contraptions wandered ghost-like through the corridors. They were like antiquated machinery, beyond fixing. Peeking into rooms, Sussman saw other gray, wrinkled, torpid or trembling forms lying in bed, distressed and stripped of dignity. Some murmured unpleasantly. They appeared to be decaying already, as though the organisms that would devour them in death were already teaming up with their present maladies. Some were no doubt younger than Sussman.

The ambulance ride had jolted him with the same force as the knife-wielding intruder. Sussman always assumed when he heard a siren that some frail senior, perhaps dying, was being rushed to the hospital, that the patient was probably miserable anyway, so despite the drama of the siren, it wasn't really an emergency but a death whose time had come. Now approaching seventy, Sussman still failed to identify with the invalid in the back of the ambulance even though it was his own aging self. He thought of all his contemporaries already suffering from a constellation of unpleasantries that included cataracts, plastic hips, limp dicks, liver spots, depression, loose labia, troubled sleep, lumps, tics, stomach acid, polyps, blockages, leaks, memory lapses, arthritic disfigurement, and cardiac stents. The mounting maladies gradually squeezed other topics from their conversation, turning them into obsessed caricatures of all the yammering geezers they'd shunned in their youth. And he was struck by the realization that a dismal scene quite similar to this one would probably be the last thing he'd ever see. If not today, some other day. He vowed then and there not to die in a hospital.

Eventually he was wheeled into a private room. Assuming ownership of Sussman's fate, a matronly nurse or doctor or someone (Sussman couldn't distinguish ranks on their uniforms) breezily mentioned they were "keeping" him overnight, possibly confusing him with a stray puppy. She seemed to think Sussman had already been informed.

"Why?" Sussman asked her.

"Excuse me?"

"Why do they want me overnight?"

The matron, as though speaking to a slow learner, explained that the doctor didn't like something or other about his injury and so he must remain for "observation, possibly more tests . . ." All across the country, hospitals, obeying their insurance masters, prematurely ejected gravely injured and acutely diseased patients. He had to run into one that wanted to keep him overnight for a lousy twisted ankle.

"Thanks, but I prefer to be home," Sussman said. Up to that point he'd been on cordial terms with the people who'd examined, X-rayed, and clucked over him. It would be rude to point out that rampant hospital infections resistant to their pitifully compromised antibiotics probably lurked in every corner, but he made his intentions clear. He was leaving. Things turned ugly fast. A posse formed. How did they all get notified so quickly? He struggled to his feet, one hand on the rail and putting no weight on his tortured ankle. He was a trifle dizzy. "May I borrow crutches or a cane or something?" he asked someone. No response. His bare ass was exposed by the hospital gown, but they ignored him again when he asked for his clothes. "What're you gonna do? Sell my underwear on ebay?"

Ultimately some clerk showed up to explain that if he left without a proper discharge his insurance wouldn't pay anything. Less than a full day out of the commune he was already bruised by random violence and by the vile nonsense of everyday life. He recalled Albania, where he'd once given a talk. It had the same aggressively complex web of procedures that existed only to exist, entwining citizens in a hopeless, baffling tangle of absurdity, although this place had fresher paint and probably vastly better food and plumbing.

Because socialist horrors had barely penetrated the Land of the Free, the bill would be in crazy-ass thousands. Which meant Sussman must surrender his dignity and stick around. But feeling sorry for himself was foolish. He once met a drunk at a party who'd been a reporter in Congo. Everywhere he went people were missing arms, legs, lips, noses, ears. All hacked off by armed, giggling fiends, and no one could really explain why. Something so evil had preceded the reporter that he was reluctant to push on and see what lay ahead in the next village. But staying where he was, seeing the same victims day after day, none of them truly healing, was also too terrible. The drunk correspondent looked old, much older than he really was, Sussman suspected. "And it wasn't a front page story very long," he said in a farm-boy twang. Until the man spoke, Sussman guessed he might be French. Most men, if they live long enough, he decided, end up looking French.

Settling back in bed, Sussman contemplated Buddha's Four Noble Truths. He'd have to wait a little longer to find out what would kill him. It was a sentiment he might get into a book if he ever wrote another. If he didn't write it down, he might lose it forever. Those thoughts that escaped, he suspected, were the worst ones to forget. *Nothing can hurt me*, he reminded himself, *unless my mind allows it to*. But just to be sure he rang the bell to try wangling another Percocet out of the night nurse.

SUSSMAN ENTERED an empty elevator and knew not why. It took him up. The stainless steel doors opened to a rooftop high above the city. Outside was glaring sunlight, but it wasn't the friendly kind. A sinister presence lurked out there. Not exactly hiding, just waiting. No buttons on the elevator, nowhere to go but out the door into blinding sunlight. And sure enough, something awful was tugging at his leg, the gimpy leg with the twisted ankle. Sussman woke to find a long-haired doctor with a multicolored ceramic earring examining his ankle. He was relieved to be out of the creepy elevator dream. In a room flooded with morning sunlight the doctor recommended an MRI, though not necessarily now. He turned out to be a *Marching with Kings* fan and gladly signed a medical release.

Sussman, in custody of his clothes again, was barely able to get his bandaged ankle through the pant leg. Zipping up his fly, he looked up to see a woman enter his room. She was African American with khaki skin, dreadlocks and a red scarf around her head. She was from the business office, she said, briskly informing him that the insurance card he'd proffered the day before had been rejected by the insurer and his Medicare status was under some kind of clerical cloud.

"I've been gone awhile," he said, hoping that might explain it. Not used to handling such conversations, he asked whether he could straighten this out later, feeling almost as befuddled as he'd been during the elevator dream.

"Don't worry, Sussman," Pick told him when she met him downstairs. She always called him by his last name, as though they were in an Ivy League study group. She'd handle the insurance problem. Somebody in green medical attire showed up with a wheelchair to take him outside. No one knew why anymore, but you had to leave in a chair. Maybe it was a long-running practical joke. With Pick carrying his crutches they moved around a couple of paparazzi from competing gossip websites. They asked him how he felt, if he'd been scared, what he was going to do next, the usual. Struggling to ignore the camera clicks, he was tempted to suggest they might find their time better spent ferreting out corruption in the military-industrial complex.

CHAPTER 4

Around the same time Philyaw was being processed into the jail at Hermosa Beach and Sussman was opening the closet to a knife-wielding intruder, newly released convict Bento was miles away, ambling through the harbor district seeking his first beer in four years. He'd already passed a few bars sprinkled among the pawnshops, liquor stores and boarded-up storefronts. He finally settled on a place called Daphne's that looked just as tired and gray as the others but with more customers. Four men in dirt-caked construction boots stood outside the entrance smoking cigarettes and talking football. They seemed unaware that if they chose they could head up to Big Bear to watch shooting stars and still make it to work in the morning. Bento had decided while he was in prison that he'd try to remind himself of such possibilities so he could drink even deeper of freedom.

Inside, he smelled twenty years of beer and burgers. It was crowded and noisy, not particularly clean. A drinking bar, late afternoon, with a few TVs scattered around to give solitary drinkers something to look at, like bright plastic dinguses stretched above an infant's crib. Lots of middle-aged customers with divorces and fading tattoos peeking out of their clothes. He found himself a stool and learned too late that a pot-bellied loudmouth next to him thought everything was hilarious. About forty working-stiff keys dangled from a ring in his belt. "Working hard?" he asked an acquaintance strolling past. The acquaintance smiled and kept moving, but the punch line came anyway: "Or hardly working?" And the man with the forty keys, though bereft of any defined audience, broke into a god-awful ear-splitting laugh. It was a recurring scenario. The man would say something corny and then find himself hysterically funny. But the laugh was eerily devoid of happiness. It was more like a *plea* for happiness that Bento guessed would remain beyond his reach. A man who had nothing to say but said it anyway.

Heading straight to an unfamiliar neighborhood was a calculated decision. Had Bento gone back to the same old streets in Anaheim they'd contain the same old friends and not a few enemies, all a danger to his freedom. Also, in some storybook corner of his mind he imagined that here along the harbor he'd slide into just the right bar stool at just the right time to strike up a conversation with just the right guy who'd send him to the secret place where they handed out longshoremen's union cards—the next best thing to winning Powerball. Bento had also dreamed of becoming a firefighter, a merchant marine officer, and the Angels' first baseman. Some people really held these positions. They existed. But one by one they'd slipped away from him.

Back in Lancaster lots of cons had warned him to stay out of joints like this. Back there if you got into a beef and fought it out you went to the hole. But out here prosecutors might wave twenty-five to life in your face for doing the exact same thing. You didn't have to kill anyone. You didn't even have to hurt anyone as long as the offense was considered "serious." And authorities seemed to think everything was serious. They were like toddlers punching shiny buttons that could melt down a man's life minute by minute, year after year. Ten years, twenty, twenty-five to life. The years tripped off the tongues of prosecutors, judges and court-appointed lawyers who nodded and went home to dinner.

Twenty-five to lifers rarely made it out. Parole boards fig-ured they'd done so much time they could no longer function out here and would just commit more crimes. So for doing so much time they got punished with more time, with all their time. Which is why, if it came down to it, Bento would let anyone in here swipe his currency off the bar and spit in his eye. What mattered was staying out in the world. And maybe in time the world would feel freer to him than it did now.

He was about to slip off the stool when the loudmouth with the forty keys left to join acquaintances in a booth. A young woman carrying a big purse and a small dish of pizza quickly swooped in from some heavenly place and took his place. Bento had seen a flash of squeaky-clean brown hair, shoulder length. He was too intimidated to make a more thorough inspection. Moments later she was cheerfully talking to him about the Dodgers playing on the screen in front of him. You could tell she felt a touch of trepidation but decided to break the ice anyway.

"We went last week and I've got this friend who works at the stadium? He calls me on my cell phone and finds out where we're sitting. He goes, 'Let me get you some real seats,' and he comes over and like gives us these tickets. So we read the numbers and we're walking closer and closer to the field, and I'm like, I don't *believe* this. Finally we end up right behind first base. I mean like I can fucken see the players' faces." *Fucken.* By pronouncing the word she'd already shared an intimacy that implied Bento was just as cool as she was.

Trying to look casual, he turned and made a more thorough appraisal. And decided she must be an actress. Regular people didn't look like that. The exquisite chin and cheekbones, flawless skin, all of it. But what would an actress be doing in this dump? Maybe she was like Eva Marie Saint in *On the Waterfront*, coming home to visit her longshoreman father whose labors had stretched one arm longer than the other. Well, actress or not, she was radiant, with an expressive face that smiled easily. She wore one of those really daring blouses that kept no cleavage secrets, and she owned lovely, round, scarily flawless, medium-sized breasts, the kind depicted in magazine illustrations but never encountered in real life. At one point she even patted them with her palm to make a conversational point, freely drawing attention to their tactile availability. She was a knockout you could talk to. Then he tried talking to her. "You were in movie star territory," he blurted out, a nifty observation about her stadium experience, he thought. Except at that point he had nothing more to say, not even anything lame. He searched his mind frantically and found only blank cartridges.

Bento ordered another beer, too paralyzed to even offer her one. They both sat there for several lifetimes that must have lasted two minutes. She was clearly expecting him to keep the conversation going, and each lost moment made everything worse, but his mind and tongue were frozen. At the same time he seemed to be exhaling some kind of deadening agent that filled the space around him with contagious discomfort. He was fresh out of anything sprightly, witty, or even mildly interesting to say. Finally a little guy on the other side of her wearing an aloha shirt and a baseball cap pointed in the wrong direction, said, "Man, isn't this the worst pizza you ever tasted?" Yes, there it was, unfinished in front of her. Something to talk about.

"Stink-adocious," she said.

A darling remark, but the little poacher didn't even pause to chuckle. "Ever been to Gino's up near Chinatown?" he asked her. Maybe Marshall McLuhan was right. What mattered was not what you said, but how you said it. The two of them began chirping like happy pigeons, all loose and free of dense, ridiculous Bento. The pizza discussion, his last small window of a conversational opportunity, closed forever as they began trading personal information. It was heartbreaking.

Bento slunk off with no good-byes. Only when he reached the street did he realize he'd left at least twelve dollars on the bar. His $200 in release money was going fast. That night he was too disgusted with himself to masturbate. Not even in his imagination was he worthy of her.

CHAPTER 5

The next morning Bento left the harbor behind him, riding a string of three buses to Hermosa Beach. Required to register as a felon within forty-eight hours of release, he found a clerk in the police station there who took his vital information and directed him to a granite bench in the lobby. On an identical bench across from him a man who was no longer young played a noisy racing car game on a tablet computer, wildly jerking and tilting the device as he maneuvered his virtual vehicle. On the wall above him was a crude canvas as big as a ping-pong table depicting a ferocious American eagle with a painted flag fluttering behind it.

And then, just like that, the wiry figure of novelist Roland Sussman swung past Bento on a pair of crutches. Bento couldn't recall ever spotting a celebrity this close before. He was used to seeing only their digital images, which must explain why the real thing looked so peculiar, as though Sussman were pretending to be his own image and only partially succeeding.

Bento had forgotten how old Sussman must be—sixty-five at least. He remembered coming to the end of *Marching with Kings,* exhilarated yet dejected because there was no more of it to read. Unlike most of the rest of the world, Bento also revered Sussman's next novel, which was set in a small college town and mentioned Vietnam only in passing. He would never be done with Vietnam, the author explained in one of his rare interviews, but he'd said what he had to say about it in *Kings.*

If Bento tried to converse with him it would only be a repeat of last night's scene with the girl with perfect breasts. He couldn't even communicate with regular people, much less geniuses. He recalled those old screwball comedies he and his mother used to watch late at night, always filled with characters who fired witticisms at a machine-gun pace. So different from Lancaster, where every word had to be weighed carefully. A guy on his cell block lost the tip of his nose over a little joke.

Just then a lanky woman cop opened a blond-wood door and called Bento's name. He followed her quite decent butt into a sea of metal desks and stopped when she seated herself at one of them. Staring into a computer screen with great determination, she banged an occasional key and finally looked up. "You know anything about this warrant?" she said.

"What warrant?"

She named a date. "Failure to appear, it says." She wore a crisp navy blue uniform that accentuated her pleasing athletic form, threatening to induce his third or fourth post-release erection, even though her severe lesbian haircut made her resemble a young Robert Mitchum.

"I was at Lancaster," Bento said.

"I know."

"I mean on that date. I was locked up." To deal with his excited penis he conjured up a vision of Dystowicz, a seventy-four-year-old murderer who lived on his cellblock and ate boogers.

"You were supposed to file a six-eighty."

"What's that?"

"Didn't anybody tell you?"

"Tell me what?"

She turned and yelled over her shoulder. "Ron? Would you come here a minute?"

Moments later Ron, a cop with a weary black face and forearms like railroad ties, was pulling out a set of cuffs and telling Bento to turn around. There was always that existential moment in these situations. Once you obeyed, you lost all your options. While Bento considered them, Ron cuffed him. Ron then marched him across the lobby toward a set of double doors, making Bento a show-and-tell for Mr. and Mrs. Beach Resident as they waited to approach the counter and take care of dog licenses and such. Sussman had moved on. Bento took a last look at the goofy eagle painting as Officer Ron flashed a plastic card over an electric gizmo and they were buzzed inside the doors.

Bento didn't have the number of his court-appointed attorney, the one who must have slipped up and failed to file the proper form. And even if the incompetent wretch were still alive and practicing after four long years and Bento managed to find him, all the guy ever seemed to do was antagonize everybody. Bento would try to clear it up Monday when he saw a judge. Not a joyful vision. The courts had never been kind to him. He tried to believe there was no deeper meaning to this new setback, yet there was no denying that society, regardless of what he did or didn't do, was once again stashing him in the same old place, and it wasn't Harvard or Wall Street. After drinking that beer yesterday he should have ignored bureaucratic requirements and worked his way south, taking his time all the way to Tierra del Fuego. Dazzle winsome *señoritas* with his gringo charm, join the gauchos out on the pampas, rope cattle and eat bloody steaks around campfires. Simple delights. Anything but the slammer again. Skip, who'd inherited Bento's books and toiletries back at Lancaster, had a name for the sticky law-enforcement matrix that never tired of surrounding guys like them: sick justice.

After his keepers put him through all the familiar procedures they placed him in a large cell with five sets of double bunks. It smelled faintly of bug spray. The crapper looked relatively okay. Stretched out on two of the bottom bunks were a snoring man lying face down and another man in a pink shirt who looked like Humphrey Bogart.

CHAPTER 6

Philyaw, hearing the clink of the cell door, looked up to see a chubby cop escort a tall, sinewy young man into the cell and shut the door on him. The kid, vaguely Italian-looking, was handsome in a rough way. He had a faint scar that crossed an eyebrow, the kind you'd see on a prizefighter. Olive complexion, clean jeans, and a short-sleeved shirt with a collar. No tattoos or hip-hop regalia. Glistening black hair swept back into a short ponytail. Looking around the room, he showed mild curiosity but little else. He didn't overlook Philyaw, but didn't pay him much attention either. Philyaw hadn't thought about it much, but they could put anyone they wanted in his cell, even the lowest, most dangerous of beasts. That sleeping guy over there could be a mass murderer for all he knew. In here he had no control over his own well-being. Just like life, only more so.

"Don't forget to wipe your shoes," Philyaw said. The kid, failing to give him the smile he'd hoped for, seated himself on the next bunk, head down, stroking his chin. The kid closed his eyes and slowly moved his head in a horizontal *no* motion as he brought a hand to his forehead and pulled back his hair, lightly squeezing his skull. "God damn motherfucking sonofabitch," he said evenly, still nodding his head side to side. He took a deep breath and turned to look at Philyaw, then pulled his head back a little as though he'd seen something unexpected. "I'm Bento," he said.

"Philyaw."

He took his hand away from his face. "Phil what?"

"Philyaw."

"Philyaw, I know you hear this all the time, but—"

"I don't think so either."

"Don't think what?"

"Don't think I look like Bogart."

The kid gave him a little grin at last. Good teeth. "I was just going to say you don't look anything like Bogart."

"What're you in for?" Philyaw asked him.

"Just waiting for the Number Twelve bus."

"They tell me there's no judge till Monday."

"That's usually how it works."

"I honked at a blue cop," Philyaw said. "That's what I'm in for."

"A blue cop?"

"Really. He had blue skin."

"Was it painted blue or what?"

"No, I don't think so. Just blue skin, like he was born with it."

"Why'd you honk at him?"

"He was blocking traffic. Plus, he was a prick."

The kid nodded. "You sure showed him."

Even as Philyaw gave him the finger he realized the gesture might be more aggressive than intended. He spotted what might have been a flicker of hostility, but it was gone so fast he couldn't be sure. The kid stretched out on his bunk and closed his eyes. A couple beats later he said, "You take the first watch, okay?"

"What're we watching for?"

"Told you. The Number Twelve bus."

It was only when the cell door clinked open that Philyaw realized he'd fallen asleep. A cop he hadn't seen before called out a name, and the kid looked up. "Let's go," the cop said.

"Where?" the kid asked him. No answer. He shook his head in disgust and rose to let the cop cuff his hands behind his back.

"Where you taking him?" asked Philyaw.

The cop snorted a fake little laugh.

"Glad I amuse you," Philyaw said.

"Some people want to get a look at you," the cop told the kid, escorting him out.

Moments later another cop approached the cell. Officer Blue again. His hue wasn't startling this time. Maybe it even made sense. His face expressionless, he peered through the bars at Philyaw. After an uncomfortable interval the cop's lips cracked just the hint of a smile and he nodded. Then he was gone. Very peculiar. Philyaw wished it didn't bother him as much as it did.

CHAPTER 7

Bento, seated at a table in a blank, windowless room, prayed any witnesses peering at him from behind the one-way window weren't imbeciles. One little nod was all it took. The world was conspiring to show him what a chump he'd been for envisioning a Land of Milk and Honey out here. When you roll snake eyes you just have to accept it. But Bento suspected his snake eyes had been rolled long ago and he'd never even touched the dice. Well, Solzhenitsyn did eight years for nothing and then got cancer. He just took it. Skip was doing fourteen years for what amounted to wrongful speech. He learned to take it too. You take it and go on. There's no meaning to it. It just is. Bento had to get his mind back to the right place, to count on nothing. It was this hope business that caused all the trouble.

After spending perhaps twenty minutes in the windowless room, Bento, still handcuffed, was escorted back through the hall. He thought he heard shouting but couldn't distinguish the source. Back in his cell, the man he'd seen snoring earlier was now sitting up in his bunk. He was a dust-caked Mexican laborer. And there were two additional cellmates, Latino gang kids maybe twenty years old, tattooed necks. They both wore tank tops and impossibly baggy hip-hop shorts whose bottoms reached their ankles. The smaller one was undeniably handsome, even with a shaved head. His partner was cursed with one of those unfortunate very low hairlines, the kind that doesn't leave much of a forehead. Even among werewolves he'd be a homely bastard. Bento would have felt sorry for him except he and his handsome buddy glared at him like he'd just shoved their grandmothers down the stairs. They were breathing a little too hard. So was the Bogart doppelgänger. Bento knew he'd interrupted a quarrel of some kind. He'd find out soon enough. Meanwhile he stepped over and took a long leak in the communal toilet. Home at last. Everybody pissing and shitting in front of everybody else like dogs or cavemen. There was no soap in the dish.

Bogey, who still hadn't greeted him, sat hunched against the wall like a fighter backed into a corner. His eyes were on the handsome kid, who at some point had moved into his personal space with what looked like baleful intentions. Bento turned to the werewolf. "What's this about?" he asked. His voice showed neither fear nor hostility.

"Not your business, motherfucker."

The formerly sleeping man shook his head, eyes squinting, signaling that all was not well. Bento, who'd already suffered more than his daily quota of man's inhumanity to man, casually walked up to Handsome, whose chin hung exposed like a sign on a hinge. Bento felt a familiar tingle of anticipation. "You guys shouldn't scare people like this," he said evenly. He knew it could be a big mistake tipping them off, but he couldn't resist. "Two scary guys like you? You need to show people a little mercy. Know something else? You really shouldn't do what you're thinking about doing. You should take a deep breath and go sit down. That's my advice. It's good advice." But Bento knew the kid couldn't back down in front of his furry partner, who was on his way over. By now the kid sensed what Bento would do but didn't know when, and while he considered the issue, Bento shot two stiff jabs into his nose, following with a right forearm to the head and a couple of left hooks to the body, all quick as he knew how. As his partner crumpled, the werewolf barreled into Bento, who turned and met him with two hard uppercuts. He really got his body weight behind the second one. Down went the werewolf, but Handsome was up again, all fear and rage, arms flailing.

Bento felt his ear strike the metal frame of the upper bunk. He stepped around to throw a combination, but the werewolf, on his feet again, got behind Bento and slid a forearm across his windpipe. Bento tried to press his chin down, but this was a strong bastard. How'd he get into this? By helping a guy. He recalled Skip telling him that you should never help anybody who won't stick up for himself. Bento worked both hands around the werewolf's thumb, but he couldn't pry it back. By now he was unable to breathe. The good news was that Bogart, now risen from his bunk, had Handsome in a bear hug. Bento reached between his legs and yanked the werewolf's leg forward, toppling them backward. Bento landed on top with a thump. The kid let go and Bento, swallowing gallons of air, twisted himself around and hammered elbows into the head and face. He grabbed a thicket of the werewolf's hair in his fists and smashed the attached skull into the floor. Once, twice. It sounded like pool balls colliding. The werewolf whimpered like an injured puppy, cradling his arms around his head and bringing his knees into a fetal position. Bento resisted the temptation to inflict more harm. Bogey and Handsome were wrestling on their feet, looking for headlocks. The formerly snoring man watched, carefully uninvolved. "Let go," Bento said. He kicked Handsome in the ass. Still no response, so he snapped a couple shots into a kidney, and Handsome pulled away, his face twisted with suffering.

Massaging his throat and ear, Bento, still drinking air, wondered what had triggered all this. Just then the chubby cop showed up with a tray of hamburgers from somewhere. "What's been going on in there?"

The werewolf and Handsome made it to their feet. "I tripped, dawg," the werewolf said, one hand over his nose.

"You're bleeding all over the floor, asshole!"

"Where'm I supposed to?"

"Over the toilet. . . . Go on. You're making a mess."

The werewolf made it over there and grabbed some toilet paper. "You oughta trip more often," the cop told him.

"It suits you." He looked from man to man and shook his head, no doubt worrying about paperwork and other possible aggravations. He turned to Bogey, who was breathing harder than Bento. "You see what happened?"

"I didn't see . . . anything."

"And you?"

The former snoring man shrugged.

"You must have seen something," the cop said.

"Dint see nothing," he said. "Why? Something happen?" It was the first time Bento heard him speak.

"I better call a doctor," the cop said.

"Don't need one, dawg," said the werewolf. Leaning over the toilet, he shook his head in disgust. The cop spent several moments watching them all like they were chimps, then walked off. His lack of concern, it seemed to Bento, had built a smidgeon of community spirit among cellmates. Bento felt looser, more secure. But that wasn't all good news. He should be at home out there, not in here.

"Stupid fucks," he said to the kids, who looked everywhere but at Bogey or Bento. "You think you're the only ones pissed off you're here? You wouldn't last ten minutes in a real jail. Little pissants." They moved to the far end of the cell. Bogart looked a little uncertain, maybe fearing Bento would turn on him too.

Bento grabbed a burger off the tray. "You did okay," he said.

"Thanks," Bogey said. "I'm way too old for this shit."

"How old are you, anyway?"

"I went to school back when cheerleaders didn't have tattoos or nipple studs or anything. At least I don't think they did. Can't say for sure. They never let me near their nipples."

"And how old is that?"

"Fifty."

The lukewarm hamburger was delicious. Bento tried not to gulp it down like a pig. The snorer was already on his second burger.

"Tell me something," Bento said to Bogey. "You weren't asking those guys questions, were you? About what got them in here? Stuff like that?" Before getting an answer, he held the tray out toward the gangsters. "You want burgers?" he shouted. They looked at each other and silently came over to fetch two each, then scooted back to their own side of the green line. They'd only been trying to do what had been done to them their whole lives and were largely unaware of other possibilities. They could become failed poets, for example. Girls dig failed poets.

"Just what," Bento asked Bogey, "did you say to them?"

He shook his head. "I get it. I was dumb."

"We're all dumb. That's why we're here. Anyway, they'd have found some excuse to fuck with you," Bento lied. "People throw you in jail, it puts you in a bad mood."

"Really."

"It's a fact. So there's another good rule—don't go to jail."

The snorer chuckled. He had a jovial face and was about five foot six with fullback shoulders. "A lot a guys," he said, "they don't like them kinda questions. I wanted to tell 'im, but it wasn't none a my business. Me, I don't care none. Ask me anything. I'm called Arturo." He extended his hand first to Bogart and then Bento.

"You look a lot like that guy in the movies," he said to the Bogart double whose actual name Bento couldn't recall.

"You mean Bogey," Bento said.

"That's the one. Okay if I call you Bogey?"

"Sure."

"Won't make you sore or nothing?"

"I prefer to get sore. It makes the time pass."

Bento explained he was paying for someone's clerical error. A box left unchecked or a space unfilled. Bogey didn't ask him what he'd gone to prison for. Perhaps he'd learned from his recent experience.

"What happened to me is my mother-in-law," said Arturo.

"Your mother-in-law?" asked Bogey.

About this time the two gang kids sidled over to check the burger situation. There were three left, and everyone signaled them to finish them off. Apparently feeling cozier with their surroundings, the kids stuck around while Arturo explained that he was a sheet metal worker who was on a job installing heating and cooling vents for a new science building going up at USC. "If they cure cancer in that building, something like that, then I helped cure cancer."

Bento: "Didn't you say something about your mother-in-law?"

"Right. She cleans a lady's house over here on Eighteenth Street. Me and another guy, we had to pick up some materials over across the freeway. So we stopped by 'cause she had my wife's cell phone."

Bogey: "You're in here for picking up your wife's cell phone?"

"No. For beating her to death with the electric coffee pot." He continued as though describing a minor traffic mishap. "My mother-in-law, she's wearing glasses I got for her last week. Drove her down, paid for everything, 'n' today she's yellin' at me for tracking in mud or something, I don't know, right in front of my frien'." He shook his head. "She's not dead exactly. They got her on—whaddaya call it when they got machines doing everything for them?"

"Life support?" somebody said.

"That's it. They gonna pull the plug probably tomorrow . . . I never shoulda got her no glasses."

Later the lights went off without warning. Bogey, speaking softly, called out to Bento in the darkness, "Kid, you got a job out there?"

"No."

"What's your plan?"

"What was your plan when you pissed off the blue cop?"

"I was on my way to work. That's what I wanted to talk to you about."

CHAPTER 8

From the hospital, Sussman and Pick went straight to City Hall, where Officer Blue and his partner led them over one at a time to view some slim guy with a ponytail who looked nothing like the intruder. Next they looked through a computer stream of mug shots that were of no use. The man with the knife had his cap pulled down so low there hadn't been much to see of his face. What startled Sussman was the number of mug shots. Were this many menacing thugs actually running around out there?

On the way home they stopped at a yuppie coffee shop where customers sat around on second-hand living-room furniture. Pick went inside to fetch rolls, coffees, and newspapers. LA had only one metropolitan daily left, but there was also *USA Today* plus some neighborhood publications. In the commune, Sussman had seen only an occasional paper. Stretched out on the sofa at home, he wasn't quite ready to read stories about himself and turned first to arts and features, where he learned that some avant-garde chef was serving berries with raw rabbit. The idea was to take in the entire experience of the berry as it tastes to the rabbit in the wild. Or something like that. The food columnist, apparently unequipped to form rational judgments, neither agreed nor disagreed with the celebrated chef.

On the editorial page a columnist concluded that the dismal fiscal situation was "everybody's" fault, meaning, Sussman concluded, that the columnist was out of ideas. Turning to actual news, he learned that two days earlier several passengers were severely injured in another crash on LA's fumbling light rail system. Papers skimmed over possible root causes. Finally he turned to his own adventure at the beach. The stories implied that the prowler must have been a moron to stalk a novelist whose last big book was published in the eighties. He wasn't sure whether the writers were angrier at him for being not so famous anymore or at the intruder for choosing an inappropriate target and then running off like a startled roach. Despite widespread expectations, America didn't end up as an Orwellian state after all. Instead it mimicked Aldous Huxley's *Brave New World*, a twenty-first century domain where Alphas and Epsilons alike huddled around the Super Bowl half-time show while the mass media pursued assorted irrelevance.

The articles also informed Sussman he was a rude, drug-seeking grouch entirely unappreciative of the considerable efforts employed in his behalf by a heroically selfless hospital team even though he hadn't produced a noteworthy book since the Reagan Administration. It seemed to him that the two groups—hospital workers and journalists—were each feeding off the other, united in their hostility toward miserable washed-up Sussman. "Jesus, what'd I ever do to them?" he asked Pick.

Pick's duties, one of the stories informed media consumers, were similar to those performed by O. J. Simpson's Kato Kaelin, except that this particular lackey had some kind of romantic connection—ex-girlfriend, concubine something. Because the sex part wasn't nailed down, that added mystery to the always compelling ingredient of celebrity violence. Sussman was reminded once again why even before joining the commune he'd sworn off Googling himself. It led to Internet scribes who assumed an odd familiarity, as though they were intimately acquainted. He imagined lonely souls pounding out LOL on their melancholy keyboards. Their comments expanded rumors and guesses into assertions that become widely accepted as fact: Sussman suffered from lung cancer, was cruel to underlings, never personally engaged in military combat (true), or, like Camus's Meursault, failed to weep at his mother's funeral. His defenders, for the most part, didn't deny these fictional offenses but tried to justify them instead. Still, Pick reminded him, wasn't it better that they believe in imaginary misdeeds rather than get the real scoop?

CHAPTER 9

Pick wondered how a cop, of all people, could parade himself in self-inflicted Technicolor like this. And why did they let him carry a gun? Shouldn't he be vacuuming rugs at some multiplex?

"Look at him again. Carefully," said Gillespie, which was Officer Blue's name. So far his partner with the cornstalk transplants had said not one word. She stepped back to the peephole to take another look at the lithe young man with a short ponytail sitting alone at a table in a small, spare room. He had fierce black eyes and his complexion was the shade of winter grass.

"He doesn't look anything like him. I told you he was massive, round. Big, big muscles. A monster with a pushed-in face, and he wasn't white."

"Neither is this guy. Not entirely. You said he had a braid? Lookit that hair. He could braid it easy. Wait, don't step away. Those tattoos you saw? They could have been temporary. What do they call them? Henna."

"It's not him."

"What about we put a baseball cap on him?"

"I said no."

"You were scared, confused. The mind plays tricks. You don't want to make a mistake. Take your time." Oddly, you could pretty much understand what he was saying even though Officer Blue barely moved his lips. An odd affectation. Maybe he was concealing bad teeth.

"I don't need more time. It's not him. If Sussman thinks it is, he's wrong." She stepped away from the window.

"So you think your pal ID'd him? What makes you think so?"

"Mr. Sussman and I are not pals."

"Why do you think Mr. Sussman picked him out?"

"That's not what I said."

"Listen, I'm not that hard to get along with."

"Where've you got Sussman?"

"He's around. Don't get silly on us, okay? We're on your side."

Here was a grown man who'd turned himself into a circus geek so he could escape a doomsday fantasy, and he was calling *her* silly. Well, maybe he deserved some credit for learning to live with his ludicrous hue. And he was sort of attractive if you went for the tall blue dumb insane types who talked like their lips were sewn together. The extraterrestrial freakishness of him was mildly enticing.

"You're trying to pin something on the guy in there, aren't you?"

Officer Blue/Gillespie shook his head and sighed, as though he were dealing with a child. Hard to tell what his partner was thinking. He must have been thinking something. Without excusing herself, Pick fished the cell phone from her purse and called Sussman. "Where are you?"

In the lobby, he told her.

"I'll come find you," she said. "If we're gone, who knows? Maybe they'll get to work and solve some crimes."

"Don't hold your breath," he said.

She turned to the silent partner on her way out. "Nice talking to you." Officer Blue followed her into the lobby. He flashed a smile. That was new.

"Feisty one, aren't you?" At least she thought he said "feisty," but it sounded almost like "tasty." Either way, Officer Blue was coming on to her.

"That's part of your job description? Describing witnesses to themselves?"

"I'm sorry if—I apologize for being short with you. We deal with so many, excuse my French, douche bags, we sometimes forget there are other kinds of people." Again a closed-mouth smile. Age-wise he was only a little older than her brother, the one she'd made up. It would be like dating the Green Lantern or the Blue Hornet. Was there really a Blue Hornet or had she made that up too? She'd have to look it up.

"Look, I don't want to frighten you, but this guy, who-ever he was, he could . . . sometimes these guys, they come back."

"I don't live there," she said. "Remember?"

"I remember. But that guy you just looked at? He's dan-gerous, believe me. You should see his rap sheet. I don't know what he's doing around here, but he's not here to do volunteer work."

"So you're going to get him first?"

"No, I'm going to be a good little cop and wait for him to commit a major crime. Too bad for his next victim, but that's how it works." He handed her a card. "Please don't lose this one. If you remember something else, anything at all, call, okay? No matter how small it seems."

"And if I don't? Remember anything else?" She shifted her feet, pointing one in front of the other, like a catalog model.

He touched her lightly on the arm and kept his hand there, half hovering, half touching. The knuckles were bluer than the adjacent skin. "Absolutely. Call anyway," he said. She'd already thought about the possibility of the knife person coming back to finish the job but was unsure whether a dead Sussman was good or bad for her. She couldn't bear to look too closely into such matters, which is why, upon seeing the blade, she'd acted on instinct alone.

SHE FOUND Sussman inside the lobby, once again examining the hideous American eagle painting he'd stopped to investigate before they went off to find Officer Blue and his sidekick.

"Look," he told her, pointing to a bottom corner where the years 1776 and 1976 were inscribed. "It was done for the bicentennial. You're too young to remember the Ford Administration." He shook his head slowly. "An innocent time. We just didn't realize it." After three years of doing his Buddhist crap he was still a pontificating prick.

CHAPTER 10

Finding the right employees to pursue his schmoes' ragged resources was one of Philyaw's biggest headaches. That's one reason he tried to chase down the chicken girl. Besides, hiring a collector from inside a chicken suit was more fun than following your standard button-down *Fortune* 500 human resources strategies. Even if it was a dumb idea in the first place, it led him to this jailbird kid and if he worked out, Philyaw could feel better about his honking arrest. The kid's failure to jump at the opportunity was a positive indicator. In his experience people who actually *wanted* to be collectors were a sadistic bunch. They became emotional and bullied schmoes needlessly, careening senselessly from power-mad to patsy and back again.

"It's not like I don't appreciate the offer," the kid said. He was stretched out in the bunk across from Philyaw, hands cupping the back of his head. He had a respectably flat middle-class accent, another plus. Street inflections were unsettling. Not a particularly fair criterion, but Philyaw didn't have to get into the collection business to know life is pretty much unfair anyway. That's why he was in jail.

Eventually, whether he hired the kid or not, this whole episode would turn into just another funny story. But because he'd helped subdue one of the gang kids, now he could tell it with a little more pride. Stupid worrying about that sort of stuff at his age. But men were stupid. How else do you explain Pearl Harbor and Hiroshima?

"I know bill collecting doesn't sound very . . . what's the word?"

"Enticing?" the kid said.

"Exactly, not enticing. Or respectable. I didn't like the idea either before I got into it. You should come down and check it out though. It'll be different than you expect." Philyaw always said that about his trade. It's different than you expect. And for most people it was, though some of them still ended up hating it. This kid had a way about him. It wasn't so much that he could handle the punks so efficiently. It was his attitude while he did it—nothing personal, just tending to a chore. He wasn't overly impressed with himself.

"Look, I can't do the job, okay? And then you'll have to fire me."

"Who's talking about firing people?"

"I can't talk to people anymore. I don't know how."

"You're talking to me."

"So?"

"Whaddaya mean so? What am I? Chopped liver?"

"It's different."

"What makes it different?"

"I don't know. Because we're in here maybe. I told you. I just did four years."

"Nobody cares."

"Yes they do."

"So what're you gonna do? Even criminals have to talk to people. You know, like, *just the big bills, the jewelry too*, that sort of thing."

"Very funny."

"It's all the same, kid. In here, out there, talking's the same."

"So you've done a day and a half and you know all about it."

"You got it all built up in your mind like some wall that's not there. We're all the same. All schmoes."

"Schmoes," the kid said, verifying.

"People on the collection list. You should hear what they call us. Hey, I'm telling you, you'll be good. I can see it. You'll even like it. Honest, it's not what you expect."

"If this job's so great, how come you've got an opening? Somebody quit, right?"

"Two openings. They formed a partnership, went off on their own. First they copied a bunch of files, of course. They'll try to steal all my clients."

"You don't look too concerned."

"It's been tried before. No big deal. It's how I got my start."

They both laughed.

"How'd you get into it? The collection business."

"I'd tried different things. Nothing hit the way I wanted, but when customers owed me, I was always good at getting it. It was a natural evolution. Might be for you too."

"I don't even know when I'm getting out of here."

"Horowitz will get to the bottom of it."

"Horowitz?"

"My lawyer. At some point I'll get to a phone."

"I can't afford any lawyer."

"It's okay, kid. It's on my tab." He was wearing down. Throwing in Horowitz should clinch it.

"Look, I don't want to fuck up this time, understand? It's really important. I need to find something . . . right, something that feels right."

Monday morning when they changed shifts the jailers let Philyaw make all the phone calls he wanted. He tried to find his daughter first, but she didn't answer and her voice mail was at capacity. Not surprising. He found Horowitz though, who got both of them out two hours later. They dropped the charges against Philyaw and had been holding the kid for not showing up to a hearing that he couldn't get to because he was in the can. Classic *Catch-22* situation. But Horowitz thrived on untangling such knots. He should have been secretary of state or something. Trouble was, he had a law degree from a school that two years after he graduated signed a consent decree to cease and desist all operations without admitting to any of sixteen counts. Also, Horowitz once ran for president—or was it vice president?—on a third party ticket with a hooker running mate. Horowitz would murder his mother to get his face on TV. In fact, for all Philyaw knew, Horowitz *had* murdered his mother to get his face on TV. But give him a case and he'd back up entire squads of opposing attorneys.

Horowitz had never actually seen this blue cop, but he'd heard about him. His name was Gillespie, and he turned blue after drinking silver compound doses to ward off some sort of Y2K calamity, which was funny because no one even remembered Y2K anymore, but it stuck a permanent idiot stamp on the dumb bastard. Other cops, Horowitz said, agreed he was a dumb bastard and once placed a live raccoon in his locker. Horowitz, though, stuck up for him. "He's alive, right? The silver must have worked." Everybody's a comedian. "Ordinarily I enjoy collecting fees," he said, "but I don't see how we can file a complaint because he stood outside your cell and gave you a nasty look. Just keep me informed, okay? It's probably nothing."

CHAPTER 11

Liz had been dancing for a full three or four minutes with her eyes closed. She did that every once in a while, taking special notice of smells, breezes, and if she turned off her earphones, ambient sounds. It helped her appreciate whatever she might see when she opened them. Wisps of clouds, all sorts of birds. She couldn't tell one bird from another though, except for gulls when they strayed this far off the beach. Some of the stores along the street had flowers planted out front, but she didn't know one flower from another either. She was shockingly deficient in so many areas, but many of her weaknesses, she told herself, were correctable.

Opening her eyes, she took a good long look at the imperial, possibly life-shortening overhead transmission lines that led straight out of a gas-burning power plant on the water a couple of miles away. The imposing cables stood tall over a middle-aged white man emptying trash into the bins alongside the Laundromat next door. He was pulling junk from two shopping carts. It was remodeling detritus—broken bits of drywall, boards with nails in them, paint cans. And he was dumping it all into the wrong places, most of it going into the blue bin designated for bottles and paper. When that was full he dumped the rest into the green organic refuse bin. He probably had some kind of vendetta against recycling rules, part of a changing world he couldn't bear—hybrid vehicles, men marrying men, coons in the White House. Liz imagined this angry white man's home with an angry white man's wife and 2.3 angry white man's kids. Probably none of them in their whole lives would ever read a book, see a foreign film, or attend a lecture. Jesus, you're a bigoted jerk, she told herself and smiled behind the mask of her chicken costume. She considered approaching the man to correct his trash disposal methods, but the fowl suit rendered all her opinions useless. That was something she didn't want to think about, how a grievous socioeconomic station could devalue everything about you, turning even incontestable statements of fact into useless blather. At least little kids thought her suit was terrific, although older ones knew it represented something not altogether amusing. On her last break she'd posed with a toddler at the counter while his mom in high heels, polka-dot slacks, and earrings the size of thermos bottles snapped photos with her smartphone. Liz never spoke when she was in costume and Buddy had asked her never to take a kid on her lap. Apparently the insurance company didn't want to take the one-in-five-million chance the child would slide to the floor and crack his skull open. "They hate to be sued," Buddy explained. Buddy rolled his eyes to express his own opinion. He often strived to let people know he wasn't as dumb as the company and assumed his superiors would never hear of these infractions. Liz had been tempted to warn him against this behavior but was conscious of her lowly status even among other employees of their fast-food purgatory. Buddy was married with three kids and always behaved properly with her, wouldn't even countenance swear words. Another employee told her he'd had gang tattoos removed from his neck.

In the windowless restroom Liz quickly removed the chicken head and wiped the sweat from her face and hair with paper towels, then checked her cell for messages that never came. The restroom, as usual, would fail any fair-minded inspection, but the chicken person did get certain perks, and one of them was not having to take a turn cleaning it. Before putting it back on, she contemplated the yin and yang elements of the chicken head resting on the toilet paper roll: smothering her as it concealed her shame. You're going to look back at this and laugh, she told herself.

Back at her sidewalk station, Liz switched on an old Miami Sound Machine samba and danced softly in place. The routine was starting to feel too familiar. Every day out here widened the inescapable hole in her résumé and took her even farther from her destination. And it was difficult to relax at night hunkered down in the clamor of Value Motel, a way station for castaways sliding toward homelessness. Couples yelled, threw things, and batted each other around while the kids out on the asphalt gave birth to rap sheets. It wasn't the kind of home her parents had envisioned for their yet-to-be-born Elizabeta when they crossed *la frontera*.

Sometimes Liz wondered whether anyone profited from the bad breaks that assailed her and her family. Perhaps the owner of the *maquiladora* where her exiled mom and dad performed mind-numbing tasks for a dismal wage. She'd looked it up on the Internet, and the company was a subsidiary of a much bigger corporation headquartered in Bermuda. How do you assign responsibility when everything is tangled in credit default swaps and exchange-traded securities? It must be that way for a reason. But it made no sense for the world to train her to safeguard books, documents, and other vessels of art and knowledge and then deprive her of the chance to do it.

Liz turned to see a man who looked like . . . yes, like Bogart. What a curious dream, she thought. But wasn't she awake? He was speaking to her, but she couldn't hear over her earphones and traffic noise. She shook her head and shrugged her shoulders, so he raised his volume to a half shout. His name was Philyaw, she thought he said. Curious name. And he began telling her about his business. She couldn't catch all of it, but it made no difference. He'd seen her in costume so he was dead to her.

An eighteen-wheeler stopped very close to them at the edge of the sidewalk, its big diesel belching and harrumphing, waiting for the light to change up ahead. When it moved on, Liz heard the man say, "You'd be on the phone a lot." He handed her a card. Western Credit Associates. Could be anything. She handed it back.

"Chickens, we don't have pockets," she shouted over the noise.

He said something else she couldn't make out.

"Is this about a job?"

Now he shouted. "Sure! What'd you think?"

"I don't need no stinking job. I'm already a crucial cog in our dynamic new service economy."

The man looked at her curiously. He probably didn't get the reference to *The Treasure of the Sierra Madre*. It seemed particularly apt, given his Bogart appearance. Oh well.

"This job you're talking about, it's not an internship, is it?" She'd once run a law library for a group of attorneys, working for nothing until they couldn't string her along anymore and had to go out and find a fresh sucker.

Bogart shrugged his shoulders, indicating he hadn't heard her. Speaking louder, she added, "More important, how come you want a chicken? Chickens aren't particularly qualified. We can't even fly."

"We're a collection agency," he said, as though that explained it.

"Look, I've got to turn the music back on."

He pointed to the restaurant. Was he going to wait for her? Christ, he started heading over there. "Wait," she yelled out, catching up to him. "Give me back the card, okay?" She pulled down a zipper. "I've got pockets underneath."

"Call any time, today even," he said. "You don't have to be coy, okay?"

When she got back to the motel she tore the card in half and threw it in her waste can. It wasn't just that he knew of her hidden chicken identity. He wanted her to help him collect debts from people who were maybe even worse off than she was. After she watched bunny-ears TV for a while she fished the two pieces out of the waste can and stuck them in the Bible drawer. Who knew what tomorrow would bring? But Bogey's proposal was just another stairway to the wrong place. She already had a crappy job, and this one offered anonymity and left her mind free.

Two days later she was taking her trash to the motel dumpster when her cell phone rang. All around her kids were yelling, radios blaring, big rigs rolling along a freeway overpass. A dog was even barking. Lately her whole life seemed spent around sounds she didn't particularly want to hear. Liz couldn't recognize the caller's number and knew she should let it go to message mode, but curiosity got the best of her. "Hello," she said.

"Ms. . . . . Huizar?" Pronounced haltingly and Anglo-Saxonly as *Hwizz-air*, not *Weez-ahr*. A female voice.

"Yes?" Liz thought she heard the word "library" in the torrent of words that spilled out. "Look, I'm sorry. It's noisy here. May I call you back in five minutes?" She raced up the steps to her room.

The woman, a Mrs. Rasmussen, was calling for a Mr. Upchurch at a private library in Monterey. Liz dimly recalled sending a résumé there weeks earlier. "Mr. Upchurch would like to see you. Can you come up Thursday?"

"Thursday, I'm not sure, but—"

"Mr. Upchurch needs to wind this up quickly, and he has a very full schedule."

"It's about my résumé?"

"Yes, of course."

Liz was supposed to do her chicken dance Thursday. It was way too early in the relationship to ask for a day off. Maybe she could just tell the truth to Buddy and plead for mercy. Passing up the chance at a real job so she could dance on the sidewalk was crazy, but a Monterey round-trip would drink more than two tanks of gas, and the woman didn't say anything about expenses. "I'll try to rearrange my schedule. Is it okay if I call you back in the morning?" Mrs. Rasmussen was displeased but finally agreed as long as Liz called by ten. Despite these troublesome aspects she decided it was safe to view this as a positive development. Funny how things always came at you in bunches. First the chicken restaurant, then the collection agency, and now maybe even a *real* job. "Fucken A!" she shouted in her little room.

CHAPTER 12

Silent pernicious demons gained on a terrified Gillespie as he scrambled across a dark room with legs like sacks of sand. Light glowed from a corner of the ceiling. It was an open trapdoor that must lead to an attic. As he struggled to get up there, his pursuers grabbed him by the ankles with hot, steely hands. The physical pain and dread were all one, an indistinguishable horror. He couldn't scream, could only blubber like an infant. Scraping skin, he wriggled through the opening. His body was still maddeningly torpid, but this new place offered a seed of hope. Until he looked around to find himself in an identical dark room, another trapdoor in the corner of the ceiling, the demons still in pursuit. Oh no, no. "No, no, no!" Someone was shaking him. He curled up in a ball, covering his head, his face, his nuts. It was real. And he looked around and saw he was home in bed but felt no relief.

Tina watched him with concern, saying nothing. Nothing new about that. She'd already edged away in case he flailed his arms like he did sometimes. He tried to ignore his shame as she casually took everything in, the smug, unfeeling cunt.

"What time is it?" he asked her.

"It's almost seven. Your cell phone's been ringing."

"Why don't you ever wake me on time? . . . Cocksucker! Gimme my phone."

"I tried . . . to. You—" She mumbled the rest of it.

"Bullshit you tried. You forgot." Tina wouldn't ask him why he didn't set the alarm. That was one of the good things about his wife. She didn't try to win arguments. But it was one of the bad things too. She left the room and returned with his cell phone, which he took outside by the pool.

Shrek must have called seven times. It was unusual for him to call even once. Gillespie always called him. Maybe they were closing in. Any pressure at all and Shrek would open up like a can of tuna. They'd love it down at the station too. *D'ja hear? Smurfy got busted for the Sussman thing!* Nothing left to do but hunker down and hope no one stumbles down the right trail. But what about the money? Gillespie had counted on it. Jesus, he'd put $500 down on the boat.

He texted Shrek: "same place—4" Seconds later he got back an "ok." He'd have to hustle.

He found Shrek, his beloved braid cut off, standing in front of his mother's house near the airport. Guys like him stood in front of their mothers' houses all over the city, all over the country, selling drugs. They were peaches you picked off a tree whenever you needed one. "You didn't write down the address," Shrek complained as soon as Gillespie pulled over. He climbed in and was struggling with his seat belt as Gillespie pulled away. He could barely get it around him.

"One eighteen, I said. One eighteen's not hard to remember." Gillespie didn't holler. Hollering could frighten Shrek into making more mistakes, stupider ones. Handling him was like trying to call cats. Dumb, nervous cats. But it wasn't just that he didn't want to scare him. The truth was, Shrek was the only friend he had left in this asshole city. A mile down the road Gillespie pulled into the lot outside a diner. Shrek went inside and brought back their drinks—coffee for Gillespie, a Perrier for himself. Gillespie always got a kick out of the fairy dust substances Shrek was faithful to.

Twenty years earlier seven people had been murdered in this diner, herded into the kitchen by crazy stickup men and shot like pigs. After such calamities places would always change hands, get a new name, a new sign out front. But Gillespie didn't forget. They never found the killers, never cleared the books anyway, though they were almost certainly dead or in prison for other crimes.

"All that money sitting there," Gillespie said. "Twenty thou at least. Just like I said. Right next door. Open sesame. What the fuck. I mean I could find a thousand guys who know the difference between one eighteen and one fucking sixteen. I try doing you a favor and this is what I get."

"But those addresses, they're all screwed up down there. It's like the people living there? They don't want you to know which is which. And you told me not to write anything down, remember? It's what you said."

He was right on both counts. Don't put it in writing. Number two rule behind don't get caught. Addresses down there were hard to find. People with serious money were secretive. Gillespie should have cruised past and checked it out. Instead he'd provided inexact information and shifted the blame. Such a sweet setup too. Gypsy jokers don't call 9-1-1 when somebody steals their drug money.

"Guess I can't go back, huh?" Shrek asked feebly. When he got nervous, as he was now, he tilted his head up as he spoke, squinting slightly as though reciting something from memory.

"You think that douche bag's still there? He probably hauled ass back to the desert soon as the patrol cars left. Look, numb-nuts, tell me something, will you? Will you tell me?"

He'd promised Shrek never to call him numb-nuts but couldn't bring himself to apologize. Shrek was looking at him funny, like he expected something.

"What?" said Gillespie.

"You wanted to ask me something."

Christ, what was it? He must be losing his mind.

"We were talking about the douche bag," Shrek said helpfully.

"Now I remember. It was—I'm not even gonna ask you what you were doing in the closet. But the knife, what's with the knife?"

"I don't know. I got scared."

"An old guy you could break in half and you got scared."

"You said it was a dealer there."

"Next door, numb-nuts. Next *door* there was a dealer. Probably got taken down by somebody else by now."

At least nobody found any DNA or fibers. In fact, except for Sussman's statement and the one from that vampire chick, there was no evidence that anything occurred at his place. The gal, she resented Sussman, maybe even hated him. That was easy to spot. *The enemy of my enemy is my friend.* He'd heard that somewhere. Maybe in a Batman movie. And if no crime occurred at Sussman's place, if no one jumped out of that closet, everyone would stop looking for Shrek. Sussman would just be an old man who fell down and made up a story. A has-been looking for attention, a treasonous asshole exposed for his lies, leaving Gillespie in the clear.

CHAPTER 13

Liz made the appointment with Philyaw two days after returning from the interview in Monterey. Dressed in a very white-person blouse and pants suit, she parked two blocks from the address in El Segundo so no one would see her Gypsy car. She must not look or behave like someone who'd spent the night in the backseat splayed out atop her belongings in a precise position calculated to avoid hard objects.

The address was in a section of old warehouses, block after block and spooky even in daylight, as forsaken as the neighborhood where she'd passed the night next to a refinery. You could park your live-in car all night in depopulated neighborhoods like these and no one minded. But it was also the kind of place where you could drag a body into a car trunk with nobody around to care. Freddy Krueger-land.

Each time she ran out of motel money she felt herself falling deeper down the rabbit hole. The scrambled feeling in her gut seemed practically permanent now. Sometimes she thought about college classmates whose families protected them from eviction, repossession, fast-food drudgery, and meal skipping. They didn't always have sparkling personalities, but their circumstances made sparkling personalities possible. If they fell they never hit the ground. Liz always knew a fall could break her neck.

At this point Philyaw the Bogart character was her only live hope. But a man who'd seen her dressed as a chicken was a tenuous, frolicsome sort of hope, like one of those wild schemes you'd see in a silly movie. Not used to her high heels, she carefully picked her way across the dirt, weeds, and sparse gravel that passed for a parking lot. She steered around a used condom. Could there really be an office around here? Finally she spotted a green door atop a tall strip of reddish brown wooden steps along the side of the building. But she couldn't make out the little sign next to the door. After climbing up there she discovered it said Pacific Asset Management instead of Western Credit Associates. Now what? That's when she heard someone else climbing the steps. A tall, good-looking guy with dark hair pulled back into a small ponytail. She was just about to ask him whether she had the right place when the door opened and a woman stepped out, colliding with Liz.

"Yeeee! . . ." The woman straightened her glasses, which had giant baby-blue frames. She was fiftyish with sparse red hair that had been chemically ravaged, three-inch heels and turquoise slacks clinging to a slender figure. Frilly blouse with tanned, aggressive cleavage.

They apologized to each other, and when Liz asked whether she was okay the woman briefly made a face, a half smile mixed with a squint, signaling just what it was hard to tell. She held an unlighted cigarette and throwaway lighter, but the collision had snapped the cigarette in two. She carefully lit the stub and inhaled deeply. "Can I help you?" she asked in a froggish voice. Exhale.

"Is this Western Credit Associates?"

"Who's there?" The voice came from somewhere inside. Philyaw the Bogart man stepped out on the landing and asked her inside. The tall guy who'd come up behind her still hadn't said a word. He followed Liz into a room as big as a basketball court, obviously an ex-storage facility. Mostly bare, it contained a dozen or so metal desks concentrated near the door, maybe half of them used by employees conversing into headsets. There were big windows up high, some of them broken. Across the room pigeons roosted on an overhead pipe. No one looked dressed for success. Books and papers were piled atop a few beat-up filing cabinets. Gray linoleum floor in the office section, rough-cut wood everywhere else. Nothing on the walls but a couple calendars and a big *Reservoir Dogs* movie poster, no frame. "You need to change the sign," Liz told Philyaw. He nodded but didn't seem terribly concerned.

"Not really," said the collision survivor. She stood in the doorway, holding the lighted butt outside. "We don't need anybody finding us."

"Nobody we don't *want* finding us," said a fat man sitting at one of the desks.

"Lots a crazies out there," explained the woman. "Even got some right here." She jabbed a thumb in the direction of the fat man. He wore an Apache-style headband and sported thick, graying facial hair carefully trimmed into a neat Vandyke that didn't match his sloppy persona. One more thing: he was shirtless.

"Please Speed, I'm begging you," Philyaw told him. "We've got visitors."

The fat man smiled at Liz and said, "Talk to Sandra."

"Forget it. I'm not apologizing," said the woman, who'd stubbed out the butt.

"I guess you might as well see this now," Philyaw told Liz. "It would have come up eventually."

The woman fished a shirt out of the fat man's wastebasket and held it up for Liz. "Does this or does this not clash with his pants?" The shirt was blue and white gingham, the trousers medium brown, almost tan.

"She's always knocking my clothes," the fat man said. "The shirt offends her, so I decided to make her happy."

"Why don't you decide?" Philyaw told Liz. "What's the truth here?"

The tall guy who'd followed Liz up the steps had seated himself at a desk and was looking through a file. "Be careful," he said. "Most people can't *handle* the truth."

Liz, still standing, rested her chin on one fist in the manner of Rodin's "The Thinker." "Are the pants brown or tan?" she asked. "That's what it comes down to."

"Brown," said the woman.

"Tan," said the fat man.

Liz looked carefully at the fat man. "Here's my ruling. In this particular instance, the shirt matches your beautiful blue eyes. That makes the color of the trousers a moot point. So although I can understand why the question was raised,"— she smiled toward the woman—"it's okay."

The woman and the fat man shook hands to applause and she helped him on with his shirt. Meanwhile Liz became aware that the room didn't smell quite right. Not awful, but not something you'd particularly want to smell either. Some of it was owing to the pigeons, but it was probably mostly from the crates and pallets of merchandise stored here when it had been a functioning warehouse. Onions, apples, potatoes. Even plastic widgets from China have a certain aroma. The smells were all mixed into a too-sweet background stench of fermented produce plus the peculiar ghost odor of cardboard boxes and the raw, cheap lumber of the pallets that once made a home here. Philyaw seemed to know what she was thinking. "It wasn't always an office," he explained. No kidding. "Sat empty a long time and . . . Well, anyway, they offered me a long-term lease so I added some paint, thought I was brilliant. Then summer hit and I had to put in air-conditioning, but we were still broiling so I paid a fortune for some half-assed roof insulation. Anyway, there's plenty of parking. I'm getting ahead of myself, but this job comes with health insurance. Starts the first of the month. We figure that beats office space in Beverly Hills with a big fountain in the courtyard."

Fat man: "It's good, too, the health insurance."

"They won't give me oxygen, though," said the woman.

Said Philyaw, "You let smokers take home oxygen and they blow themselves up. Listen," he told Liz, "I'm gonna give you—I guess you could call it an orientation. Please, take a seat." Seating himself next to her, Philyaw called over to the fat man, "Speed, whaddaya got?"

The fat man moved an earphone off and covered the mouthpiece with a meaty hand. "That lying prick who lives in Jack Benny's old house," he said.

"Is it the gay guy?"

"If he's not gay, then there aren't any gay people—it's all a hoax."

"Is he on the line?" asked Philyaw.

The fat man held up one finger in a waiting gesture.

"If you reach him, put him on speakerphone."

"Hello, this is Mr. Holland from Internal Revenue," said the fat man, impressively calm and authoritative. He sat on one of those beaded seat liners you see beneath the butts of Tijuana cabdrivers and reminded Liz of that immense *Star Wars* creature who kept Princess Leia on a leash in one of the sequels. Jabba the Hutt. "We've been trying to get him his refund. Is Mr. Millincamp there? . . . Okay." The fat man pressed a button.

"This is Millincamp," a wary voice said over the speaker.

Fat man: "It's about that $4,632.11 Mr. Millincamp."

"My God, didn't I tell you—"

"Green, Western Credit. How ya doing, Mr. Millincamp?"

"My, you're a sly villain . . . What'syourname?"

"Green. Listen, I've got a new proposition for you, Mr. Millincamp."

"If your name's Green, mine's Rockefeller."

"Look, you start to pay this down, just start is all, just a little a month, not enough to hurt you, and we'll stop calling, all right?"

"Excellent. I can send you like ten bucks and you'll go away for good?"

"Mr. Millincamp, it's like this—"

Philyaw signaled thumbs down to the fat man, who turned off the speakerphone and continued the conversation over his headset. Philyaw swiveled his chair to face the opposite direction and signaled to Liz to do the same.

"Forget everything you think you know about collecting bills, okay?" he told her. "What we do here isn't what you— what we're dealing with is schmoes."

"And there are three kinds," said a light-skinned black man seated nearby. He spoke with a soft cushiony voice that surrounded you like an old leather chair. He was fleshy but not fat. Both his eyelids and the big bags under his eyes were intensely dark, almost pure black. Set off against his tan complexion, they made him look like a serene raccoon.

"Yeah," said Philyaw. "Speed's talking to our favorite kind. At least they're my favorite. The guys who were out to screw you from the beginning. Never intended to pay. They can, they just don't want to."

"It's their hobby," said the black man.

"Do they ever get away with it?" she asked.

"Funny part is, mostly they do," said Philyaw. "Babe Ruth, he was born to swing a bat. This guy Speed's talking to, if he's the one I'm thinking of, he's the Babe Ruth of deadbeats. He once went to this big charity banquet run by, what'shisname? Eddie, who's the guy—You know, he was in the Coen brothers movie where they escape from the chain gang?"

"John Turturro?" said the black man with the light complexion.

"No, the leading man. You know."

"George Clooney."

"Right. George Clooney. It's to raise money for starving people in Somalia, I think it was."

"South Sudan," Eddie said.

"Right. The banquet's like $2,000 a head. This guy . . . Millincamp? He's the one, isn't he?"

"No," said Eddie, "Millincamp's the one who lives in Jack Benny's old house."

"I know that, but isn't he—"

"Weitzel, he's the one ordered banquet tickets from Clooney."

"You sure?"

"Hundred percent."

"Thank you," Philyaw said. "This guy, what's his name? He gets a whole table."

"Weitzel," said Eddie.

"Yeah. He's a, you know—likes to act like a big shot. So he gets tickets for all his friends so they can schmooze with the stars. He buys up a whole table, and everybody drinks the wine, eats the food. I think he even bought some crap from the silent auction. Isn't that right?"

"Yup," Eddie said. "Got himself a jersey signed by one a the Lakers. Somebody who got traded though."

"There you go. All kinds of collectors' stuff. Outbidding people who really woulda paid for it."

"The next week he files Chapter Seven," Eddie said.

"Yep," Philyaw said. "The guy, he's got money, I know he does, but it's hidden, see? He knew he was going to file the whole time, had a bankruptcy lawyer in his pocket before he reserved the table. I mean, can you believe this guy? Ripped off a charity. A goddamn charity!"

"They're Phil's favorites, guys like that," Eddie said.

"I told her. See, they're professional deadbeats. All the time you're trying to collect, they're laughing at you, running up new bills somewhere else. These people aren't even human enough to be considered schmoes. Start chopping off fingers and they still won't give up a dollar. Screwing you, to them it's . . . it's their life."

"Their religion," said Eddie.

"Exactly," said Philyaw. "If they're not swindling somebody they can't get out of bed in the morning. They're going to screw you and that's just the way it is. They're a waste of time. But," he said, and paused.

"We don't let them off easy," said the fat man, off the phone now.

"At least not every time," Philyaw said. "And if we smell assets somewhere, we get our lawyer to file for a judgment. Then we hire skip tracers—specialists—to find the money. They take a big chunk, but at least we get something."

"Phil's got a special name for the super deadbeats," the fat man said. "Ask him."

"Let's save it for later. Don't want to overwhelm her the first day."

Phil's wording strongly implied that she was already hired, but no one had mentioned wages, for example. That's how the law firm worked her wage-free internship.

"Later when?" Liz asked. "After I take the oath?"

"Oath. I like that," Philyaw said.

"The oath's just part of it," Eddie said.

"Every time I try to get out," injected the tall cute guy with the ponytail—

"They pull me back in!" they all shouted in chorus.

Liz knew all this was for her benefit and that she ought to be flattered, but she couldn't forget that underneath it all they made a living off the misery of others. "When you collect, how much of it do you get to keep?" she asked.

"Half, usually," said Philyaw. "Sometimes I buy the debt at a discount or make other kinds of deals, but usually it's half."

"Some of these doctors had their way, it would be nothing," said Eddie.

"They've got corkscrews for hearts," Philyaw said. "They call you and say, 'Forget about the Dingle account' or whatever. Right away I know this Dingle, he must have paid up."

Liz didn't understand what they were talking about and wasn't sure whether to admit it. Her puzzlement must have showed. "See, the schmoes, they're supposed to send the money to us," Philyaw explained. "But sometimes they send it to the client instead. We still get the commission. We're supposed to, anyway. So when I hear, 'Forget about this guy,' right away I know what happened. 'Doctor,' I say, 'you'll never believe this, but Dingle called and said he mailed you a check yesterday.' 'Really? I'll watch for it.' Like he has no idea. You take Sears, somebody like that, they don't try to rip you off. But these doctors?" He shook his head.

"Chiropractors are the worst," Speed the fat man said.

"You're just bigoted," said the guy with the ponytail. His name was Bento, Liz would soon find out, and he was only recently hired. But he'd already proven himself a natural, everyone said.

"Not all a them though," Eddie said. "Chiropractors, I mean. Not all a them are crooks."

"Maybe, but they're still quacks," said Speed.

"No worse than fortune-tellers," said the redheaded woman, whose name was Sandra. As she spoke she kept her eyes on a TV screen on her desk. It was tuned to a glittery bracelet on the Shopping Channel, volume muted.

"An astrologer told my mom a bunch of weird stuff that all came true," said Speed.

"Most of 'em are okay, chiropractors," Philyaw concluded.

"Okay they cure you?" Sandra asked him. "Or okay they don't try to chisel us out of commissions?"

"Commissions is all I know, sweetheart. The rest is silence."

"What the hell's that mean?" asked Sandra.

"How do I know? But it's Shakespeare, I think. I'm trying to show Liz here we've got some culture."

The last words of Hamlet, Liz almost said, but decided that would be showing off. "I guess you have a lot more business these days, since, you know, so many people are broke," she said.

"Used to be," said Eddie, "you didn't have as many schmoes to chase, but it wasn't so hard to collect. Now? Lotsa money owed, but you gotta fight for every dollar."

"It'll get harder after the massacres," said Speed the fat man.

"Who's getting massacred?" asked Sandra, eyes on the screen.

"People dying because they can't afford medicine, that's a massacre."

"C'mon, no politics today, okay?" Sandra said. "It just gets everybody mad. Try to be a little more shallow."

"Politics," said Speed, "is how they can make loans at 360 percent and not go to jail."

"We don't take those customers," Philyaw told Liz. "Payday lenders, he's talking about."

"You said three kinds," Liz said. "Three kinds of schmoes."

The question, she saw, pleased Philyaw. He opened his mouth wide for an instant in a half smile, half grimace as though he were examining his teeth in a mirror. It was something she'd seen the real Bogart do.

"Right," he said. "After the lying, thieving deadbeats, you get the second kind. They're not just broke . . ."

"They're one step from the curb," said Eddie. "Pawning stuff, maybe collecting cans. You don't waste time on them."

"You go on to the next schmo," said ponytailed Bento.

Eddie: "Like a guy I talked to last week. Some kind of computer guy. Used to fly out to Aspen on weekends, stuff like that. Now he gets these little jobs sometimes—he's practically crying telling me this—but his laptop blew out on him. He's trying to work out of the library."

Speed: "He might even be homeless by now."

Liz felt a little sick to her stomach, as though she'd swallowed something sour and noxious. Maybe they'd figured her out already. Saw through her thrift store blouse. It's their business to see things like that. "What did you tell him?" she asked, controlling her breathing.

"I don't know," Eddie said. "Wished him luck, told him to keep in touch. I mean, what can you say?"

"You loaned him money, didn't you?" Sandra said.

"Bullshit."

"Swear on your kids." She shook her head and turned away from the TV screen. "Like I said, you loaned him money."

"Didn't."

"Not yet," said Sandra.

Philyaw looked suspiciously at Eddie as he told Liz, "This place can be like an ER. We see people cut up, smashed, burned. You gotta leave it here . . . Sandra, you ever take this stuff home with you?"

"All I take home with me is office supplies."

"Anyway," said Philyaw, "the third kind, he's the one that keeps us in business."

"God bless 'em," Eddie said.

Philyaw: "He's got a job, he'd like to pay his bills, but he's over his head, can't handle credit. Hasn't got a clue."

"Might even pay 5, 10 percent off the top just to get his paycheck cashed," said Eddie. "It's what they charge, those currency exchange joints."

"A guy in that situation, he needs somebody to educate him," said Philyaw.

Speed: "First thing, we steer him into a credit union to cash his checks. Then we sit down, see what's coming in, going out, how much he's in the hole, utilities, rent, all a that. And figure out a plan, a budget, you know?"

"I did that for a guy once and he was paying okay and everything," said Eddie. "One day he calls and says, 'Okay if I send you a little more this month? I'm all caught up.' He wanted my permission."

They were trying to come off as a squad of Mother Teresas, but Liz wasn't sure she bought it. "When people don't pay their bills," said Philyaw, perhaps reading her mind, "it's like shoplifting. Everybody else pays their tab." Maybe he even believed it. He didn't seem like a monster.

After thirty or forty minutes Philyaw prodded her into making a collection call. "It only takes a minute. Go on. You're Miss White. Just dive in. Don't think about it. You can think later."

"We don't think," said Eddie.

"We calculate," said Philyaw, handing her an information sheet.

Eddie: "It's like riding a bicycle, kid. Just get on and you'll figure it out."

She looked from one to the other. "Which is it? Dive in or pedal?"

"We got another joker," said Eddie. "Like Bento."

"Okay, I'm Miss White, right? Is everybody color-coded?"

"Simple names, easy to remember," said Philyaw. "Jones, Vance, nothing that announces race, creed or color. No Gomezes or Booker Ts."

"Or Chungs or Goldbergs," said Sandra.

"Sometimes these discussions get, you know, kind of heated," said Philyaw. "Mostly we want to make it easy for them. When they call and ask for Miss White, she's always here. Whoever sits at that desk, that's Miss White. The desks around here are like restrooms. Boys, girls."

"Don't they ever notice? When you switch people, I mean."

"Never," said Speed.

"Just remind him he's got a payment due," said Philyaw. "The phone number, the amount, it's on the bottom of the sheet." Liz punched the number into her phone. Eddie put the call on speaker phone.

"Hello." A man picked up. Liz heard in his voice that whatever bad news she might give him would be no surprise. After identifying herself, she said, "You have a sixty-two-dollar payment due Thursday?" She didn't feel as revolted as she thought she would. It was only borderline unpleasant, like mediocre sex.

"Yeah?"

What now? Philyaw scribbled on a slip of paper. "We're just calling to remind you, sir," Liz said.

"All right." He wasn't happy about it, but he wasn't happy about anything. When she hung up, they were all looking at her intently.

"Well," said Sandra, "there goes that cherry."

Liz wanted to smile but couldn't. "Why'd we even make that call?"

"Because he needs to be policed," Philyaw said. "Some people need policing. But listen, you got to get that question mark out of your voice, okay? It's not, 'You have a payment due?' It's, 'You have a payment due!' Understand? Forceful. Confident. Very sure of yourself. We always know, okay? We don't ask anybody's permission. We're the Big Kahuna. Godzilla."

"Godzilla's badder brother," Eddie said.

"And don't lend them anything," said Sandra.

"Let me show you something about our files," Philyaw said.

As Liz followed him toward a computer she moved closer to him and half whispered, "Can I talk to you?"

He led her outside onto the landing. "Mr. Philyaw," she said—"

"Phil," he said.

"Phil, I'm going to do something—it's something you're not supposed to do in interviews, okay? I'm—I think you're a nice guy. You picked me off the street, and I'm grateful."

"It's not like that at all. You were doing honest work."

She shook her head.

"I mean, you weren't turning tricks. Which, by the way, wouldn't exclude you," he said. She saw his instant embarrassment. "Not you personally. You know, hypothetically speaking."

She nodded, trying to reassure him.

"Okay, what's this thing you're not supposed to do?"

"I already did it. I told you you're a nice guy."

"Thanks. You're the first. Are we done out here?"

He was trying to show a hard-hearted cynicism that wasn't in his heart, like Bogart, who told the troubled bride to go back to Bulgaria.

"Making that call, Phil, it felt . . ."

He nodded. When he saw she wasn't going to finish the sentence, he said, "We have to make collections sweetheart. Otherwise we're all unemployed."

"Look, what do you call them? The deadbeat schmoes out to get you from the beginning. They . . . you said you had a name for them."

"Madoffs," he said.

"How many have you got?"

"Hundreds. We could get more if we wanted. The other agencies, they throw them back eventually."

"Are commissions bigger? For Madoffs?"

"Yeah."

"So they're mostly just thieves, right?"

"Not mostly. All. They're lying, thieving bastards."

"Then they're the ones I want. Give them all to me. The con artists, whatever. Let me have them before you give up. I want all the assholes."

"But they're my hobby."

"You *said* there are hundreds. Keep some for yourself too."

"I don't know, kid. They're tough cookies, Madoffs. I don't want you discouraged right away. A lot of agencies don't take them at all."

"Then they should grow some balls."

He smiled. "But you have to pull your weight here, kid. I can only be so nice. We haven't talked salary."

"I'll follow them into hell if I have to. But sure, let's talk salary. And commissions. There's a nice big commission attached to Madoff money, right?"

He nodded, obviously pleased.

The base salary was more than twice the minimum wage, and the commissions sounded generous. She'd brought a résumé but never got the chance to show it. He just trusted a chicken dancer.

"You can wait out here awhile," he said. "Before you come back in." That was how he acknowledged her tears.

CHAPTER 14

Bento tried to ignore willowy Liz's long, slim, fingers, perfect for piano sonatas and leisurely sex. Yet her contemplative smile and oddly melancholy nature made him want to cuddle her more than anything else. He pictured Liz going home at night to change the litter box and cook sad, solitary meals, cutting all the recipes in half. Their clumsy office interactions convinced him she was especially aware of him too and, like him, knew better than to get involved with someone close enough to pass the salt.

On days she didn't go to lunch with Sandra she ate at her desk hunched over a book. Her portable electronic gizmos consisted only of a simple cell phone, probably prepaid like his, for customers low on money and credit. But unlike Bento, she undoubtedly could handle apps and other techno-mysteries. An old con once pointed out to him that prison locks you in a time machine. You don't live much differently than cons lived fifty years earlier. Yet beyond the walls, the world keeps changing.

What conversation there was between Bento and Liz was derived from hard-luck stories they heard day after day from schmoes whose ignorance of even the simplest financial principles never seemed to find a bottom. Liz was like their scolding sister, firm but never mean-spirited, and they never seemed to wear her out, even when her elementary questions about the terms of their obligations generated confusion and dead phone space. They were tots wandering through an alien forest without maps or flashlights. Hungry salespeople stuck them with dating and mating services, auditorium-sized home theater systems, ocean cruises, theme park passes, condo time shares, commemorative coins, expert credit monitoring, and finally cut-rate divorce and bankruptcy deals. Bento noticed that one of his schmoes had been paying ninety-three dollars a month to something called the Nostro Institute. This turned out to be a one-man entity. Nostro used his "spiritual and psychic abilities to perceive, uncover and remove the lies and negative energy that have been keeping you from connecting with your true, divine, higher self." All sessions were superconfidential and conducted by phone. The schmo, when queried by Bento, hadn't realized that Nostro was still charging her. She hadn't spoken with him for months. "I wonder if he's found anything new," she said.

His first week Bento made a snide remark about a schmo who'd purchased a no-money-down course on how to get rich from generic "collectibles." Eddie looked at him with his all-knowing baggy eyes and said, "You should see what the judge did to me in my second divorce. Compared to me, your guy's a genius."

Added Phil: "No offense, kid, but don't be an asshole." There were rules about how hard you could laugh at schmoes. Yet sprinkled among them were wife-beaters, thieves, lazy pricks, and lots and lots of liars.

The schmoes' biggest problem, said Speed, was that they didn't know how the world works: "Somebody calls 'em and tells 'em they won a contest, and they actually believe they won a contest."

Bento also marveled that nowhere within the K-12 curriculum did educators make room for a course on how to live in the world: how to examine labels for poisonous ingredients, how to avoid buying cars that had been submerged in floods, how to not get beaten up by your boyfriend. The list of significant information Americans didn't possess was deplorably long. They spent themselves into deep holes with $200 gym shoes and $4,000 excursions to Disney World.

They were like Pacific Islanders in postwar cargo cults. They had no grasp of what made glittery stuff appear or fail to appear, but they needed to keep it coming.

An endless supply of connivers found the slowest members of the herd and knew just what to say and how to say it to strip them clean. These hyenas could be behind you at the movie counter and you'd never smell it, never know they spent the day consuming the flesh of weak-minded consumers. One schmo told Bento how excited the registrar at the modeling school was after seeing her photo. "He says there's lots of openings for full-figured gals. The opportunities are enormous, he said. That's the word he used—enormous." Some predators held twisted views of what constituted humor. Bento made a notation to try to bargain down the bill for her. Hustlers like that sometimes settled for as little as 25 or 30 percent of the total.

Once or twice a week Phil invited Bento to a little hole-in-the wall bar inside a fraying shopping center. Bartenders loved Phil. He might look like Bogey, but he tipped like Sinatra. Even Bento's parole agent—a thundering maniac so used to dealing with powerless wretches that he hectored and insulted even mainstream citizens—treated Phil with deference. He was deluded on two levels, not only confusing Phil with Bogey but also confusing Bogey with his onscreen characters. But they invariably were loners without family while Phil had to deal with his daughter and her endless series of traffic tickets, lost cell phones, asshole neighbors, idiots at the day care center (she had a toddler), missed appointments, and an evil landlord. Phil had to run out and fix it all.

A WEEK after Liz was hired, Bento, three blocks into a four-mile after-work run, stumbled across her opening the door to a scraggly Toyota and saw her story spilled all over the seats—clothes, blankets, shoes, boxes, jumbo trash bags, all the pathetic paraphernalia people cling to at the end of their rope. Her face was astonishingly cold and surly. It barely looked like Liz's face. He managed to reverse direction before she spotted him.

The next day he placed both hands on her desk and leaned over so their faces were almost touching. "I just got out of prison," he said.

"Oka-a-a-y," she said. "What's that got to do with anything?"

"I wanted you to know so you wouldn't think I feel superior or anything."

"Fine."

"Look, I know you're sleeping in your car. Wait . . . that didn't come out right."

She swiveled her chair and headed for the door. He followed her down the steps, across the overgrown parking lot, and along the broken sidewalk. She kept going as he caught up.

"What are you? Some kind of geek or something? Spying on me?"

"I won't tell anyone. I don't want anything."

She stopped. "Then why mention it?"

"I'm living in a motel," Bento said.

"So what?"

"You could live there too."

"Not very subtle, are you?"

"No, not like that. I mean Phil fixed it for me. He could get you a room too. He's tight with the owner. Or I'll give you the bed in my room and I'll take the car."

"What's it to you?"

She started walking again, fast. He lunged ahead of her with his long legs and blocked her. "Hey, I wasn't spying on you. I just happened to see you at your car."

"When?" She answered in almost a whisper.

"Yesterday. I didn't tell anyone."

Not looking, she jaywalked across the street.

"Damn, don't cry," he said, still beside her. "Honest. It's okay."

She stopped, turned toward him, but kept her eyes down as she shook her head slowly, not bothering to wipe the tears.

"I'm going to hug you," he said.

"It's no *good* now. You should have just done it," she sobbed.

He'd warned her of the hug to defuse it of any sexual connotations, but now it seemed to remind both of them that their genitals didn't match. He pulled her close and rested his chin on top of her skull. She kept her hands at her sides, not trying to get away.

"Look, it's nothing to be ashamed of."

"When there's nothing to be ashamed of, people don't have to tell you there's nothing to be ashamed of."

"You should see where I lived the last four years."

"We better go back."

"You need a place to stay. We need to settle that first."

"Not now."

"This afternoon then," he said. "Here's a Kleenex."

"After work. We'll talk then."

"Sure." They started back toward the office.

"Where'd he find you?" she asked him.

"A jail cell."

"What? What was he doing there?"

"What was *he* doing there? How about asking what *I* was doing there? You figure I belong in jail and he doesn't?"

"Pretty much. But it does make you . . . you know, more intriguing. Like Jack the Ripper."

"I'm smarter and better looking."

"He never got caught, right?"

"He caught some lucky breaks."

"He found me in a chicken costume. Phil."

"Must have been crowded with both of you inside the same costume . . . Ha! You smiled. See? I amuse you. Admit it."

They reached the stairs. "Just till Friday," she said—payday. "I'll take the floor."

CHAPTER 15

"How many times do I have to explain it? The restaurant put the same bill through twice. You think we ran up two checks for eighty-four dollars and twelve cents on the same night in the same joint?" The schmo was some writer Liz never heard of.

"Did you dispute the charge? There's a way you can do that." She shouldn't waver like that. She'd run into so many liars already.

"They kept billing us anyway. Look, you guys have to stop pestering me. You don't want to be in my next book."

"Who says I don't?" She looked his name up again. "How many books have you written?"

"Apparently not enough."

Before trying another schmo Liz took a call from Mrs. Roubini. "Nick, he always kept a roof over our heads," she said. "But life was no bed of roses, believe me. Our washing machine broke? Two years I had to schlep to the Laundromat with a shopping cart. Two years. Can you imagine?" In previous calls she'd told Liz about all the other men she could have married who ended up rich. She also regretted not telling off her rotten sister while she had the chance. Mrs. Roubini kept a careful accounting of all the bad advice she'd ever followed and every wrong turn she ever made. She carried these events around like rocks in a rucksack. Liz found it soothing. Her mother carried similar rocks.

When Liz suggested specific government programs that might offer her assistance with rent, food, or fuel bills, Mrs.

Roubini's voice lost its quiver. "A waste of time is all. The politicians, they're just out for themselves." She liked Liz so much she'd already sent in a check for fifteen dollars, which was subtracted from the nearly $4,000 she still owed for her husband's burial. When Liz saw the shaky scrawl on the check she almost asked Phil not to cash it. Now she and Mrs. Roubini, who talked almost every day, never mentioned the debt.

Sandra also poured out the story of her life, but unlike Mrs. Roubini, she did so in ordered streams. She'd been in the auto business through most of her adulthood, keeping track of titles, registration, loan documents and the rest of automobile minutia that were integral to the sales process. But toward the end she was working for a Volvo dealer, and customers stopped buying Volvos. She found another job right way at a Ford dealership. "But by that time people stopped buying cars, period."

What she did at dealerships, Sandra said, was like juggling chain saws while you cradled a phone on your ear and answered e-mails. "If I can do it in the car business, I can do it for anybody doing anything. You want to put people on Mars? I can help. But no one has any imagination. I sent out, it must have been a thousand résumés. Finding a job's a whole lot harder than *working* a job."

When her last unemployment check was a few weeks off she signed a contract to teach English in Korea, a daring move for someone Sandra's age. It worked. She didn't starve, but after two years she got homesick and was tired of living in a furnished room. Upon her return she ran into debt again. One day Phil called to collect a badly overdue Visa bill. "I said right away, I'll work it off. We talked some, and he said come on down. What a nut he is." Most of her coworkers, Liz learned, were Phil's ex-schmoes. Liz, however, was his first dancing chicken.

Eventually, when the auto business started to show a pulse again, it came too late for Sandra. "It's okay to have some experience," she said, "but not post-menopausal experience.

You wouldn't know anything about that, gorgeous. What I wouldn't do for your figure. And that skin . . ."

"Cut it out. You look great. Sandra. Really. Now tell me about those Korean men."

It FELT like bursting a blister when Liz told Sandra about her interview with Upchurch. First she had to listen to Sandra reading her the highlights of a news story about a house put up for sale by a twenty-six-year-old actor/singer. Twice a week the local paper published items about LA mansions bought and sold by celebrities, some accompanied by elaborate photo layouts. This one had a sixty-foot indoor swimming pool with underwater speakers, a media room, a guesthouse, wine room, and maid's room in 9,600 square feet of living space.

"Underwater speakers, that's a new one. But what about a wet bar?" asked Liz. "What is he? An animal? Doesn't even own a wet bar?"

"Let me see. I'll read the rest. Five fireplaces, two master suites, sixteen-foot ceilings, five bedrooms, seven bathrooms, parking for ten cars . . . There it is. *Two* wet bars. Fifteen point nine million."

Liz noticed that many celebrity homes had been previously owned by other celebrities. They apparently spent much of their time buying and selling homes to each other. Buyers usually sent in designers and their crews to gut the place and create new paradises that fell short again.

"You ever see a bookcase in any of those house photos?" asked Liz.

"You got a sharp eye," Sandra said, "but maybe they're all into those, you know, computerized ones?"

"E-books? I doubt it." Liz always noticed books. Particularly when they weren't there.

As Liz began recounting the Upchurch interview Sandra asked her, "You ever get one of these guys who go to shake your hand, then they won't let go? They keep talking and kind of pretend they're not? You know . . ."

"Feeling up your palm?"

"So he *did* try something."

"No, it wasn't like that." Upchurch, a cool dispenser of malice, had been careful to avoid even grazing Liz with his grotesque pink fingers. He was a red-faced man of precise appearance down to the colored mustache and a mysterious jeweled contraption that held his tie in place. Could it be a Phi Beta Kappa key? Liz had no idea what they looked like. Another grievous empty space in her knowledge arsenal. But clearly she was dealing with a creature who'd done everything the same way for a very long time, from his choice of cologne to how he mixed a cocktail. After investing in the Monterey journey, she'd been determined to endure the dark, purposeless stink of his inquisition, unable to give up on the fable that it might lead her to the prize. She even fended off questions about her family in Tijuana, deposited there by Border Patrol agents when she was fourteen, which was when she went to live with her aunt. "Why didn't you go back with your family?" he asked her.

"Go back? I was born here."

"How convenient."

Every time his chubby index finger pointed to an entry on her résumé it was to express disdain. "I don't see any awards here. No awards?" It made no sense. Why bring her three hundred miles just to abuse her? She'd even invested in a leather briefcase. About halfway through the interview she started thinking about the seven hours it would take to get back. If the water pump held. Another tank of gas to take her down a twisty road. Before making the trip she managed to ask the secretary a direct question about expenses. "You'll get a fabulous lunch," she replied.

As he ordered lunch Liz suddenly understood why he seemed so oddly familiar. He was a reincarnated Foghorn Leghorn, except the original rooster had a basically kind attitude and never tried to hurt the vicious little chicken hawk. This Leghorn was out to make her cry.

Upchurch's rooster finger stopped at another line on her résumé. "San Jose State. Did you try getting into UCLA?" This will end soon, she thought. Then came dessert, and everything got worse.

Only later would she learn that Upchurch had a history of inviting applicants to lunch so he could eat off his expense account. He probably didn't even have a position open. Before heading for Monterey, Liz had left three messages for Debra, her thesis advisor at grad school, but she'd been on a cruise for her anniversary. "Oh Christ, I didn't warn you about Upchurch?" she said after it was too late. "I'm so sorry, dear. It's all my fault." Five others received their MLAs alongside Liz. Eight months later, none had found library jobs. Debra felt awful about that too, but she was still churning out librarians. In four months a newer batch would come out the gate. They'd stand a better chance. Their résumés wouldn't be stained with a lengthy interval of nothingness. Sometimes timing really is everything. Liz was coming to grips with the fact that she might never enter her chosen field. Had she remained in her internship her résumé wouldn't smell so much like last week's fish, but only rich kids could afford to work for nothing.

THANKS TO the Upchurch interview, she lost her chicken job. "You can't go asking for days off right off the bat," said Buddy, taking on a stiff persona.

"I didn't realize my poultry performance was so vital to the company," she said. She shouldn't have turned on him like that. He'd been a kind warder down there in fast-food hell. She left stone-faced. Mustn't cry, mustn't let him know that losing the job might mean losing her motel bed. She couldn't know that a slippery, gooey hot plum waited for her in Monterey. She'd told Upchurch clearly and perhaps even too firmly that she didn't want dessert. "It's one of their specialties here," he insisted. Posing as a gentleman doing the lady a favor, he instructed the waiter to bring two orders. But what did she know about hot plums and fucking caramel sauce? It seemed like she'd barely touched it with her spoon when it popped out like a live grenade. And it took her forever to realize she must pick it off her lap with her fingers and place it in the saucer. Someone else might have laughed it off as a particularly appropriate incident for a Mad Hatter's tea party. Upchurch observed her anguish with great interest and amusement.

"I'll be talking with the board next week," he said as she stood there with the caramel stain on her skirt. She knew what he meant. Exactly what her mother meant when, pressured by salespeople, she'd say, "I'll bring my husband in and have him look at it." It meant fuck off.

LIZ AND Bento had timid sex the first night and immediately shifted to platonic mode, a relief to them both. They henceforth took turns sleeping on the floor—an equitable, money-saving arrangement—and avoided talking about that embarrassing first night. Bento, she learned, was Dutch, German, and French on his mother's side and his father was at least partly Samoan. He knew almost nothing about his father but suspected he'd been married to someone else when he knew Bento's mother, who died while he was in the hole. Liz wasn't completely sure what the hole was, but whatever it was, they wouldn't let him out of it for the funeral.

CHAPTER 16

Pick could almost feel the legal noose chafe her skin. She'd ignored incoming communications for weeks. A growing stack of unopened mail sat on a kitchen counter, and she no longer signed on to the Internet. She might occasionally play her phone messages but was likely to walk into the next room, out of earshot. Maybe this Officer Blue could divert her from her increasingly morbid thoughts. In his first message he claimed he was checking on her safety, but the messages became increasingly personal, and the last one closed with "What've you got to lose?" So she popped a Xanax and called him back.

Driving toward the rendezvous in West Hollywood, she said a little prayer to Venus that he'd be safely married. Also that his shaving lotion wouldn't be too blue collar. After finding a parking space, she checked herself out in the car mirror and what the hell, unbuttoned yet another button on her blouse as she dabbed a touch more perfume across her neck. She despised her totally unremarkable features but was reassured by her ability to overcome them somehow. Well, whatever happened was likely to be memorable.

Spotting him on a bar stool, she nearly backed out of the place. He was even bluer than she remembered. They could stick him in the *Star Wars* bar scene without changing a thing. The *idea* of this escapade seemed faintly attractive from a distance, but up close it was starting to look more like bat shit.

The joint had about fifty overhead TVs showing various sporting events and perhaps a dozen customers scattered around. Music blared over cheap speakers at such volume that it was crazy for anyone to stay and endure it. But everyone seemed to think it was quite normal for the bartender to have to lean close so they could shout drink orders into his ear. Sit-and-talk places were almost extinct, swept away when bar owners discovered they could boost sales by stifling conversation. People who wanted to talk went to the movies.

It took money to insulate yourself from the sights, smells, noise, and danger of the herd. When Sussman was on his island, Pick had become accustomed to buying herself that separation. Now she'd probably wind up sleeping with her head next to a prison toilet. Not thinking about it wasn't working anymore. It was like telling yourself not to think about elephants.

Pick passed two yuppies at the end of the bar waging a penis-measuring contest over which one had the cooler phone. A couple of lesbians shot pool in the corner. There was nothing terribly Hollywood about the place. It would be at home in Davenport. And it didn't appear to be a cop hangout. Officer Blue must have picked a place where no one would know him. The two of them exchanged phony smiles and shook hands. He wore a tight sleeveless T-shirt. He had toned arms and appeared to have trimmed his armpit hair. She thought about a gun. He had to be carrying one somewhere, probably at the waist, concealed by the untucked T-shirt. Or strapped to his ankle or something. Did movies and TV depict cops as they were? Or did cops copy the fake cops from movies and TV? Another chicken or egg question. She rather enjoyed the fact he was packing heat. It hinted at danger.

They took their drinks—a Manhattan for her, another draught for him—to a booth. All the while they sneaked glances at each other. In order to make polite conversation over the dreadful music she found herself hollering like Fay Wray in King Kong's fist. Pick decided to get past the small talk.

"Why'd you call anyway?" she yelled.

"Because I want to know you," she thought he said. His voice was loud enough to get through, but the words were squeezed from a mouth that remained pretty much closed.

"Look, I don't want to be bitchy, but I've got a lot on my mind right now. This is probably a mistake."

He leaned in and yelled in her ear. "Maybe I can help."

But Officer Blue didn't look like the kindly type. In fact, he looked nuts. Sounded a little nuts too. You didn't have to be Freud to understand why someone would muffle his conversation the way he did.

He suggested they take their drinks outside. There were wooden benches out back, practically noise-free, she discovered, although from time to time conversation drifted their way from the next bench, where a drone on furlough from his cubicle complained about his carpal tunnel syndrome to a coworker.

"How'd you ever get tied up with him? Sussman?" the cop asked her.

"I decided to become a groupie," Pick explained. "A long time ago. I was bored." When she spoke, she realized her vocal chords were sore from the indoor shouting.

"Come on, really," he said.

"Really. I wasn't out to fuck just *any* writer. I was a Roland Sussman specialist." She withheld one little detail—maybe she'd share it with him later. It always turned guys on, especially working-class prudes like Officer Blue—that to get to Sussman she first had to blow a member of his entourage in a hotel stairwell. Sussman was like a rock star in those days, with a publicist, booking manager, and sycophants whose serious faces told you they trailed a serious writer. It was Pick's introduction to the commercial role of blowjobs in the celebrity world, where they were a currency considered less tawdry than a cash bribe and nearly as portable. She should have centered her doctoral thesis on it.

For years afterward Pick tried to relive the thrill she'd felt when Ken, the assistant, brought her up the elevator and, just as he'd promised, escorted her into a suite where she found herself ten feet from Sussman. Feet on a coffee table, he watched TV with three or four others. Enthralled, Pick was swept at once into a secret universe where gods might speak to you.

They were watching a French film—a videotape that was pretty much unintelligible. Lots of camera jiggling and darkness. No one introduced her, and Pick just stood there debating whether she ought to sit down too. She'd been watching the screen about five minutes, no conversation in the room, when the film took what appeared to be a violent turn, but the necessary details were missing. In darkness, the camera nervously targeted the actors' stomachs, necks, that sort of thing. Characters didn't say much, and when they did, it didn't explain much about whatever pretentious crap was going on. Finally she said to no one in particular, "What the hell is this?"

"A Claire Denis film," said Sussman, eyes on the screen. Then after a pause, "It's like being inside her dream. You just float."

"She dreams about stomachs?"

He chuckled and made a show of scratching his head. "You make a good point," he said. And without asking anyone's permission he stopped the recording. He acted more like royalty in those days. Turning to Pick for the first time, he said, "You should have rescued us earlier."

That was fourteen years ago. Even then Sussman didn't look terribly healthy and smelled from cigarettes, but he was really sexy, casting the same rueful aura up close as he did in photographs, a persistent but subdued melancholy that may have been passed down from his Russian grandmother, who, as a teenager, had been raped by a Gypsy passing through her village in the *shtetl*. The Gypsy, the father of Sussman's father, "might have been the link to whatever creative aptitude I have," Sussman told her. "Though not everyone agrees it exists." He was a mother lode of self-deprecation. In the old days Pick found it endearing but decided later he was only inviting others to contradict him and call him a genius. It's possible Sussman's Gypsy grandfather actually was a prodigy of some kind. The talent had to come from somewhere, but it would be of little use to someone driving a Gypsy wagon around one of the world's most obscure corners. Maybe that's why he was driven to mad acts such as the rape of Sussman's grandmother. There must have been millions of people like that down through time, people stuck in the wrong time or place. What if a girl who should have been an astrophysicist had to cope with life in a twelfth-century African village? She must have sensed something was missing. Maybe she believed she was crazy. Maybe everyone else thought so too. That could explain at least some of those burned witches. "Leave it to you," Sussman had quipped, "to find sympathy for a rapist." The presence of a felonious Gypsy forebear in his family tree wasn't a fact he tried to hide, but the media, for some reason, never picked up on it.

These days Pick no longer attempted to recapture the electric rapture she once felt for Sussman. But she gradually noticed that remarks she used to find droll often had cruel underpinnings. Like the time he stopped cold in the midst of a feverish session in bed and asked her, "You know what I think about when we make love?"

"No," she said, dreading the answer.

"I think about us making love, dummy. What did you think? I'm mulling over *Main Currents in American Thought?*"

Pick never forgave him for that half second when she visualized an entire catalog of her disgraceful failings, fears, and dark secrets. Her bricklayer ankles, skunky farts, an invented brother, plus she was practically an English PhD but kept stumbling across words she didn't know the meaning of.

She'd expected to be called out at last as a horse-faced banal charity fuck. Sussman inflicted all that terror just to crack a bad joke, and her infatuation took a hard turn. Now any thoughts of him were wrapped in her dread of a future she couldn't bear to analyze in any detail. She knew she ought to pack for a getaway, but once she fled, the game would be up. After coming this far with no regard for consequences, it was too late to apply rational thought now. So she treaded water in a dark sea.

"Correct me if I'm wrong," said Officer Blue, "but looks to me like you're not exactly crazy about your boss, right?"

She let out an embarrassing giggly half snort. How could she possibly explain it to this Visigoth? Even now, despite all her revulsion, if Sussman's face were to form that hopeful, poor soul look of his, she might once again be unable to resist getting him whatever it was he wanted.

"I think we've been through this before," she said. "He's not my boss, not my boyfriend, not . . . I don't even know what he is. It's complicated."

Officer Blue smiled out of one corner of his mouth and gave two quick, almost imperceptible nods, as if to say he understood everything.

CHAPTER 17

Side by side on the bench with the vampire chick, Gillespie was almost comfortable after a couple beers.

"I think it's time, don't you?" she asked him.

"Huh?"

"Don't give me that."

He tried to show surprise, which was odd, since surprise was what he truly felt. What was she talking about?

"Stop pretending. You know. You're a detective." Was she laughing at him? "Just what's the elephant in the room? You tell me." She traced one of her long black nails across the back of his hand. "Come on. Your . . . Your skin color is . . . It's kind of crazy to ignore it, isn't it? Let's just get it out there and get past it, okay? Is it a medical condition? What I'm . . . I'm just being honest. It's probably not even important. But if this makes you uncomfortable—"

Looking down into his glass, he found no more beer. Why was he blindsided whenever this moment came? "No problem," he said.

He wanted to leave, but that groupie talk of hers, it put his imagination in gear. The way she just let it out like that, so casual. And she smelled like flowers, which reminded him that his wife smelled like Dial soap. He pictured Pick's black hair spread out on a pillow. Pick. How does anyone get a name like that?

"You're upset," she said. "I'm sorry. I feel like such a fool."

"No, no, no," he protested.

"Really. Forget it. I was out of line." She stroked his forearm, staring deeply into him. She was smiling, but it was contrived, making the smile sinister. Sinister's sexy.

"I told you no problem," he said.

She furrowed her brow and the smile fled. "No problem about your skin? Or no problem *talking* about your skin?"

"Both. Neither . . . You know, no problem."

That's when the two assholes entered the patio with their monster dog. They must have come in through the back gate. The animal was some super expensive pedigree. Probably bred to corner polar bears or something. Must have been two hundred pounds. Lots of fur. An enormous science fiction beast with a cement sack for a head.

"Look," said the vampire chick. "Lord and Lady Baskerville." Gillespie wasn't sure what it meant, but it was probably an insult, so he supported it. The man holding his chain leash wore a backward Padres cap and a Rolex. Probably a movie asshole. The woman, wearing skinny suede slacks, must be his original wife because they both looked in their forties. While she went inside, presumably to fetch drinks, the husband talked to the dog, which was mean as a snake and growling in an impossibly deep octave, emitting an occasional bark that sounded more like a roar. The husband's voice was pleading, not commanding, and it was easy to see he couldn't control the thing. It only let him live because he could afford to feed it. The beast was so agitated it was already impossible for Gillespie to carry on a conversation with the vampire chick. But of course that was the whole point of walking around with an animal like that. To make everything else stop. The creature soon focused on Gillespie, apparently sensing he wasn't shitting his pants the way he was supposed to. Actually, Gillespie couldn't help imagining those fangs in him, but he also welcomed the situation. It made him not so blue anymore.

By the time Lady Baskerville brought back the drinks, the growling and barking were combined with attempts to lunge forward. Gillespie noticed that the husband had a fat ass. Nice even features and relatively normal torso, but some freak of a gene had left him with a watermelon ass. Tugging hard at a choke collar, the man with the fat ass and the Rolex told Gillespie, "Don't look him in the eye." He didn't even say please.

Gillespie slipped his hand around the nine millimeter under his shirt and said, "I look at what I feel like, asshole. And right now I feel like looking at an asshole. When I get tired of that I might look at Fluffy again, so you better get him under control." He was careful not to say anything too incriminating because he was halfway sure at this point that he might have to shoot the beast.

Lady Baskerville, who'd put down the drinks, remained standing. She looked concerned, but not concerned enough to get between Gillespie and her monster. "Nick. Let's just go," she said.

"Finish your drinks first," said Gillespie.

"Come on," the woman said. "Let's get out of here." She had the situation all sized up. By this time the fat-assed husband was just about sitting on the animal and yanking back so hard on the choke collar that a couple of times it reached around with its lion head to snap at him. The growl melted into a kind of yowl as the brute struggled for air, and the man managed to pull it back several steps. The bartender had stepped out on the patio to watch but kept his distance.

"I said finish your drinks," Gillespie said as evenly as he could. He kept his hand on the pistol that no one could see but everybody knew was there. He preferred to shoot the man but would settle for the dog.

"Let it go, Tim." It was Pick, calling Gillespie by his Christian name, behaving like they were a couple. He liked that. Meanwhile, his biggest problem wasn't the dog. With all these witnesses around, just pulling out a gun would require him to make a written report and submit to administrative interrogation. And he'd had some drinks.

"You know what? Go ahead," he told fat ass. "Go on, beat it. Maybe we'll meet up again sometime—out on the street." He already regretted saying that. "Bring Fluffy," he added.

The couple, no longer looking at Gillespie, managed to pull the beast back out the gate. It was real work. The bartender picked up the couple's two untouched drinks. "Sorry sir," he said to Gillespie.

"You ever see them before?" Gillespie asked him.

"No, I'd remember." He was very possibly lying. Like so many Hollywood bartenders, he looked like an actor. They kept calling themselves actors until they hit forty or so. Then they put little video clips up on the Internet that they shot with their friends and called themselves filmmakers. The bartender returned with two more drinks. On the house, he said.

"Thank you," said the chick, smiling at him. She pulled a Marlboro out of her bag, lit up almost in one motion, inhaled, and blew out a cloud. "Exciting," she said.

"What assholes," Gillespie said.

"Fluffy. That was funny. Maybe next time they'll leave him at home."

"I don't think so."

"Neither do I," she said.

They were like old friends now that they'd survived a situation together. He could kiss the damn dog.

But then she said, "It's a little kinky, you know. Your skin."

"We're back to that?"

"Kinky's not necessarily bad, you know."

He couldn't recall ever being teased about it, at least not the way she teased. He almost enjoyed it.

"It's got a name—argyria—just one of those things. A price you pay."

"I see . . . No, I don't. What I mean is, I don't know what the fuck you're talking about, Gillespie."

"Well, the book's not closed yet. I liked it when you called me Tim."

"Gillespie's better. You'll get used to it. Keep talking."

He was pretty sure now that he was about to get laid. He also recognized what she was doing—building him up and tearing him down at the same time. Passive aggression, they called it. Like the department pretending the skin condition wasn't an issue while promoting dumb asses over him.

"What I mean is, it's too early to call it a mistake," he said.

He should've moved to Idaho when he could afford it, where things are solid, genuine. Not chock-full of assholes who can't wait to make you feel small. When he got up there, the first thing he'd do is join a gym. They'd notice his bench presses, how he carried himself. He'd have people to watch football with—buddies. And living was so much cheaper. This time he really would get a boat, take guys out on the lake, fish, drink beer. Ex-cops were stars in Idaho. And it would be good for Tina. LA was hard on her. These days she did that whispering thing all the time with store clerks, people she wasn't used to. She had to repeat everything three and four times with all of them staring and puzzled. He was like her interpreter. Sometimes he'd look at her and think if she were a guy she'd be a candidate to shoot up a post office. Up there she could make friends with the wives of his buddies. He'd chop firewood, smell the clean air. You get the right kind of air, it's great for the skin. It might even return to a more natural color. No one calling him Smurfy behind his back, reminding him how he looked by never mentioning it. As for this Pick chick, if things worked out he could come back some weekends. Or they'd meet halfway. Reno or Vegas. Fun places.

But all that depended on getting out from under the Shrek problem. Maybe none of it would touch him, but he didn't usually have that kind of luck. He wouldn't be in this fix if he'd made the Idaho move after selling the house and getting Tina's inheritance. But right after Y2K he found Sun Microsystems, Cisco, and what was that other one? Webvan. The FedEx of the Internet, they said. Made him $12,000 in two days. Worst fucking thing that could've happened. And along came JDS Uniphase. Message boards going crazy on that one too. Tina finally asked him what the company did. She saw the name on some statements. It's really complicated, he answered. She gave him that look but said no more about it. The numbers never left Gillespie's head. Got in at ninety-one and change—bam, it hits a hundred twelve. *This is the one.* The others, they were just rehearsals. Doodling JDSU on scraps of paper and doing all sorts of computations. So many shares would bring in so much profit. He could see it at $2,000 a share without the splits. How much would he be worth then? He damn sure wouldn't sell for less than $13—no $1,400. He picked up more shares on dips and sometimes on advances too, always afraid it would get away from him, make the big move when he didn't own enough. It was his destiny, buying shares of JDS Uniphase. Maybe he'd get on the board of directors.

But how, why could he keep believing all the way down to twelve dollars and forty-two cents? Because when you sell, the money's gone. Stay with it and you still have a chance to get it back. And what if you sell and *then* it comes back? Unbearable. Don't be an asshole, message boards said. Get more, you'll never see it this cheap again. At least when he finally unloaded, it wasn't the absolute bottom. But all these years later he still checked the price every day. Going up is what scared him. He wanted it to sink all the way to zero, making twelve dollars and forty-two cents not such a bad place to sell. Anyway, it was impossible to forget about JDS Uniphase with Tina giving him those looks. She'd asked him two or three times about college accounts for the kids, but he figured that *every* dime he didn't stick into JDS Uniphase was a lost opportunity. Now JDS Uniphase was a third body in the bed.

"What do you mean the book's not closed yet?"

"Huh?"

"That's what you said—the book's not closed yet. But you were thinking about something else just now. I know you were. Tell me."

"You want to know everything, don't you? Maybe you should, you know, take it easy, slow down."

"That's what you want? To slow down?" She squeezed his knee. "Want another drink? I'm buying." They'd had four or something.

She was gone less than a minute. The bartender said he'd have the drinks brought out.

"Book *isn't* closed yet," he told her. "Look around. All that money we owe China. The hammer's got to come down, right? Everybody knows it, but no one does anything about it. Hey, I did something."

They stopped talking when a waitress brought their drinks. Another couple had taken the dog-owners' bench. They looked like zombies. Probably musicians. Pick lowered her voice to a half whisper. "Why talk around it? What did you do? Take silver? Just tell me."

"I thought I'd, you know, start a new style."

"You're funny for a tough guy." But he knew what he said wasn't so funny. It was lame. She swiped her index finger down his cheek. "Your skin," she said, "it doesn't feel blue at all."

"I don't get any colds," he said.

"Really?"

" 'Cause of the silver nitrate."

"You're still taking it?"

"No, but it's like a permanent antibiotic. And I take lots of vitamins."

"You're strong, aren't you?"

"I bench three thirty."

"Free weights or weight machine?"

"You know everything, don't you? You hungry?"

"For what?"

"For anything at all," he said. "Tell me what you want."

"I'll tell you later," she said. "For sure."

CHAPTER 18

Bento thought it must be a mistake when he opened the file and saw the name Roland Sussman. *The* Roland Sussman? But he'd been told before that overextended celebrities, usually on the way down, periodically turned up in the hall of credit shame. Chasing the high and mighty out of their cubbyholes was considered one of the job's perks. "Now this particular schmo, he got really cute," Phil said. "Left word he's in Estonia, then it turns out somebody tried to knife him. Guess where? At his house in Hermosa."

"Not Estonia," Eddie said. "Ecuador."

"Whatever. He wasn't where he said he was. He's right here."

"You know what?" Bento said. "I saw him right after that thing happened at his house . . ."

"We're not heartless," Phil said. "We gave him time to recuperate. Now go get 'im."

"Roland Sussman, I don't think he'd go around stiffing everybody," Bento said. He drew the chorus of guffaws he knew was coming.

"We ought to be like Ireland," Liz said. "They don't tax artists."

"But artists in Ireland, they still have to pay their bills," Phil said.

"Maybe he was in Estonia," said Bento, "and now he's back, that's all."

"Ecuador," Eddie said.

"Sure," said Sandra. "And maybe monkeys fly out his ass."
Bento got lucky. He reached Sussman on the first try.

Sᴜssᴍᴀɴ, ʜᴏᴍᴇ alone, was looking through his Chekhov volumes for a particular short story about a doctor's visit to a patient, but his collections overlapped, and different translators used different titles for the same story, making the search more complicated than it ought to be. As he combed through the volumes he was drawn to stories he wasn't looking for, such as the exquisitely conceived "Gusev," in which the last paragraphs intersect death and beauty in a burial at sea.

> The heavens turn a soft lilac tint. Looking at
> this magnificent, enchanting sky, the ocean
> frowns at first, but soon it too, takes on
> tender, joyous, passionate colors for which it is
> hard to find a name in the language of man.

Sussman considered Chekhov's demise from tuberculosis at age forty-four a painful loss, particularly in view of the fact that Rudolf Hess lived to ninety-three. If Sussman were organizing things he'd do them much differently. But skipping through his Chekhov volumes his instant coffee tasted delicious and his ankle felt better. He'd test it later with a walk along the strand.

When the phone rang he paid no attention. Pick had urged him never to pick up. She would, she said, sort through the messages when she came around, though she didn't come around much. And never, ever answer the doorbell, she said. "There are other Mark David Chapmans out there. You can bet on it." But lunatics like John Lennon's killer, the giant in Sussman's closet, and Michael Abram, who broke into George Harrison's bedroom and stabbed him in the chest, never care about authors. Sussman was more and more convinced that the man in the closet had no idea who owned the house or who Sussman even was.

"Writers," Sussman told Pick, "aren't important enough to assassinate."

But, she reminded him, thanks to the incident, the *Fox News* talking heads remembered all over again how much they despised Sussman, and they'd reminded their dangerous minions.

Sussman heard a voice come through the answering machine. That was peculiar. He must have accidentally switched the setting when he'd placed his cup down: "Look, Mr. Sussman, this is silly. You're not in Ecuador. You're right here. Let's talk about this like gentlemen."

Curious, he picked up. "Of course I'm in Ecuador," he said. "How dare you accuse me of not being in Ecuador . . . Are you there?"

"Uh, yes. Sorry about that but . . . you are Roland Sussman, right?"

"Yes, and who might you be?"

"I'm Mr. White from Western Credit Associates and—"

"Western what?"

"Western Credit Associates."

"What are you selling?"

"Nothing, I'm calling about some past due accounts."

"What did you say your name was?"

"Mr. White."

"Well, you've done me a great service, Mr. White. Thanks to you I'm now aware that I'm not in Ecuador."

"Thanks, but—"

"Wait a minute, you said something about accounts. What accounts?"

"You don't know?"

"Don't talk in riddles, Mr. White."

"I'm sorry, Mr. Sussman. I'm a fan. I don't enjoy making this call. Really. But I'm sitting on seven—make that . . . nine outstanding bills. We're talking about—I don't know. I'd have to add it up. We've been trying to reach you for months, over a year, actually."

"Really? Somebody made a mistake then. Everything gets paid automatically. It's all been set up. Besides, I don't ever buy anything. Check it again, okay?"

"We've done that."

"What are these bills supposed to be for? Maybe there's another Roland Sussman out there."

"Possible, but not likely. And . . . Look, I'm sorry about the Ecuador thing, but we were told you were shooting a film there."

"I am not now nor have I ever been shooting a film in Ecuador. Or any other place. Making films is one of the many things I know nothing about. Like cricket, for example. Or algorithms."

"We thought it was odd that someone was trying to stab you in Hermosa Beach while you were working in another hemisphere."

"You sure Ecuador's in another hemisphere?"

"About half of it I guess. It's on the equator, isn't it? That's why they call it Ecuador."

"Of course. I never thought of that. Mr. White, you know you're quite knowledgeable for a vampire bat employed to suck blood from the veins of the wretched masses."

"Not really. Our office is teeming with knowledgeable vampire bats who suck blood from the veins of the wretched masses. One of my colleagues has five years of high school."

"Is that a fact? But didn't you say you were a fan?"

"Right."

"Well that explains your remarkable deductive powers. I'd expect nothing less."

"Look, Mr. Sussman, let's be clear, okay? I'm really going to believe what you tell me. So . . . you're saying you don't know anything about these past due bills?"

"No. I mean yes, I'm saying I know nothing about them."

"'Cause I'm looking through all this paperwork and we must have sent you a hundred notices."

"I was away for three years."

"Really? Where'd you go?"

"Washington State."

"What happened to your mail?"

"I had someone take care of it for me."

"Who would that be?"

"A friend."

"What about your phone calls? Same friend took care of them too?"

"You're getting rather personal, Mr. White."

"Look, here's the thing, Mr. Sussman. If we're sitting on nine of your bills, there are other agencies out there sitting on more of them. That's usually how it works."

"Usually how what works?"

"Situations like this."

"And what situation would that be?"

"You'd know more about that than I would. I only know about these unpaid bills."

Sussman remembered the mix-up on his health insurance, that the company said it hadn't been paid. Suddenly his skin felt prickly, his insides unsettled. He was no longer sure about anything except Chekhov and maybe this Mr. White. And he remembered another odd occurrence two or three days earlier, something he'd made a point of forgetting.

"Mr. Sussman?"

"I'm here. I just don't know what to say."

"What about . . . You want me to check it out further? Try to find out what's going on?"

"That might . . . Sounds like a good idea, Mr. White."

"It would help an awful lot if I had the name of the individual you turned this stuff over to."

"Why?"

"Because then maybe I can give you better answers."

"Her name is Pickford Manville. I gave her power of attorney . . . Uh, Mr. White?"

"Yes?"

"Where are you?"

"Just up the road. El Segundo. You say you gave her power of attorney?"

"Right. How about mailing me copies of these bills you're talking about?"

"We've already done that. Over and over."

Sussman no longer had any choice. He had to explore a fearful place. "I'd like to see them, these accounts and things."

"Okay. Look, have you got a safe-deposit box? Anything like that?"

"Not that I know of."

"Where's your mortgage paperwork and all that?"

"I don't have a mortgage."

"Excellent. This Pickford Manville, where's she live?"

"She rents a place in Culver City."

"Wait a minute. She's the one who helped you fight off that nut, right?"

"She did all the fighting."

"I don't guess you have her driver's license number or anything."

"Not offhand."

"I'll bet you've got bank accounts, retirement accounts, right? Where are they?"

Sussman remembered the name of the firm and gave it to him, along with the spelling of Pick's name. He felt faintly treasonous.

"I could use the account numbers too, if you can find them."

"What have these bills got to do with retirement accounts?"

"Nothing, I hope. How much have you got in them?" Pause. "We're not talking about anything sacred, you know. Just money."

"So I should reveal all this to a voice on the phone."

"Not ordinarily, no."

"I've got about $5 million in my retirement accounts, more or less. Last time I looked."

"How long ago was that?"

"Three years or so. More, actually."

"It's time to look again."

"Ah Christ, maybe I should just forget it."

"Mr. Sussman, these bills are real. They're not going anywhere."

"Well how much are we talking about?"

"Fifty-three thousand and change. I added it up while we were talking. About half of it's from a jewelry store on Rodeo Drive. The rest I can't tell. Mostly Visa, American Express, stuff like that."

A slow-motion collision. That's how it felt. Sussman could see it but couldn't stop it. Glass breaking, metal giving way, everything collapsing toward his vital organs. Meanwhile the voice on the phone was telling him something else about checking out his financial status or whatever it was Sussman was supposed to check.

"You can add $380," Sussman said.

"Sorry, I don't understand."

"You can add $380 to the $53,000. Well, not really. I paid it."

"Paid what to whom?" *Whom.* Sussman was never sure about who and whom, but this time it sounded right. The kid was educated.

"I think it was two days ago a young woman came by with an unpaid bill for$380. She was the dog walker and told me it was past due. But she was very nice."

"Had you forgotten to pay it?"

"I thought Pick—Pickford—had forgotten. It seemed legitimate, so I wrote her a check."

"The dog walker."

"Yes."

"We can look into some of these things pretty easily," he said, "but you might want to go to someone else too."

"Who, for instance?"

"A private detective maybe."

"Excuse me. You're Mister who?"

"White. But please call me Bento."

Now it was Sussman's turn to grant first-name permission, but he'd never grown used to having strangers partake of these intimacies. And this Mr. White sounded so young . . . Did barbers and tailors call Churchill by his first name? Did the car valet tell Stevenson, "Here's your car Adlai"? Occasionally Sussman had made love to women who called him "Mr. Sussman." It was damn sexy, though he did feel guilty about the obvious master-slave connotations.

"Okay Bento. What other names have you got in the crayon box? Besides White I mean."

"We've got Blue, Green, Brown. Also a Mr. Vance, a Miss Carver . . . As long as they're easy to pronounce, easy to remember."

"*Noms de guerre.*"

Sussman heard a laugh. "Noms de desk. Each desk has a different name. Yesterday I was Mr. Green. But call me Bento. That's real."

"But when you have different Mr. Whites on different days, don't the people you deal with notice the different voice?"

"Not so far. At least that's what they tell me. You know, Mr. Sussman, Mr. Brown here is a whiz at this stuff. Checking records, accounts. He could be a big help."

"What's his real name?"

"You know? I have no idea. We call him Speed."

Sussman informed him that Pick grew up in San Diego and that her approximate age was forty. He didn't know her birthday. He could never even remember his mother's birthday.

"She's got an apartment in Culver City, you said."

"Right. She also has a PhD from Georgetown. Would that be useful to you?"

"Possibly."

Sussman made an appointment for seven the next evening. The one called Speed said he'd have some answers by then. Sussman realized he'd be better off if they were swindlers or veracity-challenged salespeople of some kind. That would mean his money was intact and that Pick hadn't done something unthinkable. Sussman liked this Bento, liked him right away. But he'd liked Pick right away too. He calmed his anxiety with the concept that nothing could hurt him unless his mind allowed it to. He put aside Chekhov and switched on the news. Apparently he no longer interested the media. He found that comforting.

CHAPTER 19

Wh_en Bento was back there suffering in the hole he'd have been delighted to hear the voice of a bill collector. And shortly after taking the job he began stumbling upon shut-ins starved for human interaction, just as he had been. There was only so much time he could devote to these poor souls, especially the ones who spun pointless narratives. Some were quite adept at leaving no spaces in their discourse, apparently believing this would prevent his escape. At this moment a schmo, taking his time on the road to nowhere, was trying to sell him business advice. "I just work here," Bento replied. The man's LinkedIn account described him as a consultant and "results-oriented decisive leader with proven success in developing and implementing business strategies." He looked about fifty in his online photo, which meant he must be around sixty-five or seventy. His credit score was practically down to two digits. He was still maundering through his hopelessly inept spiel when Bento got away and pondered, not for the first time, his role as collector, confessor, healer, and scolder. It's not what you expect, Phil had told him that day in their cell. And on his next call he ran into Norah Schulz:

"Poor, poor . . . Mr. White is it? Your plight is truly lamentable. Every moment you spend on your pitiable headset inflicts additional injury to your already egregiously damaged karma. You remember Scrooge's partner? What was his name?"

"Jacob Marley."

"Right. Marley. Had to carry around that big heavy chain for all his creepy deeds? Same principle. You have my deepest sympathy, Mr. White, and I'm honestly sorry you've had to take such a shitty job. I've got one too. It's at a car lot, sort of."

"A car lot sort of? What's that mean?"

"It's not worth explaining."

"Maybe we should trade shitty jobs," Bento said. "At least we'd be working new ones. But what I'd really like to trade is apartments."

"No you wouldn't. Mine's got my parents in it. And ants."

"Did you try traps?"

"My parents won't fall for them. Besides, I need all my cash to pay villainous bill collectors." All this was pronounced in a melodic, captivating soprano. The file told him Norah Schulz was twenty-seven and owed $2,000 and change on a Discover card. No photo. Probably a cruiserweight. That's usually the way it worked with lovely telephone voices. But so what? He knew of no specific rulings on social interaction with schmoes, though it sounded faintly offensive.

"If you've got a job we can clear up your credit." That tended to be the schmoes' Achilles heel. They wanted to repair their credit and climb back on the hamster wheel.

"Speaking of my job, if I don't leave in five minutes I'll be late."

"What about I call you tomorrow? A little earlier."

"Your intentions, Mr. White. They wouldn't happen to be on the creepy side, would they?"

So she was thinking what he was thinking. "Fear naught," Bento responded.

"Naught? No one says naught. And you knew the name of what'shisname with the chains."

"Marley."

"I'm guessing you've been to college, Mr. White."

"I've watched a lot of old movies. Same time, tomorrow?"

"Get lost, pervert."

"But . . ."

"Kidding. I'm kidding. I know the bill isn't your fault. But I had a little something I had to go to an emergency room for, and like a fool I let them have my Discover card. I had to. They were like Mafia leg breakers. Not amusing like you. Correction. I meant somewhat amusing."

"I find you amusing too," he said. "Also cruel, but I can take it."

"I'm cruel? You're the callous bill collector."

"True, but we've already agreed I'm a somewhat *amusing* callous bill collector."

Had she carried a policy, her insurance company would be billed for much less, but she, a hapless individual with no financial clout, must pay retail. She probably knew all that, yet she didn't gripe about it. The file informed him Norah Schulz was employed at a car rental agency south of the airport. Nothing about her background. The files told sketchy stories, summing up lives like the ledgers of Scrooge and Marley. Yet they already were sharing a measure of intimacies. It's what Bento did all day, going from one stranger to the next sharing intimacies. It was like working in a cathouse.

"Tell me what's shitty about your job," said Bento.

At this point an exasperated Phil gave him the cutoff sign.

"Look, you have to get to work. We'll talk another time, okay?" He clicked off without waiting for an answer, which he already was sorry for.

"Want to tell jokes?" Philyaw said. "Try *The Tonight Show*."

Bento knew Philyaw wasn't really upset but sometimes considered it his duty to play hard-headed boss, as though they were all being recorded for a sitcom.

Norah Schulz had no Twitter account, but Facebook informed him she'd attended college in Montana and lived in California. The rest of her information was private, except for her photo, which showed a little girl on a tricycle with her chin in the air as though she'd just been offended. Bento stared at it until he decided it was vaguely depraved to be enticed by the photograph of a little girl.

*T*HEY'RE TAKING *turns with the guy on the floor curled up like a baby. One stomps an ear with the heel of his shoe and another kicks the small of the back. One, two, one, two . . . They swing their body weight into the mayhem, and there's a rhythm to it. Kick, stomp, kick . . . like timed pistons. Bento opens his mouth to scream and a centipede scampers across his lip. He clamps his mouth tight, trying to shut it out, but it's half in, half out, and scrambling around, strong enough to do what it pleases . . . Who's down there getting the shoe leather? Maybe him, maybe someone else. It changes. No sound, not enough light. Now he knows it's someone else, someone Bento had tried to warn. Turn around and run, man, back to the last gate where the guard buzzed you in. But the poor dumb fish thought he had all the time in the world. Huh? He said, huh? No, no, do it now! Don't think. Run, run.*

The wolf pack went to work. They were waiting, the rule keepers. What was this guy? A snitch? Child molester? The centipede scurries across Bento's tongue. It feels electric. He's stepped back, out of the way as they stomp and kick the new fish. Two of the cons take over. They wear what look like Halloween masks. It's a friendly contest, like musicians taking turns on solos . . . Stomp, kick, one, two, one, two . . . Bento should have explained it to him better, quicker . . . The victim's inert, not covering up any more, completely out . . . Turning away, Bento hides his face . . . And now he's falling, flying, his feet churning without effect. Rocks below . . . but somebody's hugging him and speaking softly, chasing away the fearful unconscious. Darkness turns soft, and there's a gentle voice. He's not hurtling through the air or locked behind steel and concrete. "*Pobrecito, pobrecito,* sweet dreams will come. I promise. Sweet dreams, guaranteed, *pobrecito.*" It's Liz.

He explained it to her over breakfast. When you'd been sorted for entry into the general population you had to provide evidence you belonged with stand-up cons. Thieves? Murderers? Cool. *Mi casa, su casa.* But you must prove you weren't out there snitching or raping children, and it was all in the fish's paperwork that formed a vital nexus between the official Gulag and the convicts' system operating within it.

By the time the guards got to him, the new guy was paralyzed and half blind. The joke was, he could have passed the test. He was in for manslaughter, but he'd torn up the paperwork. It reminded him of a situation he didn't want to remember.

"It wasn't your fault," Liz said.

But mistakes were made, said Bento.

CHAPTER 20

"Y̶ou used to be afraid you were going to die," Speed told Mrs. Vazquez. "Now that the chemo worked? You're scared you might live."

"Whaddaya talking about? I ain't scared to live." Her voice was a deep mannish rumble, deformed by sixty years of Chesterfields.

"You're worried your savings won't last. Isn't that what you said? So you're more worried about your money than your life."

"You twist my words."

It was true, of course. Speed twisted words into pretzels all the time. This time he was trying to wedge his way into Mrs. Vazquez's savings. The fact that he might be the only person on earth that she trusted made his campaign particularly reprehensible. He ought to advise her to dine at elaborate restaurants, take luxury cruises, buy gifts for her grandkids and do whatever else might help her enjoy the time and money she had left. She was dogged by emphysema, an enlarged heart, diabetes, and breast cancer. A stiff breeze could kill her, tangling her estate in courtroom knots and making any payment to Speed a distant prospect. And there was a further complication: She was a fucking deadbeat. As soon as she'd received the cancer diagnosis she stiffed everybody, even her own sister. Mrs. Vazquez was a case study disproving the concept of ultimate justice. In a world this complex, good and evil couldn't possibly settle at a precise median on the scale of life. Karma was contrived by dreamers.

His coworkers seemed to believe they were on the side of the angels just because they didn't shout at their schmoes. But their overriding mission was dollar extraction, just as it was at any collection agency. He didn't need to be told that his occupation and beliefs appeared incompatible, but on occasion acquaintances told him anyway, usually after some drinks. Sure, he'd prefer to work in behalf of a kinder, gentler mission. Building a solar energy station, maybe, or collecting vegetable oil for recycling. But Mrs. Vazquez was his reality.

"People, they all live to ninety these days," she said. "I got to make my money last. What? Now I'm supposed to pay this crooked furniture store? The fabric, it's fading already."

"You know, if you don't tell the truth—"

"Who's not telling the truth?"

"Mrs. Vazquez. If you don't tell the truth, I'll have to turn your account over to someone who maybe doesn't understand you the way I do. Is that what you want?"

"You wouldn't do that."

"I wouldn't want to. You're a good person, Mrs. Vazquez. You know what's right. All we're talking here is $3,100. If you don't pay it, well, I hate to say this, but eventually it will be deducted from your estate. Your kids will pay it, and that's not right."

"The furniture people, they said no credit no problem."

"But they didn't say if you don't *pay* there's no problem."

Silence. Silence was good at this juncture.

"Okay, let's start eating this elephant."

"Huh?"

"Figure of speech. You don't eat an elephant in one sitting. You do it a little at a time . . . They taste good, you know, elephants."

"Go on," she said.

"Once you go elephant, you never go back. You haven't heard that?"

"You always make fun."

"Only with people I like, Mrs. Vazquez. Just send it in, okay? Then we can talk about pleasanter things."

"Once I pay we won't talk at all."

These words didn't just pop into her head. She must be expressing a long-standing fear. He knew what he had to say next.

"What are you saying? Of course we'll talk."

"You'd call me anyway?"

"We're pals, right?"

"I gotta go out Tuesday," she said finally. "Maybe I can buy a money order."

"You still have our invoice, right? You didn't lose it?"

"How much it says? I can't find my glasses."

"The payment's for $286. You'll send it in?"

"You gonna pray for me?"

"Oh Christ, pray to who?"

"You'll pray for me? Promise?"

Nietzsche said there's no such thing as moral order in the universe, that we must create our own.

"Okay."

"Okay you'll pray for me?"

"Okay I'll pray for you, goddammit."

She chuckled. "That's no way to promise."

Funny how you can bend your moral code just a little at a time and wake up one morning to find yourself playing footsie with Beelzebub. And now there was news that Roland Sussman, one of the last of the good guys, was just another schmo. A super schmo, really. Mrs. Vazquez would never fall into such an obvious sucker trap. And where was Sussman while his gal pal was looting his assets? In a Buddhist commune learning all about karma.

SPEED RECALLED very little of his storied exchange with the control tower in Ramstein on what turned out to be his last air force mission. He remembered a previous mission more clearly. Angry spirits swirled around the plane, but he knew he mustn't talk about them. They were none too pleased that Logan was clipping his nails in the cockpit. Multitasking, he called it. Logan was pleased no one was shooting at him and relieved that they were already on their way back, above the reach of weather or enemy malice, making them curiously godlike. They'd brought munitions and PX items into Al Asad in Iraq, dumped it off, and picked up the boxed-up cargo of corpses destined for Dover with a fourteen-hour stopover in Ramstein. Speed was particularly rancorous because he felt relieved along with Logan. Logan was a true believer who'd become even further enamored of Operation Iraqi Freedom after an intelligence officer laid it all out in a one-hour class he took back at Lackland.

"What was the guy's name?" Speed asked him.

"I don't remember."

Click. Another nail fragment fell to the briefing book cover. Logan's eyebrows were set on pronounced, hairy Neanderthal ridges and the eyes beneath were sunk so deep into his skull they were barely visible. It was an inhuman face and disturbing, no doubt, even to the mother who bore him. The guy could act in a *Planet of the Apes* sequel without cosmetic assistance. Speed couldn't stop stealing glances at his implausible face, as though maybe next time it wouldn't look so peculiar.

"Okay, what was his rank?"

"The intelligence officer? Major, I think. I know I told you that."

"Some insignificant desk jockey who was such a fuck-up they assigned him to lay out their bullshit propaganda to your little group of cargo jockeys or whoever the fuck else was there."

"They were all officers. Including a couple bird colonels. And he *was* a major. I'm almost certain."

"So this pissant who you're pretty sure was a major tells you something he's been told by somebody whose job or identity you don't know and now it's an unassailable truth, is that right? And now I can't even question the conclusion of this anonymous possible major."

"This stuff gets sent down from the top. Even you know that. How come you need to know his rank anyway? You're just pissed off you got called back. You don't know shit."

"I know we're taking a load of bodies back to Dover. They left young and healthy and they're coming back in dead pieces."

"If we'd listened to guys like you we'd a lost World War Two."

"You think so? Because right after World War Two we listened to guys like your major or whatever he was, and we recruited Nazis to work for us against the Russians."

"We don't have all the facts on that."

"Fucken right we don't. If they let us have the facts we wouldn't be flying this cargo back to Dover."

"Shut up already with all your Bolshevik bullshit. And you're not the only guy who reads stuff, you know. We're not all idiots."

"Ask the guys back there who the idiots are."

"Show some respect."

"Sending them out to be killed for nothing, I guess that shows respect."

"If it's as bad as you say, how come you can talk this kind of shit? Why don't they have you shot or something?"

"If you reported me, I'd be in some kind of trouble."

"You calling me a snitch?"

Speed thought awhile and answered no. Logan was an asshole, but he was an asshole with character.

"You know why you can talk that shit? Because you live in a free country, you dumb bastard."

"Bullshit," said Speed. He was all out of shrewd retorts.

"Just watch your charts, okay?" Now there was just the sound of the engines and the aircraft slicing through six hundred knots of air resistance. Finally Logan added, "Nobody forced you to take that ROTC money."

"I was a dumb kid. If I had any brains I wouldn't be stuck in this fucking hearse with you, would I?"

"Cheer up. Three more hours and you can get wasted in K-town."

Match point. They both knew it. Speed needed a drink. That's what it came down to. The swirling spirits laughed.

On the next trip he sneaked a bottle into his ditty bag, and thereafter it became routine, like brushing his teeth. But he got careless, and after the dust-up with the control tower somebody—but probably not Logan—squealed about the bottle, and he was drummed out with a general discharge. A little stain most people wouldn't notice, but the discharge conditions lacked the word "honorable."

WHEN SPEED clicked off on the call to Mrs. Vazquez he noticed Liz, looking concerned, motioning to him from her desk. Covering her mouthpiece, she told him, "Listen in on line six." He pressed the button and heard a young man's voice:

"I've seen how it works. Soon as I leave they'll change the lock. I tried, but I had to sell off my cameras. One by one. Borrowed all I could, sold all I could, called everybody I could think of, people I hardly know even. It was awful, but I did." Liz sat mute, and after a while, he said, "Got my back-pack here and everything, but I can't . . . Anything I don't take, it's gone. You know, I'm a regular person. Really, I am. Where do I go? A park? But I *have* to go. There's nothing here to eat."

Liz told him her real name and said, "I'll bring you something to eat."

"Thanks, but today's the day. Maybe . . . maybe I'll see you down the road." The line went dead.

Speed lumbered over to Liz's desk. "Call him back," he said. But the call went straight to message. It was the schmo's voice in the message but sounding businesslike and a tad jovial, as business voices should: "Sorry no one could take your call. We're either in the lab or out on a shoot. Please leave a detailed—" He sounded just as he'd described himself, like a regular person.

"Shit," Speed said. He wanted to soothe Liz, place a chubby palm on her back, but he was a walrus and he knew it. It was only natural that she'd sought comfort from Bento instead. Speed had been inside their apartment, a sunny two-bedroom near the office. Phil cosigned the lease, they told him. They made sure everyone knew about the separate bedrooms, but sometimes Speed suspected it was all a show, that they shared carnal nights. Something he tried not to think about.

CHAPTER 21

Bento turned twelve before learning he was part Samoan. She'd have informed him earlier, his mother said, if she thought it were worth mentioning. She could be quite talkative but rarely gave straight answers, and he used to wonder what other surprises she might spring on him. Easily slighted, she got fired a lot and wasn't a great tenant either. It seemed like they skipped out of their lodgings every few months. How she found new landlords to accept them was a mystery. She'd always try to make an adventure out of it, but Bento wasn't fooled.

He started working when he was thirteen—busing tables, bagging groceries. Tall for his age, he met age requirements by flashing false ID he'd picked up in Chinatown. When he was nineteen he bought an ounce of weed from two dealers who tried to rob him. He slammed one full in the face with a paint bucket and the other across the side of his head, taking off with a roll of cash and a pound of what they claimed was Northern Lights weed. But he immediately ran into three motorcycle cops, and they quickly connected him to the fight with the thieving dealers, one of whom had suffered a broken cheekbone. The DA made Bento out to be Baby Face Nelson.

The Orange County Jail reeked with subterranean madness and hopelessness, and the prosecutors, who had all the time in the world, used it as a torture device to extract confessions. Bento waited them out five months while his case inched through the pipeline.

"Why'd you hit them with a paint can?" asked Liz.

" 'Cause I didn't have a flamethrower."

"You know what I mean."

"I had a week's construction wages on me."

"Was there paint in the can?"

"About half full."

"Okay, how did the police know about the dope deal?"

He explained that the two dealers were snitches. After he foiled their rip-off they called their police pals. He was, he conceded, an idiot.

"But you're a cute idiot," Liz said helpfully.

His court-appointed attorney had been a middle-aged man with gorgeous hair and a chipper, devil-may-care persona. At first Bento misinterpreted his smile, thinking it reflected a positive attitude about the case. He never showed up at the jail to interview Bento, who saw him two or three minutes at a time, just before hearings. The hearings themselves were mostly about small points of evidence that might or might not be trickling in. Usually they didn't trickle, so the judge would set a date for another hearing. His lawyer and the prosecutor never spoke on the phone. Their only communications channels were within the hearings themselves and sometimes in the corridor outside the courtroom, when they might or might not do a little negotiating before going inside.

After one particular hearing the judge tried to set the next one ten days ahead, but Bento's lawyer, consulting his calendar, said he'd be busy in a trial and requested a three-week delay. He failed to consult jailed Bento, who at that moment realized that everyone in the courtroom—the lawyers, the judge, the bailiffs, the court secretary, everybody—viewed his freedom as an expired commodity. All that remained were details. He'd been halfway through a semester at community college when he was busted. Unable to follow withdrawal procedures from inside the jail, he flunked his courses. His job was vaporized too. The entire system seemed designed to fling him into a pit and pull up any ladders that might lead him back to where his life used to be.

THE MANACLED defendants being herded from place to place were usually guilty, but the word *guilty* was a flexible term that involved all manner of predicaments and perplexities. Most of them were charged with drug crimes, so there rarely were any victims.

One day Bento's lawyer came into the holding room and his customary smile was wider than usual. The DA was offering immediate release in exchange for time served, but he'd have to plead guilty to a felony count and accept a "strike." Bento wasn't even sure what all that meant, but his lawyer assured him it was the best deal they were going to get. "It's a one-day sale," the lawyer said.

Bento took the deal. Afterward he became more reliant on weed to help him float above the miseries inflicted by his diminished status. But he didn't space out or become vegetative on marijuana the way so many people did. In fact, he often turned mischievous, perhaps searching for a childhood that had been squelched. Almost two years after getting out of jail he swiped a bicycle out of an open garage door. He only meant it as a prank. The bike had two flat tires, no chain, and rust that got all over his shorts. It seemed terribly humorous at the time. He was wheeling the thing down the driveway when a middle-aged man yelled at him from a balcony. Still laughing, Bento dropped the bike and jumped into his friend's pickup. It became just another funny story—but only for a while because the friend got nabbed for something more serious and turned over on Bento, identifying him as the dangerous bicycle thief. The statutes treated the attached garage as part of the home, so Bento, who already had a violent strike on his record, was charged with burgling a home while the residents were on the premises. The DA's office applied the same statute that gets used against home invaders who smash their way into a living room. After Bento was picked out of a lineup, his new court-appointed attorney said the DA was pressing for twenty years but would let him off with ten if he moved now. If he waited too long, the prosecutor would have to prepare a court case, and that would upset him and make him less charitable.

Every time Bento was taken to the courthouse for a hearing he expected the light of reason to shine at last on this panoply of absurdities, but no one was laughing. He felt as though mad extraterrestrials were dissecting him in a soundproofed flying saucer from whence earthlings below couldn't hear his screams.

They tossed around years like they were tossing Frisbees in a park, he told Liz. This time he sat in county jail fourteen months. It felt like three or four lifetimes. His last thought before sleep and his first thought upon rising was the twenty-year sentence waiting to roll over him like a ten-ton boulder. An hour before his scheduled trial he was offered four years and three months along with a second strike.

Bullshit, he told his lawyer. No jury would put him away at all—and certainly not for twenty years—for grabbing a broken-down bike and wheeling it thirty feet. "But they'll probably agree you stole the bike," his lawyer explained. The sentencing hammer wouldn't come down until after the judge sent the jurors home.

"So I'm thinking, 'You'll be forty-two when you get out,' " he told Liz. "I visualized it very clearly. In jail you hear stories all the time about guys who made the mistake of going to trial." Once again, Bento took the deal.

"You did four years for almost stealing a bicycle?" Bento could see she was trying to hold in her laughter—or tears. Possibly both.

There were much worse jailhouse stories than his, he told her. Sometimes they went in the opposite direction—unimaginably cruel scumbags treated with inexplicable gentleness or walking away over absurd technicalities. And sometimes justice was, like the real estate business, all about location. DAs and judges in one county might routinely pursue sentences twice as long as those imposed next door. Kafka got the criminal justice system almost right, Bento said, but Salvador Dalí came closer.

THE LOCKSMITH, a chubby Filipino, was drilling out the lock at Apartment B. "What's going on?" Bento asked him. The locksmith warily asked him whether this was his apartment.

"No, just wondered what's the rush, that's all," Bento said. A wave of relief passed over the man's face. This particular tenant, he told Bento, made a startlingly tidy departure. Even scrubbed the toilet. "I'd let you in to see, but—" His voice trailed off.

"That's okay," said Bento.

"If you're interested in renting it, you can call 'em in the morning."

Bento carried the bag of Chinese food back to Liz's car. Her photographer schmo no longer had an address.

CHAPTER 22

Hermosa Beach was one of those gritty art colonies that had been invaded and occupied by the moneyed class. Higher rents chased away the artists who'd provided the seductive ambience, transforming a spunky commercial strip into an antiseptic strip of exclusive shops. The original cottages were replaced by twenty-first century castles that spilled out over every inch of the little lots. These monster replacements were crowded together like clowns in a jalopy. Many were second or third homes whose owners traveled from mansion to mansion at luxury locales around the globe. From time to time you could spot family members moving around and about their palaces. Multicolored signs stuck in the ground by security companies warned potential interlopers that armed rent-a-cops stood poised to ventilate them.

Bento, after parking Liz's car, walked past a mansion shaped like a Picasso toilet. On a flowery patio atop its uppermost roof a middle-aged man and woman, both thin as death-camp inmates, jogged on side-by-side treadmills above the roaring sea. They shared an unobstructed view of thirty miles of coast from Malibu to the Palos Verdes Peninsula. It was a privately owned panorama that would be there after the last Rembrandt crumbled into dust. The entitled couple appeared neither pleased nor displeased. Wearing audio gadgets in their ears, they listened to separate or perhaps identical frequencies while jogging alone together. They could have stepped downstairs and run along the beach instead, but down there they'd be mistaken for schnooks who didn't own a designer mansion overlooking the surf. Bento recalled reading Thorstein Veblen's observations on conspicuous consumption. A century earlier the cogent Midwestern economist pointed out that the utter uselessness of jewel-encrusted walking sticks and hundred-room manors was what made them so attractive to Gilded Age tycoons. What better way to advertise the bizarre aggregate of their wealth?

The sun, poised to sink beneath the horizon, glowed with golden intensity as knots of beachgoers watched the last lick of flame disappear beneath the sea in a primeval ritual of death and eventual rebirth. Handfuls of bathers gamboled in the ageless surf while beyond the breakers a few die-hards in wet suits sat on their surfboards waiting for the last wave of the day. Bento turned inland half a block before coming to Sussman's house. A dog barked as he approached.

Roland Sussman, in slacks and a collared polo shirt, opened the door, restraining a fair-sized yellow dog by the collar. They shook hands after Bento let the dog sniff him. "Hello," said Sussman, who didn't bother to introduce himself. When you have a celebrity face, Bento decided, that makes sense. Face to face, he was handsomer than most of the pictures Bento had seen. Canny blue eyes and a nose that wasn't all that big, but had a hook in it you could hang a shirt on. He had a slight limp but otherwise moved effortlessly, not like an old guy at all.

Speed already sat in the dining area with a beer and some paperwork spread out in front of him. The home was less luxurious than Bento expected. Early evening sunlight still streamed across the rooms, the translucent shafts revealing the barest hint of floating dust. Declining a beverage, Bento joined Sussman and Speed at the table. The dog curled up next to them.

"It's beautiful here," Bento said.

"What I liked about it right away," said Sussman, "was that I could look at those dumb-ass castles around the corner and tell myself I wasn't spoiled."

"What kind of car do you drive?" asked Speed.

"There's a '99 Chevy in the garage. I don't know if it starts."

Speed nodded, neither approving nor disapproving. "You know Ms. Pickford Manville drives a Porsche?"

"She's driven me places," said Sussman. "I don't know what it is, but it's no Porsche. A Toyota or something."

"That's her show car," said Speed. "The one she lets you see. Like one of those Potemkin villages."

"Only in reverse," said Bento. "The Russians wanted the villages to look prosperous."

Speed said that the cadaverous couple Bento had seen next door cofounded a multilevel marketing enterprise with participating entrepreneurs on every continent and were moderately famous. Sussman said they ran in place out there every day. "What do they sell?" he asked.

"I don't know," said Speed. "I guess the product isn't the point. The point is to sell it to someone else." Their home, he said, had been featured in some architectural magazine.

"On my way here," said Bento, "I stopped by a guy's house, but he wasn't there. He went homeless today. Today was the day. They were changing the locks. He was one of our schmoes."

"Schmoes are people on the collection list," Speed explained. "Sorry."

"That's okay," said Sussman. He likened the homeless schmo to a typhoon victim. "You hear eight hundred missing or dead. Eight thousand, whatever. Then you make breakfast, do the crossword puzzle."

Speed: "You talked about that in *Marching with Kings*. I read it I don't know how many times."

"Some other time we can discuss my wit, clarity, good looks, bottomless genius, all that," said Sussman, blending sincerity with self-mockery. "But . . . it just creates distance. Feel it?"

Bull's eye, thought Bento. Only later did he consider that Sussman might have been reciting something he'd already said to readers on similar occasions. Still, they were almost certainly his words. A person can't plagiarize himself.

"I guess we have to discuss it," said Sussman. And they all knew what he was referring to. He invited them over to the cushiony furniture across the room. Bento noticed that Speed had reached that state of corpulence that requires the fatty to walk like a penguin, arms extended to the side so they don't brush against the hips. Bento and Sussman took the sofa. Speed, after plopping onto a matching chair and ottoman, kicked off his shoes. His gray socks looked nice and clean. He had good hygiene for a slob.

Speed gave Sussman a cogent summary. Most of it came from Liz, who suspected that eventually she'd penetrate what looked to her like a complex web of straw deals involving the Cayman Islands and a dummy corporation in Delaware, all designed to loot Sussman's assets. When Speed had asked her how she learned this, she said, "I'm a librarian. I can find anything."

Sussman's woman friend lived not in middle-class Culver City, but snotty Brentwood, where she apparently held title to a $2 million place across the street from Marilyn Monroe's final residence. Five bathrooms and a tennis court, the Porsche in the garage. She'd taken at least one five-star trip around Europe. Sussman could be down to his last $120,000 and owed the IRS more than that. He was probably too late to stave off foreclosure on his home, which had been mortgaged during his absence. His situation was analogous to Manuel's in *Captains Courageous*. After the mast cracked and fell he looked okay, but beneath the water line he was a crushed grape. Sussman asked a few questions, but it became harder to know what he was thinking, as though he'd drawn a curtain across his ideation.

Speed, who'd procured a joint from somewhere on his person, asked Sussman, "When's the last time you talked to this Pickford Manville?" He took a giant hit and passed the joint to Sussman, holding the smoke in his lungs with ballooned cheeks.

"Maybe a couple weeks."

Speed exhaled. "Why don't you call her, see what she says? Skip the middle men. Just tell her you want it all back. What've you got to lose?"

"I'll have to think about it, but thanks for your help. Both of you. All of you. Thank your friend Liz, too."

"You are going to do something, right?" said Bento. "I mean, you can't let her get away with this."

Sussman looked perplexed, as though confronted by a giant math problem. Saddened, Bento yearned for a more just world. He wondered how people would behave if they really believed everybody got what was coming to them. He remembered his cellmate's dream about the demons chasing him to a trapdoor in the ceiling that led to another room with another trapdoor. "I know I'm going to hell," Lopez said. Maybe you can change, Bento told him. Too late, he replied. Narcissistic Lopez could mourn only for himself. He'd left a long trail of victims beaten, abused, double-crossed. Bento knew of other cons who'd dreamed the trapdoor dream, the same ghastly eternity of pointlessness and terror. All were psychopaths. Some of the other cons thought they made the dream up, but Bento was sure it's what Lopez saw.

"Got anything else to drink?" he asked Sussman.

CHAPTER 23

"**I** don't eat breakfast," Pick told him.

"That's not what I asked you," Gillespie said. "I asked where's *my* breakfast."

"Not my department."

In one quick motion he grabbed her wrist and twisted it behind her. She tried to stomp on his foot with her naked heel, but he slid it away in time, still pulling on her arm. He placed his other hand on her breast and eased up on her arm.

"Don't *do* that," she said, and he slipped his fingers beneath her robe, kneading the nipple roughly. "Let me," she said, and began massaging her breast beneath his fingers while searching for his lips with hers. He slipped off the top of her robe, and she shoved herself at his erect cock, rubbing it against her and kissing him, her tongue licking his teeth. Pulling her mouth to the side, she gasped, "Wait a sec," and stepped back. Thunk! She kneed him in the nuts. He was instantly nauseous, his knees weak. "Get your own fucking breakfast," she said, yanking the robe back on her shoulders. *Oh the cunt, the lousy dirty little fucking cunt.* She stalked out of the bedroom, and he sank to the carpeted floor, grasping his ambushed testicles with both hands.

She returned with a mug of coffee and a plate with some kind of sissy cheese and crackers on it. By that time he'd managed to seat himself on the bed. Setting his breakfast on the end table, she said, "You okay?" Without waiting for a reply, she added, "I've been sort of, you know, on edge lately. Don't be angry. Please?"

Gillespie was actually strangely placid, perhaps because he was thrilled to sleep in such a place. Just the lemon-colored bedroom was practically the size of his whole house. But Christ, this was Sunday morning, and she didn't own a TV. No football. He'd work on that.

"Hand me the coffee, will you?"

"You're not going to do anything, are you?" she asked him.

"Hand me the cup and you'll find out."

She studied him a moment and passed him the cup. He sipped it, handed it back, went to the bathroom and checked himself out shirtless. Looking good. He added some extra sprays of cologne and went back out, sprawling the length of the fabulous sofa in her bedroom, which looked out on the pool. He thought about the house he and Tina sold before Y2K. It had a pool too, though the deck around it was cracked. He shouldn't keep beating himself up over that house, but it was difficult with Tina always sulking about it, watching, knowing, and staying silent in her peculiar accusing fashion. The mortgage payments he used to think were killing them amounted to half the rent they paid now. Real estate, stocks, silver, gold, didn't matter which. He'd end up buying high and selling low. Couldn't stop himself. He panicked at both ends. But maybe his luck was changing.

Pick sat down with him. She'd thrown on shorts and a floppy shirt. Their bodies barely touching, they both looked out on the pool, the tiled deck, the elaborate landscaping of flowers and tropical plants. He touched the back of her neck and gave her a light massage, pulling on her shoulders with both hands. She turned to face him and caressed his thigh. Wherever her boundaries were, they were well beyond his. He reached around and rubbed her back with one hand while unbuttoning her shirt with the other. It was a rich maroon, not the black she usually went for. When he got the last button she slipped it off. He tried guiding her down on her back but pushed a little too hard. She gave him an angry look that he enjoyed. He straddled her and began playing with his cock over his jeans, just a little, almost like his hand had accidentally strayed there. She slowly pumped her pelvis and he unzipped and stroked his cock. "Is that what you want?" she teased, laughing at him. He liked her face, the paleness of it. His cell phone went off and he struggled to reach it on the end table with one hand while stroking furiously with the other. She grabbed the phone first, listened a moment, and said, half serious, half gleeful, "Can you hold a sec? Your party's almost ready to come on my face."

The fucking crazy bitch. It could be Tina, his mother even. He snatched the phone away. A Global Tel Link recording from a pay phone. Somebody locked up somewhere trying to call him collect, and he knew right away it was Shrek. He prayed hard he was wrong while the phone company voice read off a round-robin of selections—press two for this, five for that, but Gillespie hadn't heard the first part. State prisons and local jails all had different number schemes. Press the wrong digit and it could even suppress all future calls from that particular institution. He waited while the recorded voice told him this was a recorded line and all the rest of it, and then he heard Shrek, pronouncing his own name in the few seconds he was allotted. Now back to the recording. Oh Jesus, fucking Christ, oh no. Oh God, please. He didn't even know which number to press. The call clicked off.

"Get off me," he heard her say. He was mute, motionless. "This isn't funny anymore," she said. She was right about that. He picked up one leg and she scrambled out from under him. "You asshole," she said, rushing to her boxcar-sized bathroom. He almost sympathized with her, but he had more important stuff to worry about. Shrek was sitting in a lockup somewhere, but there was no central computer network for all the different jails in all the cities around the county. And he might even be in another county. But if he was in LA he'd be taken to county jail downtown. The only thing to do was wait. And suddenly Gillespie had a throbbing hard-on. Something about the end of the world was very conducive to sex. Imagine how easy it would be to get laid if a giant comet was heading straight for earth.

The bathroom door was locked. He jiggled the handle. "I'm sorry, Pick. That was a really important call," he said across the door. No answer. "I'll do anything you want. Please. Open up." No answer. "Baby? You want me to beg? Okay, I'm begging." He jiggled the handle again.

"Got another blue hard-on? Take it to a freak show. Or your wife. Take it to her."

"I'm not taking it anywhere but you."

"Get on all fours."

"What?"

"You heard me."

One thing you could say about this bitch. She knows how to take your mind off things.

The door opened and his phone went off again. Sonofabitch. "Sorry baby, I really gotta take this." She banged the door into him, the full force of it on his nose, but he managed to hold on to the phone. Drops of blood hit the white carpet as he sat there listening to the recorded message. Shrek again. At the North Hollywood Station. Standing over him, she started yelling something. From his floor position he jerked his index finger across his lips and slapped her across the thigh to shut her up. Okay, this time he heard the rest of it. He pressed the three.

Shrek whined how they were screwing him, but it was like coming into the middle of a movie. You still couldn't tell what it was all about.

"Start from the beginning."

"I was way behind on these student loans? And—"

"Jesus. Student loans? You're worried about that shit? Nobody goes to jail for student loans."

"I know, but—"

"Don't tell me about any crimes, understand? What're you being charged with?"

"It's . . . they said carjacking."

A ten-year rap. Doomsday for Gillespie. All the little problems he used to have were nothing now. No way the guy wouldn't roll over on him. Giving them a cop, he might even walk. When would they show up? Hours? Minutes? Hours probably. She handed him a wet towel and Gillespie held it to his nose. He was hard again.

"Don't say anything over the phone. Don't say anything about anything. I'll get to you. Hang tight." He slipped the phone back in his pocket and kissed her hard, squeezing her forearms and pumping against her. Blood smeared on her face. In no time at all it worked out just the way he wanted, like all those videos he'd seen on the Internet. Jizz all over her face and hair, in her eye even. And she laughed and laughed and kept laughing as she headed to the bathroom and turned on the shower. He spotted a blinking light across the room.

"Hey," he shouted. "You know you got messages on your machine?"

Leaving the shower running, she came back to him and did the strangest thing. Grabbing him by the ears, she said, "I'm not sure I ever told you, but my brother Marty died in Iraq. Cheney killed him."

What the fuck? Gillespie said he was sorry.

"But it makes me do dumb stuff once in a while." She still had him by the ears, and her laughter turned to sobbing, tears mixing with Gillespie's juices and blood. "I need your help. I'll pay you. If you help me I'll pay you."

"What kind of money we talking about?" he asked.

CHAPTER 24

Sussman figured he'd already won the lottery when they didn't send him to die in Vietnam. It was a blessing to live long enough to get cheated by a friend and fade into old age and then nothingness. Ten out of ten GIs killed in action would agree. Viewing the inevitable torments of life within a broader context was something he'd been training his mind to do for years, yet he was always surprised when it worked. The shock and fear had almost passed. He wouldn't end up like Jerzy Kosinski—a fine writer who'd survived the Holocaust but eventually stuck his head in a plastic bag when he could no longer scoop up checks at Elaine's.

"When Samuel Clemens went broke," said Bento, "he went out on a lecture tour and paid off all his creditors." Sussman knew this Bento kid from somewhere, but when you really like someone, it can feel like you'd always been acquainted, and in a way you always were.

"That's kind of you," Sussman said, "but I don't belong in the same sentence with Clemens. Daffy Duck, maybe."

How could Sussman take credit for accomplishing tasks he barely remembered performing? He wasn't even sure he was still the same Sussman who wrote the book that made him famous. And fame was fleeting and certainly relative. If Clemens could be resurrected to deliver one of his talks next week, much of the population would prefer to play *Grand Theft Auto*. Lecturers in demand these days tended to be bilious blowhards like Terrance F. Feldman of the *New York Times*. Sussman wondered whether Speed and Bento knew all about his storied meeting with Feldman in a hotel lobby just before Sussman dropped off the earth to Orcas Island. Of course they did.

The renowned, round-faced columnist was being followed around that day by a denim entourage of UCLA business students. Sussman never learned the nature of their connection to Feldman, who was decked out in his trademark bow tie and starched white shirt. He seemed to believe that when two illustrious figures such as he and Sussman met by chance they should exchange more than perfunctory greetings. He proposed they have coffee. Sussman was curious to know more about this *Times* scribe coming straight from a visit to the famous, faintly ominous Rand Corporation down the street in Santa Monica. They walked past lovely french doors to an aromatic patio festooned with exquisite flowers and tropical plants. Sussman had been told that Jordan's Queen Noor was among the hotel's guests that day. He also recalled two slender, fashionably dressed women, probably Russian, who sat next to a fountain and smoked throughout their meal, taking bored drags between bites.

Feldman, a prominent member of the chorus that cheered America into the Iraq disaster, remained aboard the slow-motion train wreck for years. But his columns mentioned it less and less as the war sank deeper into its own self-generated bullshit. Yet Feldman's reign as policy seer rolled on undisturbed. He still churned out books, columns, and lecture tours advising readers what to think. Lately he'd been counseling Americans to embrace what he saw as a dynamic new age of transnational economics created by bold, digitally connected knights of finance and technology. It was, he wrote, the next great stage of human development. Although Feldman implied that you had to be really smart to recognize which way the wind blew, he also said that it was as plain as the nose on your face.

Sussman wondered how this impervious, middle-aged narcissist summoned the nerve to keep dishing out instruction.

Shouldn't he be out in the street doing penance? Perhaps with a begging bowl. Sussman, feeling frolicsome, asked him the precise amount of his speaking fee, which was rumored to be in Bill Clinton territory. He noticed only a flicker of displeasure as the soothsayer drew his verbal sword and commenced cutting to pieces pitiful Sussman, who suddenly felt less like an artist who'd written the definitive Vietnam novel and more like a stammering schnook. On another day Sussman might have stood toe to toe, but he must have been at the wrong end of his biorhythmic spectrum. The business students rolled their eyes with multiorgasmic rapture as Feldman crushed oddly tongue-tied Sussman with polysyllabic pomposity that probably came straight from the pages of his latest book. The only break in the assault came when a waiter in a black suit came around for their order.

After the subdued Sussman finally slunk away, Feldman rushed to write a celebrated column that dismissed him as an idiot savant who'd gotten lucky with one mediocre novel chronicling a war Sussman never saw in a place he'd never visited, a novel that misconstrued, as far as Feldman was concerned, the deeper complexities of the national interest and failed to understand where we'd been, much less where we were all going. He didn't even bother to dismiss the two Sussman books that followed *Marching with Kings* and were received with decidedly mixed reactions. The column hit like an encyclical whose time had come, the final seal. Even many of Sussman's readers—disgusted that he'd failed to give them whatever they'd dreamed his next novel ought to be—joined the lynch mob.

The fresh savaging of his reputation assaulted Sussman's taut psyche at a tender time, and he checked into the commune as a battered survivor seeking refuge from the dogs of intelligentsia. He was barely acquainted with the two communards who invited him to their little island settlement, and though he didn't quite admit to himself that an inane crapmonger like Feldman could wield such power over his life, he grabbed the lifesaver without checking the place out. The residents were shocked he actually showed up. No one had mentioned money, but by the time he arrived, their search for tranquility and higher spirituality was constantly interrupted by the disappointing sales of home-baked bread and handcrafted knickknacks. His hosts, behind on the rent, showed him to a room with a soft mattress and a badly stained rug. They gave him the last of the overcooked eggplant culled from a nearly empty pantry. The next morning he wrote them a check that became a monthly event. The residents began treating him like their personal rock star.

"That's exactly what I went up there to get away from. At least that's what I thought," Sussman told Speed and Bento. He didn't mention that the communards' worship was tinged with resentment conveyed so subtly that it faded in and out like Lewis Carroll's Cheshire Cat. No one among the fourteen members claimed any special status, but a leader had emerged, and after a while he concluded that the flat ban against alcohol, tobacco, sex and drugs smacked of tyranny. Sussman agreed that the place was short on fun, which after all wasn't specifically prohibited by Siddhattha Gotama's dharma. Three residents departed, but four others took their place. Two were nicely proportioned females. Sussman, soon revolted by his weaknesses, reminded himself that we're mostly born to fail, like all those Darwinian mutations that didn't work out. A typical destiny was reached by millions of spermatozoa turning in the wrong direction or showing up at the wrong time. But he needed time to reabsorb that lesson, to think everything through. It's what he was supposed to be doing, why he went up there in the first place.

The commune's isolation was real. The little settlement took up a tiny corner of an island whose other inhabitants tended to mind their own business. The communards remained solidly opposed to TV, Internet, and all the handheld electronic addictions that were rapidly turning the world into a vast village of fuckwits. Sussman had once turned down a similar though less libertine living arrangement after a small press published his collection of short stories. The stories, which preceded *Marching with Kings*, were noticed by a literary foundation that considered writers a breed of homeless denizens. It periodically offered selectees a bed and writing desk at its woodsy New England location. He thanked the well-meaning twits but pointed out that writers don't generally need a place to flop. They need cash, just like everybody else.

SUSSMAN FELT the three years on Orcas were well spent, that he'd actually made strides toward freeing himself of anger, jealousy, Schadenfreude, and other regrettable attributes that had dogged him for decades. He still became dispirited from time to time but was gradually becoming a human being he didn't revile. He even made small attempts to resume his writing, mostly just unconnected thoughts in search of a theme and a story. *Marching with Kings* was inspired primarily by guilt over spending most of his army hitch at Fort Riley, Kansas, smoking weed and filling out supply forms while a steady stream of kids passed through to Vietnam.

PFC Sussman was an old man of twenty-three, drafted after college. Most of the other draftees around him were nineteen-year-olds too poor or too honorable to buy their way out of the war. At night he took them to places where girls from nearby Kansas State University could be found. But the girls mostly despised the kids with GI haircuts who they assumed were eager for a chance to bayonet Asian babies. Or maybe what they really despised were boys too unsophisticated or too poor to hide out in college. Where were those girls now? Old ladies somewhere, perhaps divorced, playing golf, bragging about grandchildren. And where were all the boys who passed through Fort Riley? Thousands upon thousands of them.

"You feel sorry for us, don't you?" one of them asked Sussman. A kid with a trace of Midwestern twang and hair of dark straw. Sussman had barely noticed him. He was tall with a face that disguised nothing. Sussman made no effort to remember his name because he didn't understand at the time that he'd carry the memory of the kid to his grave.

"Yes," replied supply clerk Sussman, astonished that this kid had so effortlessly perceived what was in his heart. Sussman was at that moment driving several of his wards into town in an old station wagon he'd bought a few months earlier from a mortar squad kid going over.

"Don't," said the kid. "There's not one of us who wouldn't trade with you if we could. You didn't do anything wrong."

By then everyone knew the war was bullshit. The nineteen-year-old Midwestern rifleman on his way to possibly die in it was a bodhisattva, an enlightened being concerned not for himself, but for Sussman. He was there to point the way, and Sussman prayed the kid made it through his tour okay. If he could just do that he'd be fine. All the ingredients of a good life were already his. And now Sussman worried for Pick as the teenage rifleman had worried for shirker Sussman. If Sussman had children he might feel obligated to get some of the loot back for them, but Pick was his child in a way, just as Sussman was a child of the rifleman. Maybe she hadn't planned to screw him but just lost her way and ended up in Brentwood. He hadn't always been terribly kind to her, and anyone who'd betray a friend to acquire more wealth must be bubbling inside like a volcano. A lost soul.

Yet Pick could also be inspiring, particularly when she talked about her invented brother. It was a generous story, a parable invented to illustrate a truth. Soldiers in Iraq really were electrocuted in Cheney's Halliburton-built, war-profiteering plumbing, and they were all somebody's brothers, fathers, or sons. The electric-shower death of an invented brother was infinitely more truthful than analysis from intellectual sociopaths like Terrance F. Feldman.

THE LAST time Sussman saw the tall kid with straw hair a sergeant out on the company street was chewing him out in 100-degree heat for a smudged belt buckle. The rifleman, standing at attention, made no effort to hide his amusement. Sussman looked into the eyes of this kid who was still ten thousand miles from the war and he saw *Marching with Kings* laid out like a scroll. All that was left was to write it down. He perceived it as the Biblical Joseph perceived his brothers, with fear, boundless affection, and ultimate forgiveness. Sussman didn't feel blessed by this vision. He wasn't sure he wanted to carry the burden of it, but he couldn't resist its power.

CHAPTER 25

No sense even dreaming of a run across the border. Blue gringos can't melt into Mexico. Meanwhile, to keep from going crazy, Gillespie worked on his abs in the garage. Reviewing what she'd told him, her brother got electrocuted taking a shower in Iraq, which somehow was Dick Cheney's fault. And this was supposed to prove that when Sussman claimed she'd embezzled a bunch of money from him, he was making it all up. "No one knows him like I do," she'd said. "He's a total pig. You have no idea. He's an uncaring evil shit, a phony and he knows it. Once people know the truth, who'll believe him?"

Didn't sound like much of a plan. She'd also stopped paying Sussman's bills, which meant he'd be onto her soon if he wasn't already. If she hadn't been so greedy she could have stayed under the radar. But now she'd be caught, just like Gillespie. Taking her money would accomplish not much more than adding felonies to his rap sheet.

Before her confession he'd assumed she inherited her money, a snob like her. This was a broad who could keep her nose stuck in the air while sucking a guy's dick. Now he understood he'd been underestimating her nerve and overestimating her sanity. It takes guts to steal what you want. The world just doesn't want to give it up. It wants to keep you down in your hole—in Gillespie's case a faded stucco box with no space to put anything. Like living in a junkshop. The garage was the only room he could stand to be in. How many assholes had he busted with bigger houses, prettier wives, nicer cars? How'd everything get so unfair? It all traced back to those flakes on the City Council. If they hadn't stopped paying overtime he probably wouldn't have sicced Shrek onto that score. And it was just *dope* money. It's not like he'd raped kids or stuck up a gas station. Is the world any better off if biker gangs keep their drug profits?

The older kid was watching him again, sneaking around without saying anything. What's wrong with that kid? Plenty, feared Gillespie, who'd lost count of his stomach crunches again. Still hadn't worked up much of a sweat. Finally the kid spoke in a low voice, half whispering like his mom: "You're supposed to take us to soccer practice."

Damn, Tina had told him twice before she left for work. "Okay," he said. But it wasn't. Nothing was okay. And then the phone in the house rang, four rings before his daughter picked up. Can't they just answer it?

"Da-ad, I don't know who it is!"

"Ask 'em for Christ's sake!"

"You better come!"

Gillespie recognized the voice right away as a cop voice before the cop identified herself as an LAPD detective. He decided not to thank her for getting back to him. Mustn't sound overeager. Just routine business. Yeah, she said, they had the guy in custody he'd asked about. For a carjacking in Studio City. She had a kind of naturally sweet voice, a gentle delivery, but the words weren't gentle at all. That's how she made it into a cop voice.

"Well, he's helping us clear up some cases here, and we hate to see him jammed up like this," Gillespie told her. That shouldn't sound so unusual.

"We're talking about a piece of shit who yanked a teacher out of her car and knocked her on her ass. What's he giving you? Shoplifters? Unless he can bring you another John Dillinger, taking this shitbird down is more important than whatever information you're getting from him, okay? In fact, we notice he fits the description of a suspect from your neck of the woods. The Roland Sussman thing? Home invasion? Probably the biggest thing in Hermosa Beach since forever. You must want to clear that one, right? I'll shoot you a mug shot."

"Sure, that's great, but I kind of doubt it's him 'cause—"

"Why's that?"

"That's what I was trying to tell you."

"Well detective, if you're not—"

"It's *sergeant* detective."

"How you make sergeant in Hermosa Beach? Rescuing cats?"

"Fuck you."

"Is this a bad connection or are you talking with a rag in your mouth? I can barely understand you."

"You understand me all right."

"Wait a minute, what's your name? Gillespie? I heard of you. Aren't—"

Gillespie didn't hang on for the rest. He already knew he was the dumb bastard who'd turned himself blue. Oh Jesus, everything that can go wrong, it goes wrong. How much longer before they break down Shrek? They might be pulling it out of him right this moment. He'd get years off his sentence for delivering a cop. And for a cop no one wanted around anyway? He could walk. The worst part was sitting around and waiting it out, having to act natural, to keep living the same bullshit life and hoping to dodge the bullet somehow.

GOT TO soccer practice ten minutes late, so the kid had to run all the way around the field even though, as he told the coach, it wasn't his fault. Fucking kid. The girl just sat on the sidelines and smiled. What's so fucking funny?

Next he had to meet with Rosen again. A moron who couldn't solve a crime on his own if the perp carved a confession on his ass and mooned him with it. And these days he was a one-note commander—all Sussman all the time. "So how's it look on this suspect they've got up in the Valley? We ready to ship him down here?"

Normally Rosen didn't care what Gillespie was up to. He assumed, like all the others, that Gillespie was a loon the department had to hang on to because the liberal establishment protected people with issues of race, color, gender, and all the rest. The department couldn't wait for him to finish his twenty and beat it so he'd stop embarrassing everybody. They only made him a detective so he wouldn't wear the uniform around town.

"I really don't think it's him," Gillespie said, "but even if it is, which I doubt, they still want to keep him for carjacking."

"Boss won't like that." The boss, the chief, was too important to talk to anybody directly. Like a pope, only he made fewer appearances. But he was the reason Rosen, who was assistant chief and commander of detectives, was bugging him. Rosen had squinty little eyes like a turtle. Photos of his wife and turtle kids behind him. Wife not bad. Like just about every other male officer in the department except Gillespie he'd pumped his body into a thick tube of liverwurst. Gillespie preferred the sinewy look.

"The witnesses see this guy yet?"

"I'm setting it up, but—"

"I know. You said it's probably not him. But I'm not asking you that."

"I know, but—"

"What'd I ask you?"

"Whether the witnesses saw him yet."

"No I didn't. I asked you when they'll get a look at him. And don't say next week, Sergeant."

"It's not what you asked me."

"Goddammit, when do they get a look at him?"

"If I have to spend all damn day in your office? Not soon."

"Out." Rosen didn't raise his voice, which meant he was extra angry and would probably look for payback. Gillespie should apologize. But he didn't.

CHAPTER 26

Skip never understood how dangerous Hillenbrand was. Or if he did, he couldn't bring himself to care. His indifference was partly an unintended consequence of something Bento told him. Funny how a person can hear different things day after day and it washes over him without consequence. But Bento made this particular remark while the two of them were high on an especially potent batch of fermented pruno slop, and the vile mixture helped create the kind of moment Newton had under the apple tree, except Newton probably wasn't sloshed.

Skip was one of those guys who never learned to accept his sentence, not even for a minute. It ate at him like one of those creepers sucking the life out of a tree. "Don't you see?" Bento told him. "Now you're free."

"Free," he said derisively.

"You've been truly fucked, right? So what else can they do? You've already exceeded the quota."

He understood how Skip, looking at skinny little Hillenbrand in his dorky glasses, could decide he wasn't particularly threatening—except the experiences of other convicts had already proven such thinking was a serious mistake.

"I'm telling you, don't have anything to do with that guy. Don't even make *eye* contact."

"But remember that time you said I was free? How can I be free if I walk around on tippy-toes? Make up your mind."

Just because your mind is free doesn't mean you have to be stupid, Bento told him, but Skip thought hanging around with stone killer maniac Hillenbrand was a kind of adventure—like jumping the gate at an amusement park. He'd also decided Hillenbrand wasn't really that creepy, that he even enjoyed a good joke sometimes.

Actually, Skip's bizarre frame of mind stemmed less from what Bento theorized about freedom and more from the atrocities perpetrated by his ex-girlfriend. She stole everything he owned. He'd personally packed it all up in his car because enough was enough, and she and her junkie friends just drove away with it while Skip did a shift at Jiffy Lube. Employees had to park way over at the edge of the mall lot where he couldn't monitor his naked belongings. All he had left was his garage uniform with another guy's name over the pocket, his shoes, wallet, and cell phone, no charger.

"Listen, you fucking cunt bitch whore, I will kill you, understand? Give me back my shit or I'm gonna fucking kill you."

"First, I don't know what you're talking about. Second, you go around killing people you'll go back to prison. That what you want? On your knees all day with unsanitary things in your mouth?"

She had a mouth on her, that ex-girlfriend.

"I want everything back right now or you're gonna die, understand? Die! And I'm gonna enjoy making you dead."

And so it went, all poured straight into her Radio Shack recorder. When the jurors and everybody sneaked glances at him in the courtroom Skip tried not to look homicidal. But he also didn't want to look like someone who'd go around blowing guys like she'd said. It was an awful two days. The DA's zero-tolerance response forced a trial, but with no deal to be had, his lawyer acted like the proceedings were being conducted in a foreign language. The ex-girlfriend, who'd taken a few acting classes, managed to look like a Girl Scout who needed the jurors' protection.

Bento told himself he mustn't let his prison time define him, yet sometimes it felt dishonest not to reveal it. So he found himself telling Speed and Sussman about Skip, who'd sold Hillenbrand a contraband cell phone. And sure enough, Hillenbrand figured he'd been screwed in some weird way that made no sense at all. And Skip got really foolish, disrespecting him in front of others.

"Now me he never liked," Bento explained. "Who knows why. On the other hand, who'd he like? Anyway he figures if he makes a move on Skip he'll have to deal with me eventually. So what does he do? The unexpected. Him and some goon who either owed him a favor or was hired out, because Hillenbrand had no friends. They jumped me behind the power house with these iron rods. Bam, bam, bam. I realized, hey, this is no fight. These guys, they're going to fucking kill me."

"You couldn't run?" asked Sussman.

"They had me cornered in a small space, and I was already hurt. So I moved in closer, trying to smother their swings. Like boxers do. And I get both hands around Hillenbrand's throat. I'm shoving him up against his goon, jamming both of them against the building. The goon, he's having trouble getting at me without hitting the psycho, but I'm struggling just to stay conscious. I can't squeeze hard enough so I try to get his ear in my teeth, but—"

Sussman: "Whose ear?"

"Hillenbrand's. I missed. Got his eye instead. I can feel it, and phaww," making a face, "I want to let go, but it's all I got and I force myself. I bite down hard, hard as I can, grinding. I taste all this blood and hear this . . . I mean this really horrible shrieking next to my ear and I just keep . . . biting down. His eyebrow, his eye, everything's in my mouth. This is all happening fast. Next thing I know all this stuff— eyelashes, blood, skin, everything—it's still inside my mouth, but . . . it's not attached to his face anymore, and I'm all alone, puking. I spit and spit, but . . . eeeww. Jesus, that was bad. I bit his eye out."

Sussman broke the silence. "So you failed as a cannibal."

"You can't let a little setback like that define you," said Speed. "Next time you'll swallow."

"You'll lick your plate," said Sussman.

"Bastards," said Bento.

CHAPTER 27

It occurred to Sussman that he'd been grievously robbed by someone he trusted, but here he was joking with this kid to make him feel better. Maybe he wasn't such a fraudulent Buddhist after all. But you didn't have to be a deep thinker to understand that whatever assets might or might not have been stolen from him were a small matter compared to two thugs trying to murder you with iron rods and no one there to help.

Bento wasn't proud of the outcome, but he didn't seem tortured either. It was a set of facts, like your weight or place of birth. It was also no accident that he didn't say why he'd gone to prison. Once you admit to chewing off someone's eye and spitting it out, you'd think there can't possibly be any secrets left. But there was plenty of mystery surrounding this kid. Even his ethnic origins were unclear. Aquiline features, tall, straight black hair and an olive complexion. Probably not 100 percent Caucasian. There was an indefinable dash of something else. You want to know, but you don't want to ask. His fat hippie friend was another enigma, not your ordinary loudmouth. These guys were *material*. You never know when it might turn up, but it was one of the best parts of being a writer. You could run straight into a cactus—or a crazy blue cop—and it hits you: wow, what luck!

"That turned out to be my last prison fight. Afterward even the craziest motherfuckers stayed clear of me. Nobody wants pieces of their face bitten off."

"What happened to the psycho?" asked Sussman.

"I never saw him again. When he got out of the hospital they transferred him to another prison. They talked about prosecuting me for a while. And that's no joke. You run into guys all the time doing time for something that happened inside. But I got off lucky—three months in the hole."

"The eye," said Speed. "What'd it taste like?"

"Like chicken."

Sussman nodded and passed around another joint.

SUSSMAN WAS named Roland because his parents were forty-five cents short in a supermarket checkout line. His pregnant mother picked up an item to return to the cashier, but the man standing behind them put a dollar on the counter. When they thanked him, he quipped, "Just name your firstborn after me." He, the original Roland, probably didn't understand that his dad was too superstitious *not* to name him Roland. He and his pals would go to a ball game and lay down bets on whether a pitcher would complete the inning, how many times an outfielder would scratch his nuts in one inning, everything and anything. In those days the Cubs played only day games and half the guys in the ballpark were operating beyond the confines of nine-to-five life.

"Are you gonna call her?" Speed asked Sussman. They were at the door.

"I don't know."

"Then maybe you should get a lawyer. Know any good ones?"

"The only one I can think of is the guy who arranged the power of attorney for Pick."

"He might not be such a good choice."

"What about you guys? You know someone?"

"I know a guy named Horowitz," Bento said. "He's sharp."

"Maybe you could call her too," said Sussman.

"Horowitz is a he," said Bento.

"No, I mean Pick. You're bill collectors, right? Maybe you could call her for me." Sussman wasn't sure why he said that. Maybe he wanted to regain the respect of his dead father, who never would have been such a chump in the first place.

Speed: "What exactly have you said to her?"

"I left her a couple messages asking her to call me."

Speed nodded, drinking in Sussman's ridiculous answer. "Collection agencies charge half," he said. "Lawyers are cheaper."

Apparently the wording of the power of attorney complicated any criminal prosecution. All three agreed that cops might very well call it a lovers' quarrel. Sussman couldn't bear to call the cops anyway, especially on a friend.

"Our boss says people out to screw you from the start, they probably will find a way to screw you," said Bento. "It's what they're good at. He looks like Humphrey Bogart."

"Who? Your boss?"

"I mean exactly like him. You ought to put him in a book."

"Somebody should," said Sussman.

"I mean it. Tell him, Speed."

"Exactly," said Speed.

"You think they're related?"

"Nobody knows," said Speed.

"Why don't you ask him?"

Speed: "It never comes up. The longer it doesn't come up, the harder it gets to ask him. You know Bento's right about Horowitz. You need him or somebody like him. You can't let her take any more than she's already taken, okay?"

"Okay."

"If it's okay, how come you're not asking for his number?"

"Horowitz?"

"Yes, Horowitz."

"Okay, may I have his number?"

Speed went to hunt it up on Sussman's Internet.

"You know, I saw you once before," Bento told Sussman. "In the police station. I think it must have been right after the break-in at your place. You were on crutches."

"And I saw you. I remember now. You were in a little room, and they were trying to pin it on you. There was a cop with blue skin who wanted to put you away."

"It's the way they are, a lot of them. If you've done time, it's their job to lock you up again. Before you create new problems."

"But you're calm about it."

"Would it help to get upset?"

"How old are you?" asked Sussman.

"Twenty-eight."

"You *know* a lot."

Sussman would call this Horowitz and probably end up relying on him and hope for the best. Funny how you can recognize your faults at the same time you repeat them. Of all the people Sussman had relied upon, Pick was the most capable. She'd once managed an entire shopping center. It was sad to watch her stride through life with her droopy little breasts and the name Pickford because her parents thought having a Waspy last name for a first name could be socially useful. But she knew from the start not to treat him like the Lincoln Memorial. He required only a touch of worship, he used to say. There was, she responded, a joke within his joke, namely that he wasn't joking at all. One of many clues Sussman had ignored.

CHAPTER 28

The schmo hesitated when Bento asked him to turn down his thundering TV, as though he feared it would cut off his breathing. When he got the gist of what Bento was saying, he began to weep. "I know you've got a job to do," he said between sobs. He repeated that several times. When Bento finally got rid of him he decided the crying schmo might have invented a brilliant new escape strategy.

"Nah," said Eddie. "One place I worked, they had contests to see who could make the first one cry. There's nothing new under the sun, kid. The thing that hath been, it is that which shall be."

"What's that?"

"Ecclesiastes," said Eddie, "but I don't know where exactly."

Bento heard Liz telling Mrs. Roubini, whose account was overdrawn, that she had to worry about herself first and her bills later. Phil just shook his head. On another day he might have found it amusing, but apparently he'd just had some new unspecified trouble with his daughter, Sonia. She came around once in a while, usually to pick up money, invariably tugging her daughter, who, unlike her mom, always had a big grin for everybody. Phil's daughter might have been pretty, but her face was remarkably unexpressive, almost like meat. And she treated it like meat, stretching her earlobes into hideous oversized appendages by inserting metal circles into them with circumferences like table coasters. It was difficult not to stare. Combined with the boredom in her face, her cockamamy ears were a statement of industrial-strength nihilism. Nihilism without purpose.

Sonia's features remained impassive even the day she showed up to sell kitchen knives out of a sample case. Everyone had to order something to be nice to Phil, who looked like he was being crucified. They all pretended she'd found a career that was just perfect for her and her deadpan face and mutilated ears. Bento ordered one little knife and it was forty-five bucks plus shipping and handling. And he still hadn't received the knife. Even during her sales pitch the daughter was aggressively unfriendly to everyone but Bento, who was awarded brief toothy smiles and small talk. On sales day she wore towering heels and an off-white skirt that clung so tightly to her thighs she could take only baby steps.

SANDRA SHOWED up with department store shopping bags. She'd lugged the stuff all the way up the steps so she could show off her purchases. "Jesus," said Phil, who stomped over to her desk and began griping before she sat down. "Why can't you be ten minutes late like everybody else? It's getting worse and worse. We've got schmoes calling and no one to take their money. And Liz, she's telling people *not* to pay. I mean what the hell, Sandra."

Sandra spoke to him in a low voice. Bento couldn't make out what she said, but it clearly was no apology. She was no one to trifle with. In fact, there was no one in the office who could be trifled with.

"You know what?" Phil yelled. "That's it. You are fucking fired. Fired, you understand?"

Bento's phone buzzed, but he threw his headset on the desk and rose to his feet. Phil looked over. "And where are *you* going?"

Bento steered himself over to Phil and spoke softly into an ear. "I need to speak to you privately."

"Take the call first," Phil said. He was a teapot ready to go off.

Bento returned to his desk and picked up the call. He knew this schmo. "Mr. Lester? I'll need a minute or two. Call you right back, okay?" Phil followed him over to the unpainted, uncarpeted warehouse section of the room.

"If you don't unfire her I quit," Bento said.

"Is everybody here nuts? I've fired Sandra four or five times. She knows she's not fired. Look." He turned his head. Bento followed his gaze to see Sandra curled up on her special ergonomic chair in a sort of half-yoga position, watching the Shopping Channel and talking, probably with a schmo.

"Then why'd you tell her she's fired?"

"It seems to help me. I don't know."

"You're right," Bento said. "Everybody in this place *is* nuts."

THE CAR lot was almost fifteen minutes away, next to a Spanish Pentecostal storefront. But it wasn't exactly a car lot. It was a jalopy lot that rented or sold beat-up vehicles, about a dozen on the premises at the moment. Gas-eaters all, they had nicks, scrapes, dents, an occasional missing hubcap, and a faded, dispirited look that no simple washing would cure. Signs offered sales, rentals, and long-term leases.

Bento recognized her immediately from the little-girl picture as Norah Schulz exited the little office and walked straight to him. You could see there had been no excessive grooming on her part, but she resembled a young Catherine Deneuve anyway with lustrous skin and a tiny waist. She was a blonde Stradivarius in a junk pile. Just as she opened her mouth to speak, her words were swallowed by an emergency siren. She shrugged. The lot was backed almost against the San Diego Freeway, whose swirls of exhaust, dirt, and traffic noise shortened the lives of nearby residents and would shorten the life of Norah Schulz too if she stayed here long enough. But it was easy to see that for her this place was no more than a pit stop. Anyway, the whole enterprise had the look of something that could evaporate at any moment. Come back in a month or two and you might find a strip joint or a muffler shop.

A tattoo ran incongruously down her taut right shoulder, a cartoon figure of a peppy Rosie the Riveter in hip-hugging shorts, rolled-up sleeves and a red kerchief tied around her head. Rosie, fists on hips, was ready for anything—perfectly in synch with the Facebook photo of feisty little Norah on the tricycle. Stray hairs ventured down the forehead of adult Norah, nearly covering one eye. Her smile widened just a bit, and as though reading his mind, she tossed her obstinate hair with a flick of her head. It didn't work, bouncing right back to its starting place. Wow, Bento thought. What a babe.

"Are you looking to rent or buy?" she asked him, apparently for the second time.

Must speak. Must not shut down. "I'm not sure," he said after too much hesitation. "What's the better deal?"

"That depends on how long you need it and . . . let's face it, your credit history. Look around. If you see one you like, I'll tell you the truth about it as far as I know. If we find anything's seriously wrong we don't let them off the lot."

"But there's something wrong with all of them, isn't there? That's why they're here."

She laughed a genuine laugh. The teeth were Hollywood white but not completely straight. "They're the runts of many litters, but don't underestimate them. We buy cheap and sell below market. We check histories too. Some places try to stick you with cars that were wrapped around utility poles. They also sell the same cars over and over . . . you know how?"

"They set up payments the customer can't possibly keep up, and their repo men set up the snatch while the ink is still wet on the sale."

She looked suddenly thoughtful, squinting one eye and tilting her head, as though seeing him for the first time. "Do I know you? There's something—I don't know—familiar."

His first reaction was to deny it, a con's reaction. "A little," he said.

"I know you a little? Refresh my memory."

"I'm . . . Remember Mister White?"

"Mister—You're Marley?"

"You're not upset, are you?"

"Hell yes, I'm upset."

"Please, I—"

She looked at him as though he were a glob of puzzling goo. "Maybe you should beat it," she said.

"I can't even get a car? I need one. Honest."

She took a deep breath, and he watched her appearance alter itself, switching to a more ironic mode, harder to pinpoint. It was an involuntary reaction to his amatory interest. She was like a flower that now had a different relationship to the sun. Her eyes, he saw now, were brown.

"Can you even afford one?" she said.

"The sign says you can finance anybody."

"We can, but we don't."

"My name's Bento." He wanted to shake hands but decided a no-touch policy was wiser.

"This doesn't feel right. It's a bit . . . I don't know. I don't want to say icky, but—" The situation was delicate. He must proceed without error. Liz had coached him on what he might say, but they both knew following a script would *sound* like a script. In close he was on his own. Be bold, Liz instructed, but not smug.

"You really want to penalize me for wanting to meet you? What if you'd bumped into me at a swap meet or something? That would probably be okay, right? If we'd met by accident?"

"If you weren't stalking me, you mean. It would be less un-okay, I guess, but I don't shop much."

"Me neither. And we did run into each other by accident. Over the phone."

"So what do you do when you're not sneaking up on people with unpaid bills?"

"Let me see. I read a lot." That didn't come out right. It sounded like bragging. But he'd paid his reader dues. *Anna Karenina* cost him almost eleven dollars with postage—earned in the kitchen at twenty-eight cents an hour. Maybe if society weren't so determined to deprive him of learning he'd have spent it on cigarettes. Because he'd pleaded guilty to a drug crime, Bento was ineligible for student loans or Pell Grants. And thanks to the wisdom and virtue of the American congress he could never live in public housing or get an FHA mortgage either. The government wanted to make absolutely certain he'd never climb out of his ossuary.

"Show me your library card," Norah Schulz said.

He tried not to gloat as he pulled it from his wallet and handed it over.

"Bruce from Torrance," she said, handing it back.

"Everybody calls me Bento. Can I see yours?"

"As if you didn't already Google and Facebook and Twitter me at all the virtual rape sites. What do you need with my library card?"

"Look, I don't normally do this kind of stuff. I'm not a smooth operator. I'm still nervous about it, but—"

"You didn't spot the Valium stand on the corner?"

They don't take plastic, he almost said, but decided it wasn't so terribly clever.

"How'd you know I'd be here today?"

"Just guessed. I thought maybe we could meet for coffee. If I leave you my card, will you call? Please?" Bento had never owned business cards before. He was terribly proud of them.

"You're supposed to call me, remember? To collect your money. Anyway, I was just a voice on the phone. What made it so important to find me?"

"I liked the way your mind works. I found it—find it—really attractive."

"That's it?"

"That's it."

"And now I'm supposed to swoon?"

"It would be helpful."

"What's with the ponytail?"

"I was drunk. What's with the tattoo?"

"You don't act scared to me. Anyway, I suggest you go home to your wife."

"Come on. There's no wife."

"I wasn't about to propose anyway. Let me see your driver's license."

"You're going to run a check."

"Didn't you?"

"I didn't take it that far. It didn't seem right."

She held out her hand, palm up, waiting. Such a pretty hand. No jewelry.

"You won't find much," he lied, fishing it out of his wallet. He hesitated. "You can study it over coffee, okay? Name a place."

"Let me see it now or this ends right here."

He was ruined. He knew it. She'd take it back into her little office, copy it, and look him up later. There was nothing virtuous or admirable in any computer readout with his name on it. But he handed her his license. "It's expired," Norah Schulz said.

"I renewed it. They just haven't gotten me the new one yet." He produced the receipt from his wallet. Meanwhile an elderly black couple, strolling through the lot for the last couple of minutes, now hovered over a silver minivan that looked like it spent much of its life parked in a desert. Norah Schulz handed him back his documents. Saved. "Have you got a few minutes?" she asked him. He didn't.

"Sure," he said.

Fifteen minutes later the couple left without a car, though they promised to return the next day. Meanwhile Bento leaned against a ten-year-old Nissan reading a two-months-old *Time* he'd found on a coffee table inside a cramped office. When she finally got back to him she asked, "Do you like Shakespeare?"

"Sure."

"The comedies?"

"Some more than others."

"*Twelfth Night?*"

"Which one's that?"

"I think it's the one with the shipwreck."

"A girl cross-dresses?"

"I think so."

"Sure, that one's okay."

"They're doing it in Culver City Friday night. Wanna go?"

"You have no idea how much I want to go. Does this mean I got the job?"

"Quiet. They put it on in a park. It's free, but it's got costumes and everything. Shakespeare by the Sea, they call it."

"Sounds . . . It sounds great. Really."

"You bring the wine. I'll bring something to eat."

He asked where they could meet.

"Why? You don't want to pick me up?"

"I don't know if I'll have a car Friday."

"You own a credit card?"

He nodded.

"Good. This Nissan? It's the best car on the lot. Rent it for a week, and if you like it, you can buy it or we'll arrange a lease."

She took him through the paperwork in five minutes. At the tail end she offered him two kinds of insurance. "One is for thirteen dollars a day from a company that honors its policies. The other costs four dollars a day."

"And it doesn't pay claims."

"I didn't say that. Not exactly."

"I'll take the phony four-dollar one."

"A wise choice," she said.

"Bet you say that to everybody."

"Yup. Look, we're not con artists here. We try to give customers a decent deal. A lot of them really appreciate us. You can't live in this nutty town without a car. People can't even get to job interviews." He guessed Norah was from somewhere else. LA people rarely mentioned the transportation horrors as anything unique. They were just there, like the Watts Towers or the Hollywood Hills.

She gave him the keys, wrote something on the back of her own card, and handed it to him. Her personal number. Promised Land. He'd pick up his car later. Driving Liz's Toyota back to the office, he felt the way he did the day in seventh grade gym class when he hit a pitch over the center fielder's head, way back into the sun.

CHAPTER 29

Gillespie, after finishing one of his secret phone calls out at the pool, reentered the bedroom. He looked concerned.

"Why so blue?" Pick said.

He grabbed her wrist and squeezed, pulling it toward him. With her other hand she dug her nails into his forearm and he let go, pulling back his hand to deliver a slap. She covered up, but it was just a feint. He snickered. He never let out genuine laughs, but a little violence sometimes brought forth a smile. He still didn't understand that joking about his complexion was a way to diminish its control over him. No sense trying to explain it again. After looking up argyria on the Internet she was even more convinced how deluded he must be. It had been known for centuries that silver, ingested in a liquid form known as colloidal silver, wards off some diseases but also discolors the skin. Only the wealthy could afford to take it so they became known as blue bloods. After penicillin and other antibiotics came along a blue complexion became the private preserve of fools and crackpots.

"They're gonna show you a mug shot of somebody because of that . . . you know, that deal over at Sussman's place. We need to get going."

"To the station? Can't they just e-mail an attachment? Which century do they live in?"

"Listen, this won't be the guy, okay? You give them a strong enough no, maybe we can skip the lineup, unless Sussman IDs him. If he does, we'll worry about that later."

"I don't understand."

"All you need to understand is this was not the guy. When you see the picture? You never saw this dude in your life."

Then she understood. It was a giant blast of data compressed into a few words. "Oh my God," she said.

The only sounds now were the humming of the pool filter coming through the open french doors and a barky little neighbor dog. Finally he said, "Hey, don't look at me like that."

"You had something to do with it, didn't you?"

He looked at her like she was wearing a tinfoil hat. "'Course not. He's one of my informants, that's all."

"And you've been hiding it. All this time."

"Look, you know how you offered to pay me? Well, this is part of the deal. You help me, I help you. C'mon, get dressed and I'll take you to the station. I told 'em we'd be there in less than an hour. Just remember what I said. It's not him."

"They know you're here?"

"I told 'em I could find you."

It seemed like she was never dressed anymore. Not completely anyway. Yet lately he'd been leaving his own clothes on, baring his uncircumcised member only when circumstances called for it, and even then baring nothing else, freeing it to poke out of his fly like a stiff eel. With him mostly dressed and her in various stages of undress, the contrast had become a kind of a rite that paid homage to his masculinity. Or maybe she was reading too much into it. Maybe it was more about the shape of his phallus, which, he must have been aware, was distinctly unattractive. When flaccid it was a fat stump that made gender a riddle. Lower primates had a similar condition. Pick was silently appreciative he kept the thing covered up until ready for use, like the gun beneath his shirt. Meanwhile, whatever was eating at the two of them still led to sex, but sex was a diminishing solution, giving their paraphilia a more desperate quality and proving once again there was no secret key to the universe. Every time you found one, it eventually stopped working. She was also tired of having to prove that her lack of sexual hang-ups didn't make her his fool.

"Listen to me," she said calmly. She'd learned that in a long-ago speech course. Speak softly and they'll strain to listen. "I really don't care what sort of deal you and that monster have together. I just don't like being lied to. And I especially don't like it when you act like I'm stupid for not believing you. I'm a fucking PhD. Do you even know what that means? *I'm* not the bimbo here."

She threw on her robe and stuck her chin out, daring him to slap, but he just bit his lower lip. Strange, the things that frightened Gillespie—that a commie government would steal everyone's guns or the world would expire when clocks marked a new millennium. Yet he refused to accept, for example, the slow Apocalypse of a baking planet. His mind was stuck in reverse, unable to acknowledge what was genuine but eager to embrace remarkably absurd myths and dark wishes that, unlike the foundations of paranoid beliefs, had no relationship to facts.

"Here's something to think about, okay? What if Sussman made up that story about the geek? What if he pressured you into going along? His career was on the rocks and douche bags like him, they figure a little publicity never hurts."

"That puts me in trouble too. And it still doesn't solve my problem."

"You'd be cooperating. A cooperating witness. You want to show everybody what a liar he is, right? Think about it while you get dressed."

"You must be more desperate than I am."

"Don't you worry about me."

"And I don't like you calling him a douche bag."

"That's practically all you *talk* about—what a douche bag he is. That and your brother. Sorry, didn't mean that, the last part."

She pulled out some underwear, threw it on the bed, and spent a minute at her dressing table touching up her lipstick.

Tossing her robe on the floor, she entered the walk-in closet, searching for suitable police station attire. "The person and the body of work are two different things!" she shouted out to him. "It happens a lot. Dos Passos, Hemingway, Picasso . . . Assholes, every one of them."

Gillespie, though a barbarian, was probably no less understanding of literary mastery than that ignorant corner of the literature establishment that viewed Sussman's work as disturbingly accessible. Also, it failed to be humorless. She'd long since faced up to the living paradox embodied in Sussman, a classic genius hypocrite. His condition was by no means singular. Einstein and Shakespeare were also cruel to their women and more or less got away with it. That wouldn't happen this time. She deserved the comforts she'd debased herself to acquire from such a deceitful man, but hanging on to her compensation would be challenging in a world with so little justice at its core. It was difficult not to flee the horror that had to be approaching, but she couldn't bear to leave the rewards behind. She wasn't sure whether she thought about it too much or not enough.

ON THE way to the station Pick found herself pouring out more details about her brother, Marty, about the praise his teachers used to heap on him, how his beatific aura made it harder for her in school because of the inevitable comparisons, but she never held it against him. Like everyone else, she loved Marty. As a teenager he took bag ladies out for coffee. And she just now decided he'd signed up for the army on September 12, 2001. More and more, when she was particularly upset or fearful, she added garlands to the tale of a sweet brother who'd adored her. She knew that contriving too many details could trip her up later, but she so loved them. The way she dressed and carried herself made it difficult to obtain anyone's sympathy, but the tale of Marty altered all that. Even Gillespie was respectful. The young men killed by Cheney's cut-rate showers were thinking about breakfast or whatever soldiers thought about when they were lucky enough to be back in a safe area with hot showers when sweet Jesus, the voltage ran through them and for that last minimoment they smelled their hair and flesh burning and hit the concrete dead. To this day no one knew just how many soldiers lost their lives to defective Halliburton wiring. She'd looked it up many times. The Pentagon failed to keep a trustworthy total.

Pick decided Marty had been buried at Arlington on a rainy day and that many of his friends flew across the country to be there, including the very real Arnold Isaacson she'd pursued in high school who later, she learned, changed his name to Arnold I. Saxon. Sussman, upon learning about the new Saxon, said he should have gone all the way and called himself Arnold *Anglo* Saxon. "That'd be taking the bull by the horns," he said.

Her mother, Pick told Gillespie, declined to accept the flag from the astonished officer. All of it could be true, she decided, just as *Grapes of Wrath* was truer than cable news and *Catch-22* was more accurate than your average presidential library.

SUSSMAN WAS exiting as she and Gillespie approached the building from the parking lot. She entered only after he pulled away in his car. Four cops waited for her inside the room. Gillespie made five. They strained to be polite, offering her coffee and a designated chair. Pick reminded herself she wasn't a criminal and must not act like one. In fact, she was a victim and a hero. The one in charge was a man named Rosen who looked like Richard Dreyfuss before his hair turned white, but this Dreyfuss head was stuck atop a Schwarzenegger body.

Two photos, eight by tens, in color, lay on a table. And yes, that was the geek all right. Same little nose, same Jupiter-sized head, but the profile showed there was no braid anymore. She studied them awhile, pulling them closer and farther, finally setting them back.

"It's not him," she said. A wave of displeasure enveloped the room.

Rosen, showing no expression, said, "How can you be sure?"

"It's just not him."

"He matches the description in every way."

"If it were him I'd see it. It's just not the one."

Silence. Gillespie offered no help. She'd looked into Kazakhstan, Dubai, and other spots without extradition treaties. But they all came with negative baggage. The post nine-eleven world was so much smaller, everyone tracked and stamped like supermarket oranges.

"Get him down here," said a cop who hadn't spoken before. Pick had barely noticed him but now saw he had plenty of stars on his collars.

"Right boss," said Rosen. "Let's get him someplace where Ms. Manville can smell him."

CHAPTER 30

Liz made Bento ditch the shorts in favor of jeans. His legs were still eggshell pale from too many summers without sun. After much trial and error, they settled on a charcoal gray shirt. A flapping tail, Liz insisted, remained the mandatory fashion. She also made sure his beard had at least three days of growth. They'd washed and waxed his rental car the day before, but looking at it again he stopped kidding himself. The finish was still on the drab side. It's good enough, said Liz, who followed him to the car. She gave him a hug. "Great cologne," she whispered into his ear.

"I love you," he said.

"I know."

The sun was low when he pulled up to a standard little one-story stucco home just south of the airport. It was surrounded by a mix of flowers, mostly bougainvillea, with a pint-sized lawn. As he stepped out, an airliner passed close and low, its jet screech loud enough to inflict pain. Norah opened the door in blue shorts, tennis shoes, a white, short-sleeved blouse, and a compelling smile. Bento noticed a few stray blonde hairs falling over her left eye. It was good to be alive.

He followed her into a modest living room, its TV tuned to a local news channel on low volume. A middle-aged woman who looked like she knew something Bento didn't rose to greet him. She was what they call a "handsome" woman—pretty but past menopause. Faintly African American, no wedding ring, a pleasant smile. Norah introduced her as Gloria.

"Ned, come out here," Gloria called out. Norah's father was nearly as tall as Bento, with wavy gray hair that covered most of his ears. Firm grip. He also smiled a kind of secret smile as he studied Bento, tilting his head to the side. Bento had seen Norah use the same gesture.

"Norah won't tell us how she met you," he said. "It's aroused my curiosity." The father seemed comfortable in his own skin. Maybe a little too comfortable.

"You are such a jerk!" Norah told him, but she didn't seem really annoyed.

"Don't tell him," Gloria urged Bento. "He deserves to suffer."

Bento, looking at the father, pressed his palms together, making a little Buddhist teepee of silence.

"We met online," Norah said. "We're both committed to Satanism and world peace . . . Bento, grab that, will you?" A fair-sized cooler sat on a small dining table, along with picnic blankets. Bento was touched by her painstaking preparations but too tongue-tied to say it until they were inside the car. He asked if she had room in the cooler for wine.

She found the bottle in the backseat, studied the label, smiled, and made a space for it in her cooler. Later Bento would learn you weren't supposed to chill red wine. She was too nice to say anything. Had he been a standard middle-class guy she probably would have teased him for his ignorance.

"Thanks for not mentioning how we met," she said.

"Bill collectors are like priests. You can tell me anything."

"If my dad knew a collection agency was after me he'd try to lend me money, and he's practically as broke as I am. They're underwater on that stupid house. If it were three blocks away they'd have torn it down."

"Who'd have torn it down?"

"The city. Houses too close to airport noise get torn down. Eminent domain. They decide for you. Nice, huh? We can still make the death list if they make any runway changes.

Meanwhile the airport buys us double-pane windows. But forget all that. You all psyched up for the Bard?"

"Thou art more lovely than a summer's day," he said.

"You talk funny."

"Rough winds do shake the darling buds of May—"

"Oh shut up," she said, pleased.

"I love it when you tell me to shut up," he said.

"You know what I like about you?"

"Beats me."

"You don't ask the standard twenty questions. 'What school did you go to, what was your major,' all that crap."

"I prefer to find the existential heart of you," he said. "It'd help if you get liquored up."

"Silly boy. Changing the subject, there are mostly families at these things, but it's fun. You'll see."

"Changing what subject?" he said. "I didn't know we had a subject."

"Good point. But I guess this is sort of a date. And date conversation, it's mostly, I guess, jokey insinuations, vague double entendres, stuff like that. Till they get married and stop talking to each other."

"Then let's skip the irony part," Bento said. "Let's speak, you know, straight talk. No ambiguity. You game?"

"You mean the whole night?"

"Why not?"

"Sure." Pause. "I feel naked without my irony."

"Me too," he said.

"And it's way too early to get naked."

"Agreed."

"Wait a minute," she said. "What'd I just agree to?"

He pulled into a large parking lot next to the park and turned toward her just as she pushed her hair away from her eye. She smelled faintly of flowers. All around them pedestrians of various ages paraded past, toting camp chairs, coolers, and other picnic paraphernalia. Her lips were open just a tad. Her eyes looked straight at him and off in the distance at the same time. They leaned toward each other and kissed, touching only lips, maybe a smidgeon of tongue. He wasn't sure whose.

It was an untroubled, far less nervous Bento who carried the cooler out toward the bandstand.

H<small>ER LEGS</small> crossed in yoga fashion, Norah briskly pulled stuff from the cooler—baked chicken pieces, potato salad, and fruit, plus napkins, towelettes, silverware, and corkscrew. Her fingers were strong, almost stubby, built for hard use but with a touch of baby fat. She was exquisitely sexy but only vaguely aware of her power. She seemed to have decided long ago, *So what? It doesn't really amount to much.* He would try to engrave this angel in his memory, so no matter what happened from here on in, he'd always have this fleeting image to call on, *what I'm seeing right now.*

The unpaid actors were terrific, evoking laughter and goodwill just as Shakespeare planned it four hundred years ago. Bento and Norah had one blanket beneath them, and when it got chilly and dusk turned to dark they draped the spare over their shoulders. With faint traces of chicken-grease on their fingers they held hands.

B<small>ACK IN</small> Norah's living room the sun was rising. She leaned forward, lips close. "Tell me the truth. Is my breath okay?"

He sniffed seriously, as though inspecting a milk carton. "Like you just brushed almost," he announced.

"Really? It feels like yuk."

"If your breath is yuk, give me yuk or give me death."

"Wait a minute. You said *almost.* It's really awful, isn't it?" She pulled back. "You lie about anything else?"

"Your breath is fantastic, I swear. But I lied about some-thing. When I agreed we shouldn't, you know, rush things."

"Things? What things?"

"Sex things."

"Ohhhhh." She nodded. "So you didn't mean it?"

"No."

"Me neither."

"Damn," he said.

"Rain check?"

He took her in his arms. "It's not raining now."

She kissed his cheek. "They'll be up. Wait for better cir-cumstances, okay? I'm barely awake anyway."

"Okay, I'll just sit here and wait."

"Oh shut up."

Norah owned the jalopy lot, and it was marginally prof-itable. She'd ended up on Bento's collection list only after surrendering her own apartment in the Marina so she could help her father and Gloria stave off foreclosure on a home that would never be worth much anyway. They'd borrowed against it in a doomed attempt to keep his business from going under.

Norah grew up mostly with her mother in Missoula, Mon-tana, where her mom's boyfriend liked to slap her ass and fondle it with fat, insistent fingers until she could break away. The state university was in Missoula, and there wasn't enough money for her to live elsewhere, so she spent years holding off the creepy boyfriend while she raced toward her degree in design. She escaped in a fourteen-year-old VW bus, head-ing out in the dead of winter. It was night, absolutely still except for the sputtering of the engine. Old VWs don't gener-ate much heat, and the cold was so extreme she grew light-headed. There were few signs of life in the darkness, but she knew the area was sprinkled with fascist militia strongholds. Her heart beat faster as she gently coaxed the bus over black ice on the curves. Even with the pedal to the floor the engine coughed. Going up the pass there were times she feared she might roll backward. If her bus stalled she was sure she'd never survive the night in such outer-space cold. Finally at the top of Lolo Pass she came to a diner with all its lights on. It stood like a supernatural presence, as though she'd found a bright oasis on the far side of the moon. Seating herself at the counter, she ordered coffee, shaking so badly she could barely get the words out. The middle-aged waitress told her it was forty-five below out there but wouldn't say much after that. It was as though there were only two people left in the world and the other one had no interest in talking to her. After finishing a second cup, Norah, still at the counter, cradled her head in her arms and waited for morning.

Eventually she and her weak engine made it all the way to Santa Monica. She walked barefoot out on the warm sand, watching the surf smash the beach, thrilled by its power. Sinking to her knees, she sobbed with relief and passion, tears streaming. She was home at last.

A week later she bluffed her way into a job as an animator for a small computer games company. She'd always been a good design student, but now she discovered she was a master of illusion. It was a force within her. When business improved, the company hired more artists, and training them was one of her duties. Four of the trainees were grim-faced souls from Moldova, which has the highest per capita intake of alcohol on earth. They had manners of stone, never apologizing or expressing gratitude.

After a while the owner decided hiring immigrants for the office was moving the mountain to Mohammad. He got rid of them one at a time as he forged contacts with Indian business entities and sent more and more work there. But video games referenced all sorts of cultural factoids that the Indian artists, like the Moldovans before them, found unfamiliar despite their bewitchment with all things American. Chief artist Norah was on the phone half the day with terribly polite neophytes in Bangalore who always said they understood what was needed but often didn't. Although unaware of it at the time, she was training her replacements. Somehow she'd failed to read the signs.

"Just talking about it I know how dumb I sound, but I couldn't imagine being fired," she told Bento. "Crazy, isn't it?" She defended her boss. He was a nice guy, but all his competitors were making similar offshore deals, and if he failed to follow the mob he'd be outbid every time. "I'd have lost my job anyway," she explained.

BENTO TRIED several times to reveal his convict past to Norah, but he couldn't get the words out. How should he tell her? When? "I think soon," said Liz.

But he'd worried for nothing. Norah ran a background check as soon as he left the car lot. "I was so smitten I felt creepy doing it. I almost didn't." After their Shakespeare date she was just as worried as he was, worried he wouldn't tell her. So when he did, she was jubilant. He couldn't remember anyone ever being so happy to learn he was a two-time loser.

"You were smitten? Really?"

"You must not be paying attention," she said. "Don't you remember? I asked to kiss you good night."

"You still smitten?"

"Oh no-o-o," she said. "Jesus, why do you think I'm doing what I'm doing?"

"Just being polite maybe."

"God, you're dumb."

He kissed her. "Wait, wait, stop, don't move, don't talk. Shhh. Ah, too late."

She shuddered and grabbed his shoulders. After a while she kissed his ear and said, "No, right on time."

CHAPTER 31

"Look, Mr. Bizzup, all I'm asking is do the right thing. Save us both a lot of trouble. Okay?" Silence ensued. All right then, Philyaw could outwait the bastard. Whatever it took. But a full minute passed, the granddaddy of phone silences. Did he detect breathing? Hard to say. He looked at his watch. Wait one more minute. *I can take it if he can.* And Philyaw heard:

"Do I need to send it special delivery or anything?" Bingo! A paying schmo.

"No, not if it's postmarked today," replied magnanimous Philyaw. "I suggest you mail it directly from the post office though. I'll make a notation here to prevent anyone from coming out there in the meantime. So you've got till next Tuesday."

Bizzup thanked him. The oddest part about him was his measured, baritone delivery. If you didn't know any better you'd think he was at least reasonably intelligent. Yet he believed he'd been discussing his long-overdue MasterCard bill with Detective Rogers of the Bunco Squad.

"I'm just glad we caught this in time," Philyaw/Rogers told him. But as he clicked off on the call, he had to meet the charge of Eddie, who scooted his wheeled chair across ten feet of floor and arrived next to him.

"Phil, what the hell you doing, man?" He spoke in sotto voice that wouldn't be picked up by their colleagues, his sad eyes boring into Philyaw like a power drill. He had eternally morose eyes. They made you answer him even when you'd rather not. They could almost make you forget he'd worked at agencies that collected the same bills over and over again from Alzheimer's patients. The line of acceptability moves with circumstances. Sonderkommandos in the death camps clung to life a little longer by lifting valuables from the gas victims, yanking the gold from their teeth, and turning everything in to the SS. Were they correct to eke out those extra weeks of life? If you've never been dead, it's hard to know.

"Look," Philyaw said, "you have no idea what's going on here."

"Ever read the Book of Job?" asked Eddie.

"Just give me the highlights."

"The Lord, he tells Job he's talking like a fool 'cause he's got no understanding of what the Lord knows. That's what you're saying. But in case you haven't noticed, you ain't the Lord."

Philyaw wished he could unburden himself to Eddie the way women talked with other women. Tell him how other kids go away to college and come back with degrees and his came back with a junk habit. Her latest scheme was to get his granddaughter home-schooled. He'd try to kill the plan by offering some kind of gift, although he knew better than to spell out a quid pro quo. It was like bribing a politician. But there was probably nothing he could do to get his little Bradwell her vaccinations. They're the cause of autism, said Sonia, who knew better than any scientists. Much of her agenda was designed to drive him crazy, but even though he understood that, it still drove him crazy. "Maybe the Lord should take a minute to look at the phone bills for this place," he told Eddie. "The Mother Teresa method, it's not working anymore. I don't know if it ever worked. Schmoes just don't want to give it up."

Philyaw read the *Wall Street Journal*. He knew the recession was over. But it didn't seem that way inside the offices of Western Credit Associates. The economists who said things were on the mend measured data that had no relevance on the street. Their jovial assessments only made schmoes more miserable, reinforcing the suspicion that everything must be their fault.

It felt fragile out there. So many schmoes were trapped, like miners tapping forlornly to a faraway surface they'd never see again. Philyaw could pick them out on the street. Sometimes they exploded like cabbies who finally lost their minds in traffic, screaming out the window to no one who cared. Philyaw suggested counseling to one of them. "Listen asshole," he replied. "I don't need no one to *talk* to. What I need is *money*." Philyaw could use both. Money and someone to talk to.

THIS WAS one of those days when Eddie dressed like a partner in a Wall Street brokerage—sharp creases, power tie, gleaming wing tips. From time to time he liked to remind himself and everyone else that he was an adult. It occurred to Philyaw he might try it himself once in a while.

The two of them poured coffees and went out on the porch. "I was thinking," said Eddie. "You know how Liz found that pot shop of Weitzel's? Every collector on earth after his ass and who nails him to the wall? Liz. She's an A-bomb, man. I don't want to tell you your business, but you gotta use her properly."

"I want you to tell me my business. I count on it. But we *are* using her, and I can't have you arguing with me in front of everybody. We've got to get some money outa these schmoes, understand? It's crunch time." Philyaw loved this coffee. He made a mental note that no matter where the future took him, he'd take this coffee pot along.

"You're asking me to compromise my soul, man, everything I believe."

"Eddie, I've compromised my soul plenty of times. It's not so bad, honest."

Eddie chuckled.

"I'm not kidding."

"I know," said Eddie. "But we don't have to get down in the mud. We got *Fortune* 500 clients, man. We're smokin'."

"Look, if we go under, I'll come out okay. I always know when it's time to jump. But Sandra, Speed and the rest, what about them?"

"You're not just talking about them. You mean me too. Like what would an old guy like me do if he lost his job?"

Phil didn't try to deny it. Meanwhile an idea showed up. "You know what you said about Liz and the A-bomb? I'm thinking if she can find a $3 million chain of medical marijuana shops some guy's holding in a custodial account for his poodle, what else can she find? Maybe when Horowitz files judgments, we should forget about skip tracers and sic Liz on them. Maybe we're letting too many Madoffs slip through. Her first day she asked for all the hard cases. Maybe she was right."

"But we can't just forget about routine schmoes, and we don't have enough people as it is."

"Exactly. We need to hire another collector. We're gonna expand."

"That takes money," said Eddie.

"I've got this emergency Berkshire Hathaway stock. I'll sell it and double down. If it doesn't work, at least I'll keep the house." Philyaw knew better than to mortgage his home to bail out a business. That's how you wind up sleeping at the Salvation Army.

"You sure this is a good idea?"

"Of course not," Philyaw said.

CHAPTER 32

Hearing Pick's voice on the phone reminded Sussman
of the handful of fistfights he'd fought as a kid. The grown-
up responsibility of confronting others with their wrongdoing
was eerily comparable to punching another boy in the face.
So he found himself curiously relieved that her call had nothing to do with the embezzlement, a subject that she apparently found too trivial to bring up. She was concerned instead
for the welfare of the knife-brandishing bruiser whose mug
shot he'd more or less identified. Pick seemed to think that
targeting him or anyone else for the American Gulag was
unforgivable. He could get ten years, she said.

"Where'd you get that?"

"From someone who knows. The sentences they hand
out get really crazy. I'm finding out. I wouldn't want that on
my conscience."

"You didn't identify him?"

"Of course not."

He was stunned. True, the cap had hidden the top half
of the man's head, but those squinty eyes, the smashed nose
and giant shoulders all matched precisely. There couldn't be
two people in a million who'd be mistaken for this guy. Sussman wasn't even sure why he'd left room for doubt. He'd told
the police he was 80 percent sure. "But I've been thinking,"
he said. "If he walks away he could really hurt somebody
next time."

"So you want to put him in preventive detention the next
ten years?"

Sussman was no stranger to the world of muggers and thieves. He'd grown up in a neighborhood teeming with half criminals. When they were kids they might shovel neighbors' walks one day and commit petty thefts or extortions the next. Whatever opportunity presented itself. Most kids drifted away from shortcuts. Others grew into full-fledged bandits and thugs, some of them mob-connected. It didn't take much of a breeze to bend kids like them one way or the other. Scientists, schoolteachers, killers. There were endless possibilities on Chicago's South Side. But whatever happened, you didn't call the cops to solve your problem. Sussman's father let a pickpocket go free at the racetrack. Yet he was a poker player who pounced on the weak like a hungry rattler. His dad read Kant, Buber, and Schopenhauer, but he did so secretly, as though it were shameful.

"You know I've spoken with the mortgage company," Sussman told Pick, "and some others."

"What's that got to do with the kid?" she shot back.

"Not a thing, but I think it's worth mentioning, don't you?"

"Sussman, I . . . just can't talk about any of that now. Try to understand." There was a bit of a tremor in her voice. It didn't quite make up for the lost five million bucks, but it was a start. Of course there was a 60 percent chance she was playing him. "I'll see you at the line-up," she said.

So she'd be there too. He drove without enthusiasm through bright sunlight to the police station, less than eager to see the giant with the mustard skin. The cops had him wait ten minutes in a fair-sized room that looked like an insurance office except most of the people working in it wore police uniforms. Pick said hello as though their relationship was unstrained and natural.

"You know, you could have at least paid the dog walker," he said. She ignored the remark with remarkably impressive dignity.

Eventually the Jewish cop, Rosen, came in and escorted him without Pick to the same little room with the one-way glass where he'd viewed Bento several weeks earlier. So it wouldn't be a traditional line-up after all. As Sussman and Rosen seated themselves at blond-wood student desks, the giant, in a blue jail jumpsuit, entered the little room on the other side of the glass and seated himself in the plastic chair. He looked like a sorrowful bulldog. It was him, all right, only without the giant braid or the knife. Suddenly Sussman heard him say, "Get away from me." It came through a little speaker near the ceiling that Sussman hadn't noticed before. Apparently the suspect was obeying instructions from someone Sussman couldn't hear. "Get away from me," the giant said again—the only words Sussman had heard from the intruder. But the suspect used a voice tone you'd use to state your address. He repeated it twice more in the same bored manner.

"What do you think?" asked Rosen. "Want to see him with the baseball cap?"

"Sure."

Rosen picked up a mic and spoke softly into it. The giant donned a red Angels cap that had been sitting on the table.

"It was pulled down to the tops of his ears," said Sussman. Rosen relayed more instructions, and the giant pulled the cap lower.

"Well, you sure this time?"

Sussman tried to suppress a smile. "No."

"What does that mean exactly?"

"I'm less sure now than I was before. The memory could be fading, but there's a good chance this isn't the guy."

Rosen looked skyward. "Is something going on here we ought to know? Let me tell you, the man who broke into your home is extremely dangerous. He'll do it again. You can count on it. To somebody who could get hurt or killed. You want that on your conscience?"

"You take care of your conscience, I'll take care of mine." At which point Rosen informed him the hulk in question had been busted for a carjacking in the Valley that would put him away for years. Which meant Sussman could rest easy. The guy wouldn't go out there and chop up a family of Quakers.

"I hope it wasn't something we said that influenced you," Rosen said, his tone suddenly solicitous. "Maybe somebody rubbed you the wrong way. Something like that."

"You mean like the blue meanie who treated me like a suspect?"

"Is that what happened?"

"My ability to recognize or not recognize your suspect had nothing to do with anyone's attitude," Sussman said. It felt good to say that because it was pretty much true, unlike most of what he'd been saying.

CHAPTER 33

Speed saw Liz crossing toward him holding something behind her back. "Please don't bring me one of your spreadsheets," he said. "What the hell's it even mean? Spread sheet."

"I have here . . ." She snapped out a letter-sized page and placed it on his desk. ". . . Voilà! Something that's *not* a spreadsheet. See? It's much more complete now. And no gobbledygook."

"You're such a sweetheart. I'm mad for you."

"Shut up about that."

The top sheet was titled, **The Brazen Rip-off of Roland Sussman as Engineered by Pickford Manville & Painstakingly Deduced & Summarized by La Zorra**.

"I guess this makes you La Zorra," he said.

"La Zorra's identity is a closely held secret."

"All anybody knows is she's gorgeous," said Eddie. "And really smart."

"This'll help a lot," said Speed, reading it over. He was reasonably certain the details were superfluous, given Sussman's inclination to absolve the guilty. "I'm really, really impressed. How do you find this stuff anyway?"

"I told you—"

"I know. You're a librarian. You can find anything."

"Not anymore," she said. "I'm an investigator. Much cooler."

"I know. When do you start?"

"We're still negotiating."

"You she-devil . . . awright, get outa here. I've got cash to collect."

Liz always walked with great determination, yet her shoes barely touched the floor. Speed couldn't decide whether he preferred to see her coming or going.

"Wait a minute. Liz?"

She twirled back and ended up with one knee almost touching the floor, a hand extending toward him in supplication. "Yes, my liege?"

"Just thought of something. You ever see *Stroszek*? It's a film by Werner Herzog."

"I don't think so"

"There's a scene at the end where the lead character drops coins into a slot in this arcade and a chicken starts to dance. A crazy-looking chicken. Then the character goes off to shoot himself."

She smiled. "Okay . . ."

"I never knew what it meant. People argue about it. Maybe Herzog didn't know what it meant either."

She tilted her head quizzically. Cutely, open and wonderfully curious. "Okay, what's it mean?"

"I don't know for sure. Futility, absurdity, the innate cruelty of the universe . . . Maybe you could share some insight, given your experience as a dancing chicken."

"I'd have to see the movie first. Not all us chickens are alike, you know. I'll look for it. What's it called?"

"*Stroszek.*" He spelled it for her but wasn't sure whether a DVD existed. "Let me know if you find it."

"If I do I'll invite you over."

"Invite me over anyway," he heard himself saying.

She looked straight at him, discerning something, puzzling it out. "Let me think about that," she said.

He knew he was old and repulsive, but Renoir painted girls who looked like Liz when he was a broken-down specter, his fingers so weak and misshapen that he had to tie them around the brush. Speed couldn't paint her, but he loved the anticipation of looking at her. Besides, a man without dreams might as well pick out a grave.

ONE OF those robot voices answered the phone, the kind that comes with the answering machine. When its spiel was finished, Speed said:

"This call is for Ms. Pickford Manville. This is Dr. Wu in the office of the Los Angeles County Medical Examiner. Please call me day or night. It's urgent. Thank you." He started to leave his number when a voice came on.

"May I help you?"

"Ms. Pickford Manville?"

"Yes?"

He read her address and date of birth and asked for confirmation.

"Wait a minute," she said, "how do I know you're who you say you are?"

"If you prefer to come down here, that's fine. Do you need directions?"

"No, Christ. What is it then?" So far so good.

"You are Ms. Manville then."

"Yes, what is it?"

This was where it got tricky. Speed could go in a number of different directions. He made his decision on the fly.

"Listen to me, you fucking crackpot. You left a red-hot trail, understand? Roland Sussman is a celebrated artist, and there's no chance you can rob him in broad daylight. You really want to go to prison so you can buy a bigger TV? You're gonna lose it all, honey, everything you stole. That's a certainty. Question is if you wanna lose it *and* go to jail."

"Who the hell are you?"

"This is Mr. Vance from Western Credit Associates. Do what I say and you might avoid serious prison time. Why Mr. Sussman's giving you this break is something I fail to understand, but we're prepared to sit down with you and work out a realistic transfer. What happens then is we read you off the list of assets that were stolen and sit them next to *your* list of assets—the real one that includes everything you shifted to your phony corporation—what's the name? Here it is. Stanford Brumberg Inc. in Delaware. All that silly crap, it's a paper plane, doll-face. It won't stay up."

Long telephone pause.

"You don't *need* time to figure this one out. Act intelligently and expeditiously and do exactly what I say. Starting now. There's no decompression chamber, understand? No time for any of your thieving bullshit. You can run, you can even hide, but when we find you, they put the cuffs on, get it? Try to stall? Same outcome. You don't believe me, call up the district attorney. Ask him if there's any way you can keep the $5 million you stole from your employer. Especially since we already have a comprehensive list of where it is now, including what you spent on stuff we can't retrieve, like your first-class hotel rooms, etcetera. That's something we need to talk about. But you try to keep any of your swag, any accounts you think are secret—like I told you, you'll spend a long time in prison. Not some tennis camp either. You'll be locked up with junkie whores. Crazy murdering bitches with sewer breath. Believe me, honey, being broke is a lot worse when you're broke in prison."

Horowitz, after looking through the paperwork, had confirmed that prosecutors would be reluctant to file criminal charges. Apparently Sussman, of sound mind and body, had signed everything she put in front of him. His best hope for recovery would be in civil court, where you hire your own lawyer and hope the jurors can follow the case.

Speed waited through a long pause before hearing a click at the other end.

CHAPTER 34

Gillespie, parked on the street in a nondescript SUV, waited outside the collection agency office. In his pocket were fifty aromatic hundred-dollar bills from Pick, neatly rolled in a rubber band. Time to take care of the Vance business. And with a little luck he just might make the Sussman problem go away—all part of the same package. Lucky for Pick, Sussman hired a collection agency instead of a good lawyer. In a courtroom she'd be about as believable as that dickwad who kept three girls locked in his basement for ten years.

Vance had to be scouted out, and Gillespie, the only blue-skinned person for a thousand miles in any direction, was a poor candidate for any kind of undercover work. Mischke would do. Like Tina, he didn't ask a lot of questions. And here he was, pulling up right on time, killing the engine on his pickup and without pause proceeding up the steps carrying a scuffed green toolbox. He looked so authentic it made you wonder whether he really should have picked termite school instead of the academy. Killing bugs and rats would have to beat standing around in a dopey rent-a-cop outfit, like so many cops ended up doing in retirement—even the ones that escaped to the country, where everything is cheaper.

These days Gillespie's Idaho idea was a stage he'd gone past. LA wasn't a bad town if you could wake up in Brentwood every day. Pick, no crazier than Tina, was an obviously better deal even if he'd have to come up with child support to make the switch. As for Shrek, he still hadn't thrown

Gillespie under the bus, which made it less likely that he would. He had more spunk than Gillespie gave him credit for. You don't know a guy until he's tested.

Lɪᴢ ᴄᴏᴜʟᴅ hear Speed quarreling with his air force buddy again. Amazing how many topics they could find to argue about. But no matter how intense it got, he rarely raised his voice, scoring points with an outward patience that didn't match the ferocity of his language. The other guy just plain hollered. She could hear him coming through Speed's headphones. All rage and indignation. It was as though Speed reserved blocks of time each day to get yelled at. Sometimes she'd look over at his blubbery presence and reflect on all those ads that depicted eager-to-please, scrubbed call center employees crowned with their cheery headsets. Phil definitely didn't run that kind of place. Just look at it. Sometimes Liz spotted bats—actual bats—roosting up in the eaves. Who knew they could coexist with pigeons? One day she came in early to make some calls back East and discovered a janitor— the only one she'd ever seen in the office. He was emptying wastebaskets. She asked him about the bats. When he pretended not to speak English, she asked him again in Spanish. He looked up and said, "Oh, you mean Porfirio and Letitia," and they both had a good laugh.

Yet when Phil offered her the chance to work out of Horowitz's office she realized how terribly fond she was of this dump. She'd decided to work the new job right here with the same old crew, the same old warehouse smells. Thanks to the promotion she could send more money to her family, maybe even buy a laptop for her brother.

"But what if *your* mom were a crack whore?" Speed asked his air force pal. "Wouldn't you appreciate a spot in Head Start? But maybe I've got you all wrong. Maybe your mom *was* a crack whore. Forgive me."

A workingman carrying a toolbox was talking with Phil about something. It was rare, having a visitor. She took a call. "I'm calling Mister Vance," a man's voice said.

"Call for Mister Vance!" she announced. "Line five."

Bento took the call. Speed, who'd taken leave of his air force buddy, was already heading out for a smoke break. Liz followed him out on the landing. "Why do you talk to that guy? The one you argue with all the time?"

He struck a match. "Habit," he said, and then lit the cigarette between his lips.

"I want to ask you a favor."

His eyes crinkled with curiosity. He looked sweet when he was hopeful.

"What're you doing this weekend?" she said.

"Whatever you want me to do, sweetheart."

She didn't particularly enjoy him calling her "sweetheart" but let it pass.

"I'm visiting my family in Tijuana. I could use someone to talk to in the car. You know, waiting at the border and everything."

"I'm very good at waiting at borders."

"I'll leave Saturday morning. Coming back Sunday."

"Bringing me home to meet the family. A wise choice."

"Behave, okay? Give me a serious answer."

"Everyone around here tells me I'm *too* serious."

"What do they know?" she said. "They're a bunch of bill collectors."

"I'd be honored. That's a serious answer." Now he looked too happy. Exactly what she'd feared because she still wasn't sure what she was doing or where this would lead. Anyway, she'd enjoy his company.

"What's your family doing in Tijuana?" he asked.

"You know, the usual Mexican things—bullfights, siestas, Chevies . . . You'll see. Go have your cigarette. I've got like two hundred Madoffs to bring to justice." He started down the steps. "Hey," she said, "you do know there's no smoking in my car, right?"

He waved his assent without turning around. The man with the toolbox, his business with Phil apparently finished, followed Speed down the steps.

Back in the office, Bento looked perplexed. "You know that call you gave me?"

"You mean for Mr. Vance?"

"Yeah. They hung up as soon as I got on the line."

"Did you check the number?"

"I called it, but I just got one of those electronic voices. It said no mailbox had been set up."

"He'll call again," said Liz.

"It was a man? What'd he sound like?"

"Not very friendly. Who was the guy in coveralls?"

"Phil says he's a termite guy. Wanted to know if anybody'll be in on Saturday."

"Do we have termites?" she asked him.

"Probably, but Phil says he doesn't know. He just rents."

Liz wondered if termite guys could chase off bats.

GILLESPIE WATCHED the brunette go back inside while the fat guy staked out a spot to smoke. Mischke, downstairs again, casually got in his pickup and pulled out. Gillespie drove off in another direction and they met up on the other side of the block. Mischke got in beside him. "I saw Vance," he said.

"You sure?"

"Two minutes after I got inside. That's when you called, right?"

"He said 'Yes, this is Vance.'"

"Exactly."

Gillespie circled the block and they began their stakeout. Neither said a word for twenty minutes.

"There he is," said Mischke. "That's Vance."

A tall kid with a short ponytail, late twenties, descended the steps two at a time. He looked familiar.

"Jesus," said Gillespie. "I know that guy. His name's not Vance though. He's an ex-con. This is getting good."

CHAPTER 35

Returning to the office after his first dental exam in five years, Bento passed Sandra coughing and smoking, standing beneath the stairs to escape a drizzle. She waved a finger in the air, nodding her head to acknowledge his presence. Climbing the steps he read a text message from Norah: she'd sold a car ten minutes after opening the doors and another just now. She was taking him out for celebratory sushi. Followed by an exclamation point and a happy face. He'd been simulating fondness for raw fish to please her. Kind of like faking an orgasm.

Just as he sat down, Sonia, looking rather sexy if you were attracted to angry, bored young women with disfigured earlobes, swept into the office and snapped gum as she waited for Phil to get off the phone. After a while he pulled a clump of bills from his wallet. Taking no count, he handed them over.

Bento took a call. "I can't wait to see you," said Norah. "You wanna hear about my big sales?"

"Tonight," he told her. "Life is good."

"It really is, isn't it?"

"Yeah, gotta go." Searching his computer screen, he came up with Leo Hull, Saint Louis. Made the list last week. Visa. Six hundred sixty-seven dollars, minimum wage job. Hull's voice was vigorous for a schmo.

"Where you at, man?"

"California," said Bento.

"Well, I'm in the projects, man . . . crackheads breaking into cars, gunshots . . . you know, all that good stuff. The other night, I'm watching the Knicks? And I'm thinking, two, three hundred years ago nobody could watch the Knicks on TV. Not even the richest millionaires. Makes us lucky, right? So how come I don't *feel* lucky?" Hull paused. He wanted an answer.

"We measure ourselves against those around us," said Bento. "Nowadays that includes people we see on TV in tuxedos walking on red carpets. You don't get to actually see the people who lived hundreds of years ago."

"That's right. That's exactly right. You're a smart dude, you know that?"

"No, I just read that someplace."

"You read a lot?"

"Not as much as I used to."

"What you doing as a bill collector?"

"What you doing in the projects?"

Hull snickered. "I'm guessing you was in prison. Am I right?"

"I guess maybe you were too," said a deflated Bento. They didn't trade any of the details. It wasn't like two Yale men crossing paths. Bento had spent so much energy to disinfect himself of obvious signs, trying not to be just another ex-con that cops and other ex-cons could sniff out in an instant. But he still gave off the telltale stink, just as Hull did. Maybe they always would.

Hull agreed to start paying twenty a month. At 30 percent interest he might pay it off in fifteen years if he stayed out of prison. Meanwhile Bento half listened to Phil and his daughter. Phil didn't want her driving her car for some reason:

"You want me to poke my head outside and show you your car? The one you drove up in? I told you, take cabs. I'll pay."

She let her breath out through her teeth. "Awright."

"Good. Where you going? I'll take you."

"For Christ's sake, I'm just going home. I don't want to leave my car in this shit-ass neighborhood all night."

Phil said something about the money for the car being earned right here in this shit-ass neighborhood. He'd fallen into the hackneyed role of a ridiculous, hectoring parent and was no doubt aware of it, which added to his annoyance. "I'll take responsibility for your car. Let's go."

Bento wasn't keen on spending time with Sonia, but wanting to do something nice for Phil, volunteered to take his place.

"You've got stuff to do," said Phil.

"I want to," said Bento. It was almost true. Besides, he loved owning a car, being licensed and insured just like regular folks.

Sonia scrunched her two lips together, which apparently meant it was okay with her. The address she gave him was ten minutes north, but the freeway had been slower since local authorities converted a carpool lane into an expensive toll lane that Speed called the job creators' lane. Those who could afford to pay whizzed through while everyone else suffered.

Sonia, still chewing gum, lit a cigarette before getting in. As he pulled out of the lot she pressed her head back against the headrest and looking toward the roof, said, "What're you doing working for my dad?"

"I don't know what you mean."

"Don't take this wrong, but it's kind of a loser job, isn't it?"

"It's very kind of you to point that out."

"You need to chill," she said, proud she'd found a cliché to throw at him. Apparently it need not match the situation. Okay, he decided, say as little as possible, get her home and get the hell away. But then she pulled out a rolled joint and lit that too. Now she had a cigarette, the jay, and chewing gum all going at the same time. Medicinal marijuana was allowed in California, but smoking it in a vehicle invited arrest. She was a front-seat tsunami.

"Would you put that out please?"

"I said chill."

"I mean it. I'm on parole."

"So that's why you took that shitty job."

"I'm telling you to put that out. I won't say it again."

The exit was coming up. He'd let her out at the end of the ramp. But she snubbed it out in an ashtray. He rolled his window down. The smell seemed to be receding, but maybe he'd just grown used to it. "What were you in for?" she said. He returned to silence, still the best plan. He'd like to turn on the radio, but she'd argue over station selection.

"I don't—"

"Listen," he said. "Will you please just shut the fuck up?"

She was quiet for a while, then said, "I don't mean to be such a bitch. That's all I was gonna say." It struck him how miserable it must be to be Sonia. Now, on top of everything else, she'd made him feel like a jerk. He reminded himself he'd be seeing Norah tonight. This too would pass.

"My dad doesn't want me driving because I lost my license," she said.

"I kind of figured that."

"It was for total bullshit." He tuned her out as she told him all about it. Heading east on Manchester, they passed a series of vapid-looking, lonely strip malls. Lots of bright colors fading into sun-bleached history. Dry cleaners and fast food seemed to dominate residents' needs. No wonder visitors didn't get LA. It was like driving through twenty thousand South Dakota towns all stuck together. But if you got out of the car and circulated you'd find an urban core beneath the crust—hipsters and dealmakers, gay hustlers, artists, science impresarios—people who, if they're born in places like South Dakota, have to relocate to places like Los Angeles or go mad. At the corner of La Cienega Boulevard he caught a red light across from Randy's Donuts with its giant doughnut sculpture on the roof letting you know you weren't in any ordinary town. He was pretty sure Sonia had just asked him a question.

"Sorry, would you repeat that?"

"You don't like my ear jewelry, do you? I can tell."

"I guess it makes a statement you want to make."

"You still think I'm a bitch."

"We all have bad moments. But if you want to behave differently, the way you do that is to start behaving differently. Anyway, I don't know what I'm talking about. I don't really know you."

"Maybe you should then—get to know me." She didn't crack a smile, which made the suggestion stretch across the front seat like a physical presence. After a while she added, "You're not very friendly."

"My girlfriend has a pretty big tattoo. I can handle your ears."

"Yeah? Cool."

Bento double-parked in front of the apartment building. It was sand colored with half-dead plants around the entrance. Brass letters that needed polishing spelled out "Royal Palms" on the stucco. Cars along the curb were on the same downward spiral as the buildings. Sonia hit a speed dial number on her phone and told someone, "It's me. I'm here." Turning to Bento, she said, "Wait here just a minute? I'll be right out."

"Isn't this home?" But even as he said it Bento realized that Phil would never let his daughter live in such a shabby place.

"It's a quick stop. Two minutes, okay?"

Before Bento could protest she was running through the intermittent drizzle.

CHAPTER 36

Someone buzzed her inside. Bento, feeling helpless as his simple errand expanded, reminded himself that he was doing a favor for Phil. Although the street was lined with apartments, he saw no one about. Three or four long minutes later she came back out carrying a dark plastic garbage bag. He switched on the door locks and rolled up the passenger window, leaving it open only a few inches. "You're not putting that thing in my car," he said.

"You kidding? It's my laundry."

"I don't see any laundries."

At this point Bento noticed someone coming up behind her. He'd apparently followed her out of the building. He was about forty, a pasty-faced white man, almost as tall as Bento. Brown dirty hair hung straight and oily to his shoulders. He was clean-shaven, and the long straight hair framing the plain pale features made him look like a homely woman. He wore new, expensive basketball shoes but was unkempt everywhere else. His eyes looked crazy. "Who's this asshole?" he said.

"Just a friend," said Sonia.

He peered inside the car, front and back, as though it were something both peculiar and repulsive. "Well then get the hell outa here," he said.

"Okay, okay," she said.

He glared at Bento, turned around and headed back to the building entrance.

"What the fuck, dude, let me in. C'mon," Sonia pleaded. She set the bag on the hood, still grasping it with both hands.

"Sonia, that guy doesn't do laundry, okay?"

"It's his old lady. God, you're just like my dad. You both must have Alzheimer's."

"I'm going," he said.

"You crazy or something?" He turned on the engine and was about to pull away when he saw Sonia look over her shoulder, frightened. The man with the dirty hair was coming toward them again, this time carrying a ball-peen hammer.

"I told you to get the hell out of here!" He banged the hammer three times on the roof. Dent, dent, dent. "Beat it, bitch." Sonia's stony-stoic face showed real fright. Bento couldn't leave her with the madman, and if he got out to confront him, the situation would get uglier fast. Someone might already be calling the cops. The hammer man went into a crouch, moving toward a retreating Sonia, which created a silent, slow-motion chase around the car. He held the hammer like he meant to use it. Bento, waiting for the right moment, unlocked all four doors with one click and got out fast, inserting himself between the hammer man and his prey. When the pursuer got close, Bento pointed toward an upper floor of a building across the street.

"Jesus, don't you see that?" he shouted.

Hammer man looked up and Bento slammed him with a one-two, remembering to turn his body into the right. They were both good shots. Meanwhile Sonia slid into the front passenger seat and slammed the door behind her. Blood poured out of the man's mouth, but he otherwise didn't seem affected. He struck the hood with a thundering hammer smash. "You wanna play, motherfucker? You wanna play?"

Bento faked a kick to the nuts and stepped in with a left forearm to the head. The swinging hammer glanced across his biceps. Hurt like crazy. Bento stung him with a jab. He couldn't get his hands on the hammer. The man pulled it back in a two-handed batting stance. Bento tried to open the rear door, but Sonia had locked the car. "Unlock the doors!" he yelled. The bloodied hammer man advanced, still in his batting stance. Bento became the prey in another slow-motion chase. He could take off down the block, but he couldn't leave Phil's daughter with the madman, who was trying doors as he followed Bento around the car. "Unlock the doors!" Bento yelled again. She must have heard him because this time the madman got a rear door open and started to enter. Bento made it over in time to slam the door on his ankle. Two, three, four times. "Fuck, fuck, fuck!" shouted the hammer man. Sonia was screaming now too. She sounded like a crazed three-year-old. The madman stumbled back grasping his ankle but still held the hammer. Bento made it around to the driver's door, jumped in, and pulled away. The madman tossed the hammer at the car. It missed and skidded down the asphalt.

Sonia was still screaming. "Shut up!" Bento yelled. He wanted to turn the corner before throwing her out, but the block was a long one. When he finally made a right turn, he stopped and reached over to open her door. Her makeup and tears were smeared into a kind of gray mud as she pulled on her hair with both fists.

"Please, please, don't leave me here, please." He pulled away and headed toward the freeway. "Thank you, oh thank you, thank you." Three or four blocks later he heard a quick burst of siren. Red lights flashed in the rearview mirror. He stopped and waited. "Shit!" said Sonia. It was only then that Bento noticed she still had the big trash bag. It sat under her feet.

The cops were in an unmarked vehicle, the portable red light on the roof still flashing. They took a full minute to do anything, keeping Bento and his passenger in suspended animation. She was wiping her face with her sleeve. Bento didn't think his arm was broken. Finally the driver got out and approached them on Bento's side. He wore khakis and a polo shirt with a little golfer silhouette on it and held up a badge and an ID. Peering inside, he snorted a big breath through his nose and scrunched his lips as if to say he smelled something interesting. He checked out the ashtray that held Sonia's roach, then stood there looking at them, as though thinking what to do next.

"All right," he said finally, "you'll be getting out of the car one at a time. You first," he said to Sonia. "Keep your hands high. No sudden moves."

There was a time when if you hit some legal snags you could ride west and start again somewhere elsewhere. Choose a new name if you liked. What a sweet, lucky time that must have been. But this could still be a small thing. Bento had to stay alert, stay cool. He'd done nothing wrong, so don't act guilty.

Now a tall cop in jeans also approached. He had a long face and really was blue, just as Philyaw had described him. Asking for driver's license and registration, he had a strange way of speaking, as though the words had to fight their way out of a resisting mouth. The first cop sat Sonia down on the curb.

Ever since hearing about him, Bento had been keeping an eye out for the blue cop, actually hoping to make a sighting, like seeing a shooting star or a mountain lion. How wrong he'd been. It was more like recognizing you'd picked up the clap. The two cops quickly established that Bento was a parolee. They needed no excuse to pull him over and search. Regular rules didn't apply. After patting him down they sat him next to Sonia on the wet curb. It hadn't occurred to Bento yet to wonder why Hermosa Beach cops were operating in LA. No handcuffs. So far so good. It was drizzling a little harder now. Their lights dancing, more police cars showed up.

"What's this?" said the blue one, leaning into the front seat. "The bag, what's in it?"

Bento thought this might be a nice time for Sonia to speak up. She sat impassively. Her makeup was still smeared just enough to make her look like one of Fellini's low-rent hookers. As even more patrol cars showed up, the blue cop's partner cuffed Bento behind his back and sat him down again, this time about ten yards from Sonia. He could no longer see or hear her. Two cops stood over him: a pudgy female and a tall Asian man. The woman, looking pleased, said, "You wouldn't happen to have prescriptions for all those substances, would you?" The bottom fell out of Bento's insides. "My, my, so much OxyContin, thousands of pills. And a pound of what will no doubt test out as crystal meth. What're you running? A delicatessen? Wait, how silly of me. There's no such thing as a prescription for crystal methamphetamine, is there? It's like getting caught with a barrel of dead babies, except you might have an excuse for dead babies. But if you can show us prescriptions for the pills, well hey, you might only have to do about a thousand years."

Controlling his voice, he told this comedienne that he had no idea what she was talking about. "That's not what we're hearing," she said. Closing his eyes, he imagined he'd gone home after seeing the dentist, that he hadn't returned to the office and none of this was happening. He could be in some unmapped dimension he'd soon escape, just as Jimmy Stewart's George Bailey got his lovely life back in Bedford Falls exactly as he remembered it in *It's a Wonderful Life*. He opened his eyes to the dancing lights.

CHAPTER 37

The beachy waitress with the lovely complexion who served Sussman at his outdoor table was so polite she made him feel a hundred years old. She took his order for coffee and a fruit platter as though both their lives depended on the outcome. What sort of fruit did he prefer? Would he like to see the peaches? If he'd wait just a few minutes she could get him in on a fresh pot. Would that be all right? And she found Lucy so *cute* stretched out on her stomach, gazing at pastel sights along the beach. It happened more and more, Sussman being spoken to as though he were a toddler or a panda. The waitress saw him more accurately than he saw himself. She beheld one of those genderless patients in a geriatric ward, or at least someone so close to being there that it made no sense to draw a distinction. It was unendurable, these savage dismissals adorned with concern and confection. And yet sitting at his pine table beneath a sun umbrella he just smiled back at her. The scarcity of his remaining days imbued them with a special fragrance. The music stops, he's standing alone, and the game goes on without him. Such thoughts used to irritate and sometimes even terrify him. Now they were comforting. The earth would endure his absence.

The waitress probably hadn't read a book since high school. It was only because he'd been on TV that anyone in the neighborhood knew his identity. And this wasn't one of those pitiable, run-down areas beset by crime and material deprivation. People hereabouts glistened with material well-being and were ignorant only by choice. As long as it was sunny and seventy-two with only a hint of breeze, what else was there to know? The days of endless, spiritless ambience destabilized Sussman's awareness too. He couldn't tell you what month it was without thinking about it first. There were only two seasons—night and day. Give him a senility test right this moment and he'd flunk.

Still, he'd heard back from his old booking agency, and the wheels were in motion for a Mark Twain tour, just as Bento suggested. There were still readers out there, and he enjoyed their company. Travel niceties would be less than sumptuous, but simplicity had charm of its own. Maybe he'd find material out there—hear a train whistle, see trash blowing into a gutter or a tramp blowing snot out his nose. He could do without grandiose hotels and pompous eateries where reciting a detailed litany of specials was a task so solemn you'd have thought the waiters were arming a torpedo. Uniformed lackeys adding and subtracting plates and glasses and moving around your silverware with such tenacious mindlessness.

After conducting a flash inspection, magic-man Horowitz had already suspended Pick's power of attorney. He also had a scheme that would allow Sussman to keep the house. That's when Sussman explained that he didn't plan to spend the last years of his life in legal proceedings, especially if he'd have enough to live on anyway. After the tour he'd curl up with his laptop and write the next book, maybe even start it during the tour. He found an old notebook of ideas he'd forgotten, and two or three weren't bad. That was kosher. After all, they were his own ideas.

"Hey, how ya doin'?" said somebody, and Sussman looked up from his fruit plate to see the two plainclothes cops, the blue one trailed once again by the partner with the crummy transplants. This time he wore a baseball cap. Good choice.

"Fine," Sussman replied, immediately irritated with himself for answering the rhetorical question that was no question at all. Why must he fall so promptly into insipid, unearned, ill-timed politeness? "Don't tell me you've been following me around," he added. These guys were up to something.

"We're just trying to do you a favor, is all," said the blue one, lips zipped together, vowels and consonants all jumbled into something that sounded like one long word. What a bundle of tiny tragedies and secrets this prick was. Sussman tried not to despise him, but he also thought, well, if somebody out there has to turn blue, this is a suitable candidate.

"That's a great dog," said the smaller one, checking out Lucy. "What's his name again?" Still trying to implement the good cop-bad cop nonsense. Without asking permission, they sat down.

"We have to be sure of a couple things," said the blue cop, "because, well, I don't mean to alarm you, but filing a false police report? It's a felony. You need to understand that."

Sussman recalled a study that proved the human species is more likely to remember negative events than positive ones. It helps people avoid repeating their mistakes, which aids survival. Trouble is, survival can be hell when all the stuff you'd prefer to forget crowds out memories you'd prefer to keep. Now he'd have these two stamped in his memory. "What," he asked, "are you talking about?"

"First, we want you to understand that you always have the right to remain silent," said the blue cop, trying to sound casual.

"Jesus Christ, are you guys for real?"

"Let's just get through this, okay? Anything you say can and will be used against you in a court of law. You have the right to an attorney. If you cannot afford an attorney, one will be provided for you. Do you understand these rights I just told you?"

"So this is on the record? All formal?"

"Well, yes."

"Good. First, I do understand these rights. Second, you— Ah Christ, are you really dumb enough to believe what you're telling me?"

"Let's not forget our manners," said the ridiculous blue cop.

Sussman closed his eyes and took a deep breath. "What's this crime I committed?"

"See," Officer Blue said, "a lot a these celebrities? They'll do anything to keep their face out there. So they stretch the truth, you know? Sometimes they even release their own sex tapes. So we have to make sure everyone understands there are consequences, okay? Because filing a false police report is a serious crime. It can get messy. Maybe you should just back off, you know? No more accusations and everything goes away."

Could Pick be in league with this freak? He'd love to know. "Listen, if you happen to see Pick, Ms. Manville, tell her she has nothing to worry about. There's no need for bitterness. I hope she finds a way out of her little hell. I really do."

The cop with the hair transplants looked confused. The blue one didn't. "You mean," he said, "you're not in touch with her anymore? It's all over between you?"

"Tell her to go and sin no more—if you see her."

"Have a nice day, Mr. Sussman," Officer Blue said, and suddenly Sussman was alone with Lucy. He wanted more coffee, but waitresses, like cops, never seemed to be around when you needed one.

CHAPTER 38

"**W**hy here?" Gillespie asked her.

"Nostalgia," Pick said. She'd arrived early and was already on her second Bloody Mary. "It's so *romantic*—the scene of our first date. Don't you remember? All those secret thoughts and passions? The conniving? Checking each other out under the radar? What do you think? Is the electricity still there? Tell the truth. I can take it." She chuckled and drained her glass. He looked puzzled. Too dumb to know she was pulling his leg. "Get us a couple drinks," she said. "I already started a tab. I'll get us seats out back."

She found the same bench they'd used the first time, but the patio was more crowded this time. She saved him a seat with her purse. When he joined her she grabbed her fresh drink from his hand. "Remember that monster dog?" she asked him.

"Yeah," he said, squeezing in. "Listen, what I wanted to tell you about Sussman, just stay away from him, okay? Let me handle it. This is tricky. It could go either way, but the thing is—"

"What'd he say?"

"Well, he's not happy, but if I play it right, you could come out okay. Just do as I say, okay?"

"I already spoke with him," she said. "He called and asked my forgiveness for any hurt he caused. Isn't that sweet?"

Poor Gillespie was confused. She watched him thinking fast, searching for another way to con her. "Really? That's . . . wow, great." Now he'd pretend that nothing had changed.

What a schmuck. "Also, I found the guy who was bugging you, the one who called himself Mr. Vance." He looked like he expected a doggy treat or something.

"No kidding," she said.

He set his beer on the narrow table, still untouched. "Yeah, you remember, the guy with the ponytail. The one you saw in the station that time. The one I said is dangerous? He was using the name Vance. I nailed him. He's out of your hair."

"Nailed him for what?"

"It's not important, but he's going away, just like I said he would."

"Drink your beer before it goes flat." She raised her head with a gay smile. "Or order yourself a whiskey, why don't you? Beer's for teenagers."

He took a generous swallow.

"Listen," she said, "you want to play cops and robbers, be my guest. Arrest whomever. Have a ball, but Vance doesn't matter anymore. Get it? Incidentally, I'm changing the locks at my place. Correction: I *have* changed the locks. Your key's no good anymore."

He stuck his thumb between his teeth, probably not aware of it. She'd never seen him do that before. It wasn't terribly attractive.

"You won't be getting the new key, understand? Let me put it like this. You're a great stud and everything, but you're married and it's time. This is where we move on to the next chapter. Separate chapters."

Now he got it, emoting waves of shock and anger but still trying to think it through.

She must show no fear. "What are you going to do?" she said. "Kill me? What would happen to your little kiddies? And your crappy little pension? That's the Achilles heel, isn't it? Of people like you. You sell your life so you can maybe start to live after you get old. And you're so-o-o close. Listen, I'll save you some trouble and tell you what you're going to do.

Nothing. Understand? You'll go back to your pathetic little life. You'd have figured that out eventually, but I'll save you the suspense. What else can you do? You're the fearful type. That's why you turned yourself blue—out of fear. You know what I'm talking about."

She wasn't sure he was breathing. Or maybe he was hyperventilating. Something extreme was going on inside him. "Money," he said, lips moving just a tad. "You owe me money."

"You've already been paid. With—"

"Five fucking thousand?"

"Yes, and certain . . . privileges. Right, sweetheart? I'll always cherish those moments, but don't you see? We have to be grown-ups now, both of us."

He grabbed her shirt at the shoulder. She slapped him. When he didn't let go, she slapped him again. All conversation around them stopped. He let go.

"You think I'm the crazy one. I'm the fool, right? Hey, I'm not the one who hooked up with a goon, a *burglar* goon. But you know what? I might just hook up awhile with some civil service drudge who can't afford to risk his little pension. I'd have nothing to fear from a pathetic little asshole like that, would I?"

It was still deathly quiet when she stood up and smoothed the material on her shirt. "The bartender has some things of yours," she said. She'd made a thorough sweep, chucking his razor, stray underwear, and other entrails into a cardboard box. "I think that covers it." She made her way out.

CHAPTER 39

Horowitz was one of the very few customers doing business in this coffee shop who actually had an honest-to-God office somewhere. Most of them prowled around like stray cats, working out of their smartphones as self-anointed dynamos of commerce and technology. Horowitz heard snatches of their conversations, and they really could sound masterful, but he suspected many of them at the end of the day returned to their old high school bedrooms.

Philyaw showed up a few minutes after Horowitz, looking like he'd just received an awful diagnosis. Nodding to Horowitz, who already had his no-frills black coffee, he went straight to the counter. Horowitz liked Philyaw, but he liked just about all his clients, including the ones who were slow to pay. He even liked Sedarski, a pitcher who'd burned out his arm in the minors and who looked like Frankenstein. After a bad day at the track, Sedarski came home last year to find his delicate Asian wife napping on the bed. She'd just picked up their two darling children from day care at the end of a long shift at the checkout counter. He was still upset with her for spilling bleach on one of his favorite shirts so he seated himself on her stomach, and as the children shrieked, rained down punches and hurled vile insults. Then he rolled off and fell into a deep sleep. But his wife called her mother, who came over, snapped photos of her daughter's bruised, bloody face with one of those fucking iPhones, and then called 9-1-1.

Everyone was so disgusted by Sedarski that the DA wouldn't offer him a deal. Horowitz had no choice but to go to trial. He could have waived the right to a jury, but the evidence was so clear he figured his only shot was to find an outrageously nonconformist or downright crazy juror. It only took one. But after the first few hours of proceedings the jurors looked ready to storm over the railing with torches and pitchforks. Unanimously unsympathetic to Sedarski's blown-out arm or substance-abuse difficulties, they spent less than two hours to find him guilty on all four counts. But he really was a nice guy when he wasn't drinking, which was practically never. It wasn't his first domestic assault, which the judge used as an excuse to impose a life sentence. Everyone was relieved. In his heart of hearts, so was Horowitz.

Horowitz, going against personal preference, usually left tie and jacket in his car before entering the coffee shop. Just about everyone in the place, including its uppermost tier of entrepreneurs, dressed like skateboarders or worse, and Horowitz didn't want to attract attention in a world where the government not only recorded the doings of its citizens but also conducted black bag jobs, sneaking into homes while the occupants were out. After looking through drawers, medicine cabinets, and all the usual places, they put everything back the way it was so residents wouldn't know police agents had been there. These activities were hidden by secret courts, secret warrants and additional layers of concealment whose very existence went unacknowledged. Ever since the panicky passage of the Patriot Act, American lives were available for dissection by any dumb-ass clerk with a security clearance. All it took was for Horowitz to take on a client that somebody in one of those Stalinist-looking government buildings wasn't fond of and they'd be shooting figurative periscopes up his butt too. It was because of this outrageous, ubiquitous snooping that Horowitz ran for vice president on a ticket with his former client Glenda Radke even though it earned him a reputation as a flake. He'd been doing stuff like that all his life—making moves he knew he'd regret even as he made them. How many times had he fired off angry letters to people in position to harm him? An attorney should know better, and he did know better but couldn't seem to act on the awareness.

Anyway, maybe the fight for his lost cause was worth some unjust stains on his reputation. And government eavesdropping was only part of the problem. From time to time he'd hired private investigators whom he happened to know owned thousands of dollars worth of bugs and taps and all the rest. They weren't hobbyists. If he could hire them, so could anyone else. In fact, if he were really conscientious he'd meet Philyaw on a park bench, which was even harder to bug than a coffee shop, but he liked the coffee in here. He also liked the way the sunlight poured through the tinted glass and the way the Japanese American owner always studiously supplied the place with mostly crappy old magazines that no one read because who the hell read magazines anymore? And he liked the way the kids behind the counter included an occasional non-kid like the middle-aged lady with punk tattoos running up and down her arms. She looked like she just stepped off a prison bus, and Horowitz appreciated it when a business hired American untouchables who reminded him of so many of his clients.

Phil took the seat across from him. "What's with the tea?" asked Horowitz.

"Coffee's not agreeing with me lately." Phil looked frazzled and beat. A baggy-eyed Bogart, which made him look even more like Bogart. Except if you tried serving tea to Bogey he'd probably have plugged you. Phil had a miniature teapot and an empty cup and looked a little confused by it all. "They told me to let it steep," he said.

"Goddammit Phil, how come you look so much like Humphrey Bogart?"

"He was my grandfather." Horowitz felt a mixture of satisfaction and foolishness. Why in God's name did he wait all this time to ask?

"You inherit any money?"

"He didn't marry my grandmother. Left her out in the cold. We didn't get a dime."

"Jeez, she should have gone after him."

"Think you're telling me anything I don't already know?"

"Sorry."

"They're both dead anyway. Fuck it."

"Let me ask you something else. Who do you think was more likely to be dealing oxy and crystal meth out of a garbage bag? Sonia or Bento?"

"You know the answer."

"But I'm asking you. What's logical? The young middle-class mother or the two-time loser with a record of drugs and violence? Bear in mind she can hide her freaky ears with her hair and she's never been arrested."

"Look, I thought she was clean, Siggy."

"I've asked you not to call me that."

"Right. Anyway, I didn't know anything about it."

Phil would have made an excellent lawyer. He knew how to talk around things.

"No one's accusing you of dealing drugs, okay? Did you get a chance to ask her about any of this?"

"She's not talking to me, but I told her Philyaws don't lie. I made that clear."

"And?"

"She laughed. Telling the truth is a joke, I guess. Look, you can forget about her listening to me. It won't happen. Some kids, they're absolutely certain you're an idiot, you don't know anything. Then they'll run into some monstrous piece of shit somewhere, they don't even know his last name, and they'll believe anything he tells them. It doesn't do any good to think about it."

"You need to understand I can't represent both of them—Sonia and Bento. I've seen the police report and their cases have to be separated. That's the first thing to do. Although right now there's no case as far as she's concerned. No charges filed—against her, anyway. But that could change."

Now Phil looked like he just received the second medical opinion and it was worse than the first one. "Then I can hire two lawyers. One for Bento, too. You know good ones."

"Sure."

"Look, what's the problem? If you don't like it, say so. What the hell's wrong with you?"

"This is a zero sum game, Phil. Somebody was attached to those pills and powder, and one of them's taking the fall. One or both."

"And?"

"That means the more you help one, the more it hurts the other. Like I said, a zero sum game. And one of them has already turned snitch. Which one do you think that would be?"

Phil just looked at him. "Let me hear you say it, please," said Horowitz. He wanted them to understand each other.

"Why?" asked a distressed Phil.

Horowitz looked straight into the Bogart eyes and waited for an answer.

"Sonia, okay?" Phil poured some tea into his cup. It looked weak. He took a sip and winced.

"Okay," Horowitz explained, "so let nature take its course and she'll come out all right. She'll say the bag was on the floor when she got in the car. She said it already."

"But if—who do they really think is guilty?"

"That won't come into play."

"What are you talking about?"

"You *know* what I'm talking about. They seized a pile of dope and they're after a conviction, and what do they find? A two-striker, which makes it a much bigger deal."

"Jesus, I never should have hired him. He'd never . . . he . . . None of this would have happened."

"You had the best of intentions, Phil. It's like saying it's my fault because if I hadn't bought you lunch somewhere you wouldn't have been coming out the door when the meteorite hit you in the head. Everything's related to everything else, but that doesn't make all of us responsible."

"Whose fault is it if I don't hire a lawyer for him?"

Good question, thought Horowitz. "Look, I don't like this, but I have to give my client the best representation I can. If I don't, what good am I?"

"How much time you think they'll give him?"

Horowitz stared at his empty cup. Why is it you could go into any restaurant and drink all the coffee you wanted for the price of one cup and these phony coffee-snob joints made you pay for each and every cup? He decided then and there to switch allegiances. In the future he'd take his coffee business to a diner with waitresses who came around and filled up your cup and talked to you like human beings. "I'd say ten years."

"How much if he takes a deal?"

"That *is* the deal. Something like that. Seven or eight would be generous, but only if he cops a plea."

"And if he doesn't?"

Horowitz spit it out. "Twenty-five to life."

"Oh Jesus, Horowitz, I can't—I can't let this happen. I can't do it." Little tears formed in the corners of his eyes. It made Horowitz want to cry too, but he willed himself against it. No one, as far as he could tell, was paying attention, but how would that look? Two guys at a table crying like saps. On the other hand, who cared what the other customers thought? They were worried about their own petty little lives. They should see the lives he had to deal with. People under pressure. Sometimes, like Phil, they discovered they weren't the person they thought themselves to be.

"Looking at the evidence I've seen so far," Horowitz said, "if I were his attorney I'd probably advise him to take the deal."

Phil was suddenly business-like, recovered. It was just a squall. "Even though you know he didn't do it."

"I don't know anything. I know less every day. Sometimes the less you know the more money you make. You just look the other way and it comes rolling in. But I know the law, I know these courtrooms. I know you can't always predict what a jury will do, but I look at the odds and I say he takes the deal. If I were his attorney. Except . . . Ah, forget it."

"Except what?"

"Except the cops are saying they didn't see any bag until they pulled them over. That means it had to already be in the car. Does that make sense to you? Their stories match, the cops' and Sonia's, but . . . well, you could call her to the stand and try to shake her testimony. Bento's attorney could. Or maybe find a witness who could contradict her somehow."

"She can lie right to your face and never blink," said Phil. "You getting more coffee?"

"I'm not going up to the counter, ordering all over again, tipping all over again, just to get what they should be bringing me anyway. I don't know why anybody comes in these places."

"But you come here all the time."

"I changed my mind," said Horowitz.

"When?"

"Just now. I can change my mind, can't I?"

"What's wrong with you?"

"I don't like my job."

"You don't like this place, you don't like your job . . . Look, I'll go up and get you another cup."

"No."

"I'm going up anyway."

"For more tea?"

"For coffee. I'd rather die on my feet than live on my knees with this fucking tea."

Returning, he walked faster than Horowitz would walk carrying two cups of hot coffee. He started talking before he sat down.

"The cops, what they're saying, it's not true is it? About what happened," Phil said.

"They've got a clean case. It's his car, his record. Sonia's just somebody who got in the wrong car with the wrong dude. But let's say she decides to tell them something else, say she actually takes the rap. Well, that's a lot of dope. To stay out of prison she'd have to bring in three bad guys. That's the way they work these deals. You turn informant, you give them three good cases if you want to walk away. She'd be wearing a wire, testifying, all that. Like an undercover cop, but without pay. Going into dangerous situations and getting people mad. People get killed doing that. As her attorney, I wouldn't advise it."

"But what about Bento? Couldn't he do that? Wear a wire and all that?"

"Possibly, but probably not. What's he got to tell them? That after four years in the can he came back and lived a straight life? That means the people he knows on the street, if any of them aren't dead or in prison, are probably all in Anaheim anyway. Another jurisdiction."

Horowitz had seen this paradox too many times. Only lowlifes can give you other lowlifes. Innocents have nothing to trade, no one to betray. He was glad he wasn't Phil right now. Trouble was, just this minute he wasn't too fond of being Horowitz either.

CHAPTER 40

Shackled with the other wretches in the inmate section, Bento watched as one of the others agreed to forgo a trial and do two years. The defendant was seated at the table next to his public defender, but he hadn't made bail and was chained up, hands behind his back. Bento didn't know the man's offense, which was typical. Contrary to the spirit and letter of the constitution, probably no one in this batch of prisoners would receive a trial by peers. The courtroom was here to put an official stamp on bargains reached behind closed doors. Here you heard only bits and pieces about the cases against them. This particular defendant was much older than his manacled peers, fifty at least, bald, a bit round, and colored in a glossy shade of brown. He had a wide-toothed smile and seemed like the kind of guy who'd take the time to give a stranger good directions.

"I see there was a previous prison sentence," the judge said, looking through papers. "What was that about?"

The prosecutor, given the name Fat Bastard by the prisoners, searched papers on the attorneys' table. Apparently finding nothing, he said, "It was just like this one. Nothing serious." Holy crap, Fat Bastard was actually acknowledging that you didn't have to commit a serious crime to go to the joint. And the judge saw no problem in that. He sees the same scenarios acted out day after day and after a while starts to believe it's not crazy, that he's not crazy. The judges who used to have heretics disemboweled must have followed similar patterns. Same old same old. From the tone of their voices these guys might have been passing the mayonnaise or asking about tomorrow's weather. There was never a hint that the poor stooges parading in and out of the courtroom were, between hearings, confined week after week, month after month in the seventh circle of hell, places where these nonchalant officers of the court would fall apart inside of twenty-four hours. The wisecracking judge, the bored little Filipino bailiff, the prim stenographer, the dimwitted public defender with the world's worst comb-over, and especially Fat Bastard himself. They'd each and every one confess to firing shots from the Grassy Knoll if it would get them out of county to take their chances in the state system and the possibility of finding edible food, catching some occasional sunlight, and escaping the pitiless bullies currently tormenting them. Of course there would be a new set of bullies at the next destination. But their congenital fear of the unknown would be overcome by current horrors.

In his few months on the outside Bento had started to think like a civilian, to trust the future. But back here at the bottom of the 99 percent, as Speed described it, he was among people led around in chains, and they had no such illusions. Bento recalled some of them who, unmarked in previous hearings, showed up later with terrible bruises, new gaps in their teeth. One even had a section of hair ripped from his scalp. The wound was still raw yet no one paid attention. Men in courthouse shackles were like lobsters destined for the pot. A species that probably couldn't feel pain anyway.

FOR A while—a short while—Bento was tempted to tell investigators the sack belonged to Sonia. For starters, it *did* belong to Sonia. But the words wouldn't come. To pin the deed on her he'd have to shed his skin and become someone else. And he would *remain* that person, a loathsome creature with a pink tail scurrying for any kind of life. And the cops wouldn't believe him anyway. It would all be for nothing, tearing out his own guts so they could laugh at him. They had to attach a body to the booty, and it was Bento's car and Bento's two strikes. They'd been saving him a cell all along.

Eventually they'd offer him a deal. Take it. That's what any lawyer would tell him, probably even Horowitz the miracle worker, who'd already come down to the jail to tell him no, he wouldn't be defending him. The fucker. Once again there were no miracles in store for Bento.

"Sonia said it was my dope, didn't she?"

"You know I can't answer that question," Horowitz replied. "I shouldn't even be talking to you."

"Then why are you?"

"I thought you deserved some explanation."

"Explanation for what? For why you're gonna help them frame me?"

No answer.

Bento: "What should I do?"

"Get representation."

"How much would it cost?"

"Nine, ten thousand for somebody good." That would be in cash. Bento considered sending a bat signal to Liz, Norah, Speed, Eddie, maybe even Phil. He could drag them down into his hole, but the results would be the same. Might as well end up with whatever court-appointed lawyer who couldn't get cases on his own, would work cheap, and happened to be in the courtroom that day. Horowitz was only a temporary shoulder to cry on before he lined up alongside the enemy. Funny how Bento used to think being tossed in a cell with Phil that day had been a stroke of good fortune.

"Those cops were following me, weren't they? Why?"

"You really should get your attorney to go over this with you."

"Then let's speak hypothetically," Bento said. A con told him that once. When you want a lawyer to say things he believes he's not allowed to say, tell him you're not referring to any particular case. You're just talking. "Why would cops be following around somebody like me?"

"They could follow any parolee, but they could also get tipped by an informant. That's what they'd probably say."

"An anonymous informant."

"Most likely the informant wouldn't be named."

"So really they could be their own informant," Bento said. "There doesn't even have to be one. Let me ask you about a hammer, a hypothetical hammer. Would these hypothetical cops say anything about a hypothetical guy swinging a hypothetical hammer? Maybe a couple of minutes before they pulled a guy like me over?"

Horowitz looked at him quizzically. "I personally haven't seen anything like that." That's what Bento figured. By acknowledging the guy with the hammer they'd have to expose a cupboard crawling with roaches.

The next day there was a preliminary hearing, and Bento, hands shackled behind him, was led into the courtroom after hours and hours of waiting in different institutional spots along the inmate trail. His attorney turned out to be not so bad, but even Bento could tell he wore a cheap suit. Your only chance of landing a really sharp lawyer was to team up with a young one whose talent hadn't yet been proven. This one was about sixty with neurotic eyes that darted everywhere. Maybe it showed he cared. For now we'll plead not guilty, he instructed Bento three times during their three minutes together. *For now.* Bento was reminded of Peter, fated to denounce Jesus three times before the cock crowed. "What are they offering?" asked Bento, who'd been down this road before.

"You're in a hurry," said his attorney. Bento didn't catch the name.

"Well?"

"We haven't got that far yet."

"I didn't do it."

"We'll talk about it, but not now."

"No, really, I didn't. I don't get high anymore and I'm not a dealer. I'm in the can for something I didn't do."

"Going to trial is always a possibility, but let me at least read the arrest report."

"Can you get the bail down?" The judge had set it at $300,000.

"I'd have to file a motion," said the nervous, aging attorney in the Kmart-looking suit.

"Are you going to file it?"

"We'll see how it goes."

Bento could insist and the guy might do it, but then he'd be annoyed with Bento, which was dangerous. And the bail wouldn't get down far enough anyway. All this was like having to rewatch a movie he'd hated the first time. Once again he didn't get enough time out in the world. The interval had passed so sweet and quick. Still, it left him with much to savor. The look and feel of Norah, the bell-like tones in her voice. When she spent the night he'd gaze at her sleeping next to him, so sweet a presence in his Salvation Army bed—and wonder why he was so blessed. She grew more lovely each time. He should have done a better job explaining to her what was in his heart.

Anyway, he'd made some good friends out there. He'd seen a Shakespeare performance. He regretted not making that trip to Big Bear to watch the stars. You never get any yard time at night. Being cut off from such a big chunk of the natural world made prison feel even more artificial, not one with the world.

But doing time was something Bento knew how to do. You mustn't think of it as a worse life, just a smaller one. The emotions are still there, but on a different scale. Triumphs and setbacks, like the days themselves, don't hold the same value. Meanwhile, beyond the walls, the smudge he'd left behind would gradually wear away as the world around him rotated at a different speed. Time for him would transpire in a gray dimension, apart and dissonant.

Little mistakes he'd made were bothering him because now there was no way he could make things right. He couldn't go back and be kinder to Mr. Hull, the last schmo of his career. What gnawed at Bento the worst was the thought of Norah sitting in that restaurant all alone, waiting for him, watching the time, texting, calling and calling, and finally at some point going home with her wound. He'd remember it again and again. He'd turn over in his bunk and feel it slash his heart but never quite kill him. He almost wept thinking about the hurt he'd left behind, but where he was going there could be no tears.

CHAPTER 41

Howevever, Bento's hibernation from emotional engagement was sorely tested when at his next hearing he spotted Liz and Norah seated together, concerned yet glowing with irrational hope. They and their optimism comprised a magic vision that threatened to overwhelm their tired yet malevolent surroundings. Still, he resisted acknowledging their smiles and gestures as the judge and his courtiers lumbered through a gray mass of clerkish issues. The next day Norah showed up at the jail and he refused to see her. Screening visitors was one of his few privileges. The next Saturday he was escorted to one of the special rooms reserved for attorney visits. Horowitz, wearing a splendid black suit, sat reading a newspaper at an institutional folding table. He folded the paper and said, "You mentioned something about a guy swinging a hammer."

"I did," Bento said.

"Hammering a nail?"

"Hammering me. Trying to."

"Those two Hermosa cops, they followed you all the way from the office. So they had to see it. How come it's not in their report?"

"You'd have to ask them."

"They're the arresting officers. You find the guy with the hammer or you find somebody else who saw him, and it could all fall apart. I mean *really* fall apart. They'd probably have to file charges against those two cops. In that neighborhood, I'm guessing somebody did see it. What do you think?"

"I'd go out and look for witnesses, but my calendar's kind of full right now."

"What about your attorney? Has he tried?"

"Don't be silly. Look, who are you working for?"

"You know, you've been here awhile."

Bento, resisting sarcasm, merely nodded.

"And you haven't copped a plea. So what's going on?"

"I won't confess to something I didn't do. I'm done with that."

Bento saw a microsecond of a smile in one corner of Horowitz's lips. There were many reasons the answer might have pleased him, not all of them kind. "Tell me more about the guy with the hammer," he said.

"I asked who you're working for."

"You know, you don't look so bad, considering. I like the mustache."

"There's no way you could change sides now. Even if you could, you're not Superman anyway. What's the deal? What do you want?"

"What I want is to call in a librarian. Librarians kick ass."

"They can find anything, can't they?"

"Damn straight."

Bento realized he'd been unable to muffle the last torturous murmur of faith in the future. Like a ringing in the ears. Was it always there or only when he noticed?

"I never met with Sonia," said Horowitz, "never accepted the case. I kept putting it off till finally Phil hired someone else. It's what he wanted, I'm sure."

"Why'd you wait so long?"

"I had to work it through in my mind. Which got shredded in law school so it took awhile. I apologize for that. But also, I get annoyed with people who don't accept visits from their pals. Or answer their mail. And you don't call anybody."

"I figured it was better if they forgot about me. I still think so."

"They're the ones who hired me, you know. People from your office."

"Which ones?"

"All of 'em. Plus Norah somebody."

"You can't take money from Norah. She's broke."

"If you must know, I gave them a rate."

"If you weren't working for Sonia, how'd you get to see the police report?"

"Sometimes lawyers go through channels. Sometimes they don't. Hypothetically speaking. Now tell me what happened that day. Start from the beginning."

"I won't rat anybody out."

"Don't give me that jailhouse shit. You've got people who care about you. Listen, let me ask you something. Say you're walking down the street."

"So we're hypothetical again."

"A car goes by. You spot some guy in the backseat grinding a lit cigarette into a girl's forehead. Do you take down the license plate and call 9-1-1? Or do you remain a standup con and go on about your business?"

"You've done this before, haven't you?"

"What's your choice?"

IT was theoretically possible to make a collect call to a cell phone from the jail, but in practice, the connections usually went haywire. So that night, after waiting more than an hour for the pay phone, Bento put in a call to a landline. When Gloria picked up, a programmed voice announced it was a collect call that emanated from county jail. There was no way to hide. At least it wasn't her father at the end of the line. A moment later he heard Norah's voice: "You swine," she said. "Answer my letters."

"Okay."

"And let me visit you."

When his mother died a part of him was relieved that she no longer suffered because of Bento. That sense of relief made him more miserable than the fact of her death. And the picture remained stamped in his mind, her getting searched at the jail so she could speak across smudged glass through black World War II era phones. She liked to imagine that her son was somehow untouched by their marginal situation, but there was no arguing with a prison sentence and the expectation of more of the same. Lying in a cancer ward, a welfare patient without visitors, she at last faced it, how the world worked.

"You didn't sign on for this," he told Norah.

"Oh shut up."

The next time Bento was shipped over to the courthouse Horowitz had already taken over. He waited for a recess and when the judge left the room, signaled the bailiff, who wordlessly escorted Bento to the defendant's table as Eddie, Sandra, Speed, Liz, Phil, and Norah came streaming through the gate. One at a time they hugged shackled Bento. When the judge returned, Horowitz locked horns with Fat Bastard, startling him with a motion to reduce bail and basing it on some statute that appeared to carry weight. Bento, drinking in everything he could see, hear, or sense, dreamed once more of going up the mountain to watch the shooting stars.